NO ONE BETRAYS THE ORDER —EXCEPT A DAVIS.

Are you willing to take the risk?
—Ethan

REZONED

THE DAVIS ORDER
PREQUEL

Copy Editing: Jenn Lockwood | Jenn Lockwood Editing

Proofreader: Rosa | My Brother's Editor, Mary | On Pointe Digital Services

Interior Formatting: Danah Logan

Cover Design: Danah Logan

Photography: Katie Cadwallader Photography

Cover Model: Taylor Isaacs

ISBN: 979-8-9867063-3-7 (e-book)

ISBN: 979-8-9867063-4-4 (paperback)

ISBN: 979-8-9867063-5-1 (paperback – discreet cover)

A NOTE FROM THE AUTHOR

Trust Ethan and Jules.

All my books are unique to their main characters. They write the story; I'm just along for the ride. They make mistakes that can have you either relate to, like or dislike (possibly even hate) them. They are raw and flawed, but we love them anyway.

You've met Ethan in *The Dark Series*. *Rezoned* is his story.

Ethan's book gives you a glimpse into **The Davis Order** and can be considered its prequel. You'll be introduced to all the Davis siblings, get to know them, and maybe even get some hints to their individual stories.

Rezoned is split into two parts: past (ten years ago) and present.

If you have read my previous books, you are familiar with my writing and know that I thrive on the small details. *Rezoned* was meant to be a novella, but it quickly turned into a full-length novel. However, I decided to cut some of the "filler scenes," as I call them, and if you notice jumps in the story, that is why.

All the mentioned regions, sites, and locations you encounter in this book are made up to fit the story.

It is **not necessary** to read *The Dark Series* before *Rezoned*.

Rezoned is intended for **MATURE (18+)** readers. It is a dark, (love-to-) hate-to-love, second-chance novel and features strong language, violence, explicit sexual scenes, and situations that may be considered **TRIGGERS** for some. **Reader discretion is advised.** *(For a more detailed list of potential triggers and tropes in this book, scan the below QR code.)*

For all the phoenixes whose wings were clipped—broken.
Who burned and yet rose from the ashes stronger than before.
Don't let anything (or anyone) ever hold you back.

PLAYLIST

"Satellites" - No Sleep for Lucy
"HOT DEMON B!TCHES NEAR U !!!"
- CORPSE and Night Lovell
"Vendetta" - UNSECRET and Krigarè
"The Saint and The Sinner" – AViVA
"Waking up" - MJ Cole and Freya Ridings
"Bodies" - Drowning Pool
"Reaper" - Glaceo, RIELL
"Another Level" - Oh The Larceny
"Back from the Dead" - Besomorph, AViVA and Neoni
"Burn" - 2WEI and Edda Hayes
"Poem of a Killer" - WE ARE FURY and Elijah Cruise
Back from the Dead" - Besomorph, AViVA and Neoni

PROLOGUE

ETHAN

PRESENT

SAYING goodbye to my foster sister is never easy. It makes my chest constrict as much as my (in her presence, permanently coiled) muscles relax. I care for Jenn, love her—on a nonromantic, platonic level. Out of the four Davis siblings, she's the only one I remained in touch with.

However, over the years, we drifted apart. Our lives don't blend well. I work security for the Altman Hotel empire, and she is *The Cleaner* for one of the biggest organized crime families in the western hemisphere. A family I used to be part of—not that I ever asked for it. Did I want to be out of the foster system? Of course. What five-year-old wouldn't want to belong somewhere? But at what cost? A price I didn't understand until it was too late.

"Can I talk to you for a minute?"

My eyes flick to Jenn, and a sour taste forms on my tongue. As good as she is in her profession, she doesn't possess the mask our brothers wear, which is why she is *The Cleaner*, and the guys execute the jobs. She is about to deliver the news I never wanted to get.

My pulse thrashes in my veins as I follow her to the driver's side of her Bugatti. She studies me, and with every passing second, I fight the urge to latch on to her arms and shake her. I don't want to hear what she has to say, but I don't have a choice.

"He found her." Her tone is level. While she visually can't hide shit, she is a professional in her area of expertise. The groove between her brows contradicts her voice. The sorrow and fear for me are etched across every inch, but no one would know just by hearing her speak.

"How?" I choke on the question.

"By sheer coincidence." She peers over to where my employer and her friends stand but continues her recap. "Cor called just before we got here. He overheard Marshall on the phone with Tony. He was on assignment in Maine and stopped at a diner on the drive back."

My fingers flex and curl as I listen. "Don't tell me she works at a diner." Why would she do that? A vision of her red hair behind the counter flashes in front of my mind's eye.

"Not work. She owns it," Jenn states. "It's all she's ever known. Can you blame her?" Her gaze jumps between my eyes.

"And you're telling me Tony stopped at her diner, of all places?" This is the most fucked-up coincidence in the history of random occurrences.

Jenn nods, and my hands fly up, fisting the strands of my cropped dark hair. I get ahold of enough to pull, causing a sting that distracts me momentarily from the pit that has been ripped open in my stomach.

"Why didn't Tony eliminate her on the spot?" Not that I'm

not glad he didn't, but she should've been dead a decade ago. To Marshall Davis's knowledge, she was.

"Marshall ordered him back to the plantation. He probably wants to figure out what happened before taking action." She chews on her bottom lip.

"Are you going to be okay?" What I'm asking is, *will you be safe?*

"He won't kill me." The corner of her mouth quirks and my snarky little sister is back.

I slant my head, not dignifying her attempt to make light of the situation.

Jenn rolls her eyes and places both hands on my shoulders. "You know Father doesn't tolerate disobedience. That's what started this mess in the first place. But Mother will not allow him to harm me. To him, I wasn't even there."

"Maybe not you, but Corbin was. *I* was. He sent me there to watch Ju—" Saying her name constricts my airways, and I have to pause. "How can he not think we had anything to do with her surviving?"

Her expression softens. "I will call you once I have more details. Cor is working on getting the exact location."

Jenn hugs me, and despite returning the embrace, I feel nothing. A hollow cold has taken over my body.

They found Jules.

PART ONE

How the phoenix burned...
                -Jules

CHAPTER ONE

JULES

PAST

"HE'S BACK." My friend, Della, skids to a halt next to me and bends over at the waist, catching her breath.

I'm elbow deep in soapy water. My hands involuntarily stop scrubbing the pot I just grabbed from the dirty pile. The rolling sensation in my stomach is accompanied by its usual humming-bird flutter as *his* chiseled face with its boyish, dimpled cheeks pushes itself to the forefront of my mind.

I'm fully aware of who she's talking about, but I don't allow my giddiness to show. "Who?" I feign ignorance, forcing my hand to continue the job my father assigned me.

"Stop acting like you don't want to jump him." She purses her cherry-red lips. "You stare at him just as much as he eye-fucks you."

"Della," I hiss. If my father would've heard that... Her words are true, but I can't help the sting they cause inside my chest. I slowly pull my hands from the suds and swipe them on my apron. Swiveling toward Della, I school my features. "He is a Davis. My father would kill me if I ever so much as smiled in his direction." After a deep breath, I add, "Plus, he's with Jenn. You've heard what Ivy said."

My friend scowls. "Ivy and the pom-pom squad don't know jack shit. Jenn doesn't go to our school—none of them do." She throws her arms up in exaggeration. "Ivy tries to get her minions off her back so she can put a move on him—any of the guys. I mean, look at these brothers." Della wipes imaginary drool off her mouth. "Ivy can't say anything about Jenn with the others. That'd be incest, so he's the obvious choice. But what she can't control is that he only has eyes for one certain redhead." Della winks.

"Shhhhh," I shush my best friend as my eyes dart behind me, waiting for my father to round the corner.

DELLA and I are seniors at the local high school.

My family's diner is situated strategically on one of the roads connecting the BC Swamp to Renneton, Georgia. Tourists always stop here either before or after their trip to get a look at the black cypress. For the past nineteen years, I've tried to figure out why people are so obsessed with this damn tree. I don't get it. Its black bark and leaves probably stem from an unknown disease or poisoned water supply that will kill us sooner or later.

Renneton is small. Not some backwater bayou town, but also not big enough to not know everyone's business.

Then there are the Davises. That family is a different story. The siblings consist of Corbin, Theo (or T as they call him), his twin Jenn, Paycen (whom no one ever sees), and Ethan.

Ethan is not related by blood, but he lives with them. Rumor has it he was adopted or fostered since he was a kid. For all intents and purposes, he is a Davis. His black credit card says so. They live near the swamp on a massive plantation. T and Jenn are my age, but besides the occasional visit to our diner, no one ever sees them. They stick to themselves.

Corbin and Ethan are older by a few years, should be in college, but both live at home. And all of them are painfully gorgeous, which is why every girl is after at least one.

Ethan always has an arm around Jenn, and the word on the street is that they were seen making out in front of the *BC Shack*, a bar that serves minors if you have the right connections.

The rumor mill spins circles around them, yet no one would dare ask them directly. The Davis family is to be left alone. That's what was drilled into me from an early age. My father, Grant Arrow, is a large man, tall and broad, but when he spoke of Marshall Davis, I could see him shrivel in front of me.

Focusing back on my friend, I shake my head. "It doesn't matter. I don't have time for a boyfriend. My only goal is to get out of here and never look back."

She shrugs. "Doesn't mean you can't have fun while you wait for the bus." With that, she leaves me slack-jawed, and I watch her retreating form.

I finish my chores, and just as I'm about to take my apron off, my father rounds the corner. "I need you up front. A busload of tourists just rolled in, and you need to take over Della's tables so she can help your mother.

Take over Della's tables? No, no, no.

I'm hiding behind the saloon door, peeking through the little round window. Jenn, Ethan, and Corbin are lounging in the far booth near the emergency exit. Ethan scooted all the way in with his back against the window. He has one leg propped up on the bench, and Jenn is nestled between his thighs. She leans against his chest while his fingers play with a strand of her dark hair. My mind starts throwing images at me. His hand on me, him curling my high ponytail around his fist before bending my head backward and devouring my mouth with his.

I bite my bottom lip as my greedy eyes rake over the rest of his body. The sleeves of his hoodie are pulled up, and the tattoos adorning his muscular arms are on full display. The ink spreads over the backs of his hands but stops at his knuckles. A feverish flush slithers up my neck, and I touch my palm to my cheek. Is it suddenly too hot in here?

"Jules," my father barks behind me, and I jump.

Fuck.

I don't turn out of fear that he'd see what just went through my head written across my face.

I push against the door but then halt abruptly. Three sets of eyes flick at me, and I have the urge to smooth my hands over my apron. Instead, I draw my shoulders back and place one foot in front of the other.

Ten feet. Six feet. Two feet.

"Hi, guys. What can I get you?" There is no point in introducing myself. They know who I am as much as their names are etched into my brain.

"Hey, Jules. How are you?" Jenn is the first to speak. While she intimidates everyone with a pulse, she's been nothing but friendly to me.

I can sense Ethan's gaze but keep my attention on his *sister*. "I'm good. I'm taking over for Della. She has to help with the—"

Loud shouts echo through the diner, and the four of us jerk our heads toward the commotion. Dad didn't exaggerate when he said a busload of tourists had arrived. Probably twenty seniors are piled into the four large booths on the other end, yelling their orders at Della and Mom.

I fight the grin that threatens to spread over my face as my best friend glowers at me over her shoulder, promising retribution.

Focusing back on my table, I meet Ethan's eyes. His irises resemble the color of caramel, and I immediately blame the comparison on spending too much time helping my mother bake.

Someone clears his throat, and a new flush sets my cheeks on fire.

Oh my god, how long did I stare at him?

"I'll take the double cheeseburger with extra cheese, no tomato, one whole pickle on the side. Whole. Do not cut it," a deep voice states, and I forcefully tear my gaze away. Meeting Corbin's obsidian eyes, a completely different sensation spreads through me: gut-wrenching fear. Where Jenn exudes warmth (at least toward me), Ethan has a devilish smirk on his lips, promising a good time—for him. But the older Davis brother bleeds danger from every pore. I've heard rumors about Paycen being feared, even by his siblings, but he cannot be worse than Corbin, can he?

"Uh, um...sure." I pull my tattered notepad from my apron, scribbling the order while simultaneously praying the cook doesn't mess it up. Who knows what'll happen if the pickle ends up on the burger?

Inhaling a shuddering breath, I address Jenn. "What can I get you?"

"I'll take the Caesar, please." The warmth in her smile thaws some of the ice Corbin has injected in my veins with his cold orbs.

"You got it." I smile.

Ethan is already waiting for my attention, a flutter spreading from deep in my core through every cell. My mouth is suddenly parched, and Ethan's nostrils flare as he watches as the tip of my tongue swipes across my lips. His eyes blaze with heat, and I feel naked under his scrutiny. He doesn't speak. In my peripheral vision, I notice Jenn smirking at Corbin.

This is getting ridiculous.

"Ethan?" I wave my notepad and pencil through the air.

He blinks and cocks his head. "I'll take you."

My brows shoot up, and I question if he really did say what I think I heard. His brother sprays his water across the table, making Jenn squeal. She starts patting her face with a napkin.

I guess he did say it.

"Ewww, Cor! What the fuck!" Jenn pulls more napkins from the dispenser.

Ethan stares at me unapologetically as Corbin helps his sister mop up the mess.

It's just him and me. Everyone else fades into the background. While my mind starts running with the idea of him *taking* me, I won't give him the satisfaction. If he intends to see me flustered, he clearly hasn't watched me close enough.

I prop my pencil to the paper. "Aaand where would you like your pickle?" Ending the question with a toothy grin, the double meaning is clear.

Ethan throws his head back and laughs.

God, why is he so gorgeous?

Jenn shakes her head and winks at me.

"He'll take the cheeseburger as well," Corbin barks, and I get the hint. *Move along.*

I quickly peer at Ethan to confirm that's what he does want. He gives me a nod, and I mark Corbin's order times two. I'm not going to inquire again where he wants his pickle.

"I'll get that put in for you."

As I walk away, I hear Corbin snap, "The fuck, asshole?"

The last thing I hear is Jenn. "Jeez, leave him alone, Cor. He's just having fun."

AFTER I PUT the order in, I walk down the corridor leading to the storage room and back entrance. I crack the door. For once, we have a little bit of a breeze, and I let it cool the flush on my face. I just need a minute to collect my thoughts. What was I thinking flirting with Ethan Davis? Was I flirting? He started it. But why did he—

An arm snakes around my midsection, and another covers my mouth, muffling the shriek I was about to let out.

Warm breath fans over my ear and my cry for help transforms into a whimper. My thighs clench involuntarily. He doesn't have to say a word for me to know who it is.

"Jules Arrow." Ethan lets go of my mouth and tugs on a strand of my coppery hair. "Little Phoenix." The whisper is barely audible, and I wonder if he even noticed he said it out loud. He presses his groin against my backside, and my eyes roll inside the back of my head. While he is half a foot taller than me, his body molds to mine like he was meant to fit there.

"Your food is not back here," I murmur while my hand finds its way to his thigh.

His nose trails the shell of my ear. "Are you so sure about that?" His teeth graze my skin, and I moan.

Full-on moan. My spine stiffens, my nails digging into Ethan's leg as I wait to be caught by my father.

His fingers splay over my apron, and his thumb caresses the fabric. I lean my head against his shoulder, relishing the sensation as I imagine no barriers between me and his touch.

"Do you know how long I've wanted to do this?" he whispers in my ear.

"How long?"

Before he answers, a ding in the front alerts me to an order being ready. Reality snaps into place like a rubber band.

I twist out of his grasp and stare at him wide-eyed.

Oh god, what did I do? Let him do?

I race to the kitchen window and grab the waiting food. I let Ethan Davis touch me. And it felt incredible. Like nothing I had ever experienced before. But he is a Davis. This can never happen again.

CHAPTER TWO

ETHAN

"WHAT THE FUCK WAS THAT EARLIER?"

I stop in my tracks, my heart jumping once before it continues to thud in its steady rhythm. I hate when I don't hear them enter. Walking out of my attached bathroom with only a towel around my waist, the second one to dry my hair obscuring my vision, I lower the towel and narrow my eyes.

Corbin lounges on my bed. Leaning against the headboard, he has one booted foot propped on my clean sheets. My jaw clenches. My brother's mood has been exceptionally pissy the last few days.

"Not sure what you're talking about." I know exactly what he means, but I don't feel like baring my soul to him.

Soul. Ha.

I lost that part of me years ago when Marshall spelled out his expectations for the provided room and board. Not that I had a choice at that point. I was already in too deep. Seen too much. It was kill or be killed. Literally.

And that's what Corbin and I have done since we were fifteen. I held my first gun when I was six, just a few months after arriving at the plantation, got my first rifle at age nine. And I have been training ever since. Knives, guns, bows, fucking axes. We had to master everything since we never know what the next job will bring. Marshall has no limits.

Corbin lights a cigarette, inhaling deeply.

I tense, watching him take another drag and flick the ash on the cherry hardwood floor.

Grinding my teeth, I'm at his side in two strides. "Since when do I let you smoke in here, huh?" I rip the cigarette from his fingers and douse it in the tumbler he also brought with him on my nightstand. "What's going on with you?"

Before Corbin can answer, my door flies open, and Jenn and T stroll in. The way they move in sync has creeped me out from day one. Even as toddlers, they would shadow one another in everything. They had a bond one would typically expect of identical twins.

T drops his ass onto the dark leather couch against the wall, and Jenn plods over to me. She's dressed in shorts and a sports bra, which tells me she just finished training. Passing me, she snatches the edge of my towel and snaps it from my hips. Pivoting midstride, she slaps my ass, and I let out a growl. Cold air hits my balls, and I suppress a shudder. Not that I give a shit about being butt naked in front of my siblings; I just don't feel like having a fucking family meeting in my bedroom. Modesty is another quality that's not valued in this house. Sex is a given, which is also how Jenn and I ended up between the sheets. Not that I objected. My foster sister is hot as sin. I prefer fucking her over the other females living on the property. And with me claiming her, Jenn is off-limits to any dick she doesn't invite to her bed, which is only one other besides me. For all I care, she can do what she wants—as long as it is her choice. While I enjoy the release we give each other, we are too combative—even in bed.

I ignore Corbin lighting up again. If he goes against my rule twice, he's in a dangerous mood that even I don't feel like messing with. Not today.

Jenn retreats to her twin's side and plops down with my towel in hand. I reach for the gray sweats I discarded on the floor this morning. Planting my ass on the side of the mattress, I wait for one of them to speak.

To what do I owe this dis*pleasure?*

"I was just inquiring what kind of game E"—Corbin gestures lazily at me—"played today."

T stretches his arms over the back of the couch, followed by crossing his ankle over his knee. "What did I miss?"

He had to stay behind for debriefing when we decided to grab food. A new contract came in, and he'd leave for a job in the next few days.

Jenn grins from ear to ear. "Oh, our brother here has a crush on a certain redhead."

"Get fucked, J." I fight the heat that explodes in my chest to keep it from showing on my face.

"You offering?" She wiggles her brows and T mock gags.

Jenn elbows him.

"Come on, Wild Bill, it's cute." She flutters her eyes at me. There is no jealousy in her statement. It was never about love when we destroyed a room (literally). Lust, yes. Love, never. Sex is an outlet for our pent-up aggression or when we come down from the high of a job.

Cords in my neck twinging, I snap. "Stop calling me that." Usually, I don't mind the nickname—we all have them—but today, it rubs me the wrong way. The Wild Bill was the axe Marshall gave me for my thirteenth birthday. He had noticed my affinity for this type of weapon during training. My aim has been unchallenged to this date. Where one would resort to a bullet or knife for the final blow, I appreciate the effectiveness of the bit slicing through muscle or splitting a bone. It's more messy, sure, but the likelihood of the target walking away is less probable than a knife wound. The WB has two handhold areas, allowing me to adjust my grip on the fly when changing my strike angle. Empathy has long been pushed aside by efficiency. If Marshall wants a job done quick, he sends me. I don't toy around like my brothers. Whether that makes me more dangerous is still up for debate.

"Jeez, are we in a mood?" Jenn folds her legs underneath herself. Her teasing has changed to boredom, which also annoys me.

What the fuck is wrong with me?

I know what—*who.* Jules. She ignored me after she all but sprinted away in the hallway. Jules served our meals and thanked Jenn for the generous tip *I* had left, but that was it. She didn't make eye contact once.

Had I pushed her too far?

Why I followed her was as much a mystery to me as it was to my siblings. The way she countered my intent to make her flush had given me an instant hard-on. No one (outside of the family) talked back to us. Not at home and especially not in town. We were Marshall Davis's offspring. Yet Jules wasn't intimidated by my bluntness.

She had fascinated me from the moment I laid eyes on her a few months ago. Was I going to act on it? No. There was no point in mingling with an outsider. Until today. Her snark had changed that. She issued a challenge.

Nothing impressed me anymore. Pussy was a distraction. Taking a life, the norm. But Jules managed to send my pulse into a frenzy. A sensation I craved to experience again.

She responded to my touch like no one ever had. It wasn't just her body that reacted; her entire soul was drawn to me.

Jesus fuck, where did that come from?

"What redhead?" T's question breaks me out of my mental spiral.

"Grant Arrow's daughter," Corbin sneers.

"Oh, fuck no. She's a *Ren.* That's a no-go zone, and you know it." T throws his arms up, peering between his blood sister and brother.

A Ren, a.k.a. citizen of Renneton. Not a part of the Order.

"I'm not going there." Agitation elevates my reply, and it comes out louder than it should have.

Jenn slants her head. "You followed her." Her accusation is out in the open.

"I went to take a piss," I lie.

"Uh-huh, that's why she would break out in hives every time she came to the table."

"Everyone out!" I bark. I've had enough. I love my brothers and sister, but right now, I need to be alone.

T and Jenn chuckle and stand in creepy twin synchronicity. She links her arm with her brother and starts exiting. Before they clear the threshold, she turns, and her serious expression makes me pause. "Be careful, E."

I curl my lips under and dip my chin. Some of the anger dissipates.

When the two are gone, I shift my attention to Corbin. I expect some more needling on today's diner visit, but instead, he says, "Marshall wants to see us at five a.m. sharp."

Fuck.

"Why?"

My brother leans his elbows on his thighs. "Your guess is as good as mine."

If that isn't the truth.

. . .

I SCRUB my cuticles with a brush that might as well be steel wool. It always takes days before I regain full sensation in my fingers.

I hate this part of the job.

A manic cackle reverberates through my mind. We just killed someone, and the voice in my head whines about ridding myself of the evidence.

The grime coating the sink of this small one-bedroom shack takes on a pink hue as the blood slowly washes off my hands. I zero in on one particularly dark droplet and follow its trail until it disappears in the drain.

About six months ago, Marshall declared that Jenn was to be trained by Corbin and me. She needed to be able to take over if necessary. Subcontext: if we ever got compromised, she would be the executioner. It wasn't likely, yet we all understood the reason behind it.

We have crews all over the country, but when Jenn is on location, she runs the show. In the not-so-far future, she'll be in charge of the cleaners. For now, she usually is with at least one of us. She is a Davis and learned from the best—her mother. Marshall didn't entrust this part to anyone who could switch loyalty. However, it's one thing to clean up afterward, but looking into *the job's* eyes as the life bleeds from its eye sockets (not metaphorically speaking today) is a different story.

"Give me the fucking tarp." Jenn's demand rings through the small space. "OVER THERE! God, do I have to do everything myself? What are you getting paid for?"

Oh joy, my sister is in a mood.

But so am I. This had been a messy one. Plus, a female. While Marshall doesn't discriminate, the majority of assignments are for males. This particular one had double-crossed him, and he ordered us to make an example out of her. She is—correction, was one of his go-tos when he needed *authentic* paperwork.

Poppy was hired to write up the freight and import documents for a shipment that would've allowed Marshall to take over the territory of one of his rivals. But Poppy decided to double-dip. She gave Carlisle Underwood the details, which allowed him to outbid us, and Marshall ended up empty-handed.

We ensured the last thing she saw was us before ending her business arrangement with *The Davis Order*—or anyone, for that matter. The souvenir Corbin took would be mailed to her associate as a warning.

Under normal circumstances, this wouldn't faze me. I've done and seen worse than my brother spooning someone's eyeballs out of their sockets—while still alive. But there is this throbbing in the back of my head that won't go away. I knew who Poppy was. I had seen her a handful of times before, but I wasn't familiar with her on a personal level. She was just a random. So why won't the tightness in my chest go away? Ever since Cor let her lifeless form drop off the chair she was tied in, I can barely breathe.

Loud clatter jerks me out of my thoughts. Behind me, Corbin drops the tools into the bathtub, getting ready to eliminate any DNA from the evidence that could link us ever having been here. We never leave a site with compromised equipment. Thank fuck we didn't use guns this time. Taking those apart before exiting is a pain in the ass. But you never know when you will hit a roadblock or could be pulled over. Our cargo is more easily explained when it isn't dripping crimson.

"Jesus fuck, Kroy, you're stepping in the blood again."

Not stopping my task, I peer at Cor over my shoulder.

He smirks. "She didn't like the eye landing on her new shoes."

I snort. "No shit."

"You mean, *aye*," he counters dryly with the perfect accent as he uncaps a bottle of hydrochloric acid and salutes me with it.

I bark out a laugh. Our sense of humor matches our occupation: disturbing. Often, it is the only thing preventing me from letting go of the last sliver of my humanity. If you are no longer human, there are no jokes, no laughter. I like laughing. It feels... good. The risk of becoming my little brother is enough for me to cling to it. In his thirteen years, I have never so much as seen Paycen crack a genuine, nonsardonic smile.

Satisfied that my fingers are clear of any evidence, I thoroughly dry my hands and glove up. The more hands on deck, the faster we're out of here. We've been gone for almost a week. It took two days to drive to our destination, then another three to scope out the area and put the plan in place. The full cleanup would be another two since we have to ensure Poppy is sufficiently dissolved and disposed of.

Jenn flew out on the jet yesterday. She didn't need to be here for the legwork and would meet up with T on her way home. Theo is staking out a long con in Virginia before heading back south, and Jenn wants to be with him. The two are never apart for long.

CHAPTER THREE

JULES

Maybe I shouldn't have ignored him?

The same thought has been reverberating through my mind for the past nine days. Every time the bell over the door chimes, my head whips around, and my heart plummets. It's not like Ethan or any of the Davises are regulars. The opposite is more accurate. Sometimes, there are weeks between their visits. But before, it never bothered me. Ethan is a flirt. Good-looking and unattainable. A wet dream when I let my hand wander under the covers at night.

Now, I am missing something. He changed the game. Putting his hands on me. His hands... The phantom touch of his fingers still lingers on my skin—even though he never made full contact.

"You're spacing again," Della hisses in my ear as she passes by with a tray of food.

My spine stiffens, and I jerk around on autopilot. Mom has started side-eyeing me the last two days. Thankfully, so far, neither of my parents has opened interrogation, but it won't take much longer.

I grab the bucket from under the counter and head toward the two tables that just cleared. Dipping the rag into the water, I'm about to wring it out when the hair on the back of my neck prickles. Pausing, I scan my surroundings without actually looking. No one has entered the diner. He's not here.

What the—?

Something shifts at the far end of the parking lot. I zero in on him, and my heart instantly beats in my throat. I can barely draw in a breath.

Ethan is leaning against the side of his Bronco. It's an older model but immaculately restored. I heard them once talk about how much time Ethan spent working on it.

My spine stiffens as I take a closer look at the guy who has had me bent out of shape for over a week. Where his posture would seem casual to the unobserving eye, something is off. His biceps strain against the short sleeves of his dark shirt. His shoulders are drawn back, and his jaw...his trademark smirk is absent. His body is coiled so tight he reminds me of Corbin.

I throw a glance over my shoulder. The diner is fairly empty; we're past the main dinner rush. I drop the cloth back in the bucket and take it over to Della. She peers up as she collects dishes from another table.

"Can you cover for me for a few minutes?" I chew on my bottom lip.

A crease forms between my best friend's eyes. "Why?" she draws out the word, suspicion dripping from the one syllable.

I don't want to reply. I don't have an answer. What am I about to do?

I hold her stare as if I will find the answer in it. She must see my internal struggle because she nods once. Taking the cleaning supplies, she squeezes my hand with the other. "Be quick."

I bob my head and pivot on my heels. I stride down the corridor to the back door, trying not to run, despite the urge. I push against the metal door and peer behind me once more. My father is in the office, and Mom already left since we'd be closing soon. Della will be okay for a few minutes. Everything is going to be fine. I'm not doing anything forbidden. Right?

I step outside, the humidity, even at night, instantly coating my skin with a sheen of sweat. One more reason I want to leave this place. I despise the weather. No matter how many times a day you shower, one step outside and you're grimy again.

The crunching of pebbles under my flip-flops sends vibrations all the way up my spine. The hummingbird flutter in my chest increases with each step until I round the corner and the Bronco comes into view.

He's gone.

The tingling behind my ribs stutters to a crashing halt.

"Little Phoenix," his voice comes from behind me.

I whirl around and find Ethan not three feet away. My jaw drops. "How did you—?" I gesture between him and the car.

The corner of his mouth twitches the slightest bit before the shutters fall again.

"That"—he steps closer—"is a secret you have to earn." His body heat mingles with mine, and his hand lifts. His fingers are inches from my face, and I hold my breath. Ethan cocks his head, his hand hovering between us. Something flitters across his features, but before I can begin to interpret it, it's gone. I watch as his hand bridges the distance, and for a second, I would swear his fingers are trembling. He tucks a strand that has come loose from my ponytail behind my ear. Where his fingers connect with my skin, an electric current begins to spread. Every cell in my body ignites, and there is nothing I can do about the onslaught of sensations.

Ethan pauses, and turmoil swirls in the depths of his caramel irises. Of its own volition, my hand lifts and covers his that is still touching my face. Ethan's nostrils flare, and I wonder if I've made a mistake.

Is he mad?

His eyes flutter closed. "I shouldn't be here."

His words are so low I'm not sure I heard him right. So I wait.

"I had to come." He blinks, and when I meet his gaze this time, everything has changed. The wall he usually keeps up, despite his quips and banter, is gone. He lets me see him. Ethan.

I inch closer until my chest almost brushes his. His hand falls to his side, but I don't let him withdraw. An unfamiliar desire overcomes me, and I reach for his fingers, intertwining them with mine. The sensation is foreign and familiar. I've never initiated the touch before today, yet it feels like we have done it hundreds of times.

I have so many questions. Why shouldn't he be here? Where did he go for almost a week? Is this a game for him? Instead, I swallow the curiosity burning on my tongue. "I'm glad you came."

He squeezes my fingers and twists my arm until our joined fingers rest against the small of my back. He applies the slightest pressure and guides me closer until our bodies are flush. The drumming of his heart pulses through me, and I fight the urge to press my ear against his chest and listen to his reaction to me. I've never experienced a pull like this. His nearness is like a magnet drawing me in, yet it's never close enough.

I swore up and down to Della that I was not interested in him. He's a Davis. My father's one rule is that we do not mingle with that family. He has never stopped me from dating—something my girlfriends envy me for—but if he finds out I am out here with—

"Why is that, Little Phoenix?" Ethan's free hand lifts and cups the side of my face.

"Huh?" My mental spiral sent me off track.

"Why are you glad I came?" The soft curve of his mouth sends tingles all the way to my toes.

I hold his gaze. "I missed you."

What?

I have no idea where that came from. Let alone why I would confess such an intimate thought to a guy I haven't spoken more than a handful of words to. But I did...miss him. Despite all logic, I did. He had changed the game. Upped the stakes.

Ethan's lids shutter, and he sighs. I watch as his forehead scrunches and his mouth presses in a thin line. Not an angry line, but as if he is in pain. He drops his forehead to mine and blinks his eyes open. From this distance, we're both cross-eyed, but I ignore the uncomfortableness. I inhale his exhales. Disentangling my fingers from his, I reach around and place both my palms against his neck. My thumbs glide up and down, caressing his burning skin. I am doing this to him. His pulse throbs underneath my touch, and the rumble in his throat is the last push I need. I tip my chin up and cross the distance. My lips hover near his, the crackling in my veins making it hard to remain upright. Ethan hesitates only a second before he eliminates the last bit of space. My lips part in a moan, and his tongue enters mine without hesitation.

Oh my god.

Both his arms are now around me, and my fingers move to the back of his head, my nails scraping his scalp. Our kiss turns frantic, and Ethan walks me backward until I hit the side of the building. The brick hard against my shoulder blades, I arch my back. I don't want to crush his hands between me and the stone, but Ethan has a different idea. His palms glide toward my ass and cup my cheeks. I tighten my hold on him, and with one swift move, he lifts me up. My legs wind around his waist, and his hard length presses against my pussy.

I whimper as he grinds against my sensitive spot. My fingers curl into the strands of his hair, and I tug. A growl erupts in his throat, and I swivel my hips to meet his thrusts.

My tongue matches his strokes, and I grow wetter with every moment we're touching. His fingertips press into my exposed flesh where my shorts have ridden up, and I nip at his bottom lip.

Ethan pulls back a fraction. "If you don't stop this, I will fuck you against the wall of your father's diner, Phoenix."

I've never liked my red hair, but with him calling me that, it makes me feel desired and beautiful.

"What if I want you to fuck me?" I try to kiss him again, but Ethan pulls back farther and lets me slide down his body until my feet hit the ground. As soon as I'm stable, he recoils. Like literally recoils. His palm swipes across his face and lingers over his mouth. He turns and takes two steps before he halts. His hand drops to his side, and he hangs his head.

The heat he ignited in me gets snuffed out by his reaction, and insecurity burns its way to the surface. I bite the inside of my cheek, forcing my face to remain impassive as he slowly pivots around again.

"I'm sorry." His sincerity takes me off guard once more.

"For?" I keep my tone hard, refusing to let him hear the quiver that wants to make an appearance and show him what he did to me.

"I was selfish. I shouldn't have come." He rolls his lips under before continuing. "But I wanted to see you."

"Why?" I struggle to keep my composure. Conflicting emotions tear at me, and I'm between begging him to keep touching me and telling him to go fuck himself—or Jenn, if the rumors are true. Not that that stopped me a few minutes ago.

I don't have time for this. A few more months and I am done here. I will leave this town behind, go to college, and start fresh. I don't need the drama.

"I—" The always confident Ethan Davis stumbles over his words. "I have no idea. You're...you're different."

"Is that supposed to be a compliment or an insult?" I snarl.

He huffs a noncomical laugh. "Definitely a compliment."

He's giving me whiplash, and I don't like it. "So, you follow me, put your hands on me, disappear for nine days, then show up, attack me with your..." I gesture up and down his body, my words stuck in my throat. I refuse to compliment him on his freakishly hot physique. "And then you tell me you shouldn't have come. This was a mistake."

"I never said it was a mistake," he interrupts my irrational rant.

He has me bent so out of shape I feel like I am about to snap in half. "Then what was it?" I fling my hand between us.

Ethan peers toward the sky, interlacing his hands on top of his head.

We stand like this until I hear the back door creak open.

"Jules," Della whisper-shouts. "Your dad is looking for you."

The clang of metal indicates that she has rushed back inside, and I curse under my breath. I sidestep Ethan. I'm not ready to be done with him, with his lack of explanation, but if Dad finds us together, all hell will break loose.

Ethan's hand shoots out and grips my wrist. The anguish in his eyes chips away at the fury his back-and-forth has instilled in me.

"You're not a mistake, Little Phoenix. You're so far from a mistake, you have no idea." His words say everything and nothing, yet I can't stop myself. The draw he has on me is overpowering.

I bridge the gap and press my lips to his in a lightning kiss before whirling around and rushing inside.

CHAPTER FOUR

ETHAN

MY MIND IS REELING.

I don't remember how long I was rooted in the parking lot. Or how I completed the thirty-minute drive to the plantation.

Jules is a local. A Ren. She is Grant Arrow's daughter. We don't fuck where we eat. I could have any hole on the property, but all my dick wants is her, her green eyes gazing up at me as I wrap her red hair around my fist, and she takes me in until I hit the back of her throat. Blood rushes instantly to my cock, forcing me to shift in the driver's seat.

Not that that's the whole reason. She is different, though. I can't put my finger on it. The entire time I was gone, she invaded my thoughts. I wanted to see her. It was like a compulsion—made no sense.

But it got worse after the dream.

The dream.

My dick deflates like a balloon when you can't tie the knot fast enough and it slips out of your grasp. I pound the steering wheel with the heel of my hand until pain receptors fire up my forearm.

"FUUUCK!"

As soon as Poppy was taken care of and Jenn deemed the place clean, we hightailed it home. We left before the sun came up, switching off behind the wheel.

It was part of Corbin's and my routine. I wouldn't feel clean until I scrubbed myself raw in my own bathroom. It was all psychological, but I couldn't help it. I concluded a long time ago that it was my last shred of humanity breaking through—the one *he* hadn't been able to break.

At about the halfway mark, I declared I'd get some shut-eye.

I inserted my wireless headphones and pulled up a random playlist. "Satellites" by No Sleep for Lucy filled my ears, and the black void slowly pulled me under. I stopped dreaming when I was fifteen.

Until that day.

After my first kill, I woke up screaming for weeks, apprising the entire compound of my fragile mental state. Eventually, Marshall was fed up. He didn't take me in to raise a pussy—his words. One night, he dragged me out of bed, packed me in the car, and drove me to a place I will never forget. I've tried. It was the one visual that remained whenever I closed my eyes.

We drove for fourteen hours. When my father parked his SUV in front of a two-story, single-family structure, I hoped for a fraction of a second. Was he kicking me out? Was this some type of orphanage or foster home? The house looked like your average suburban residence.

We exited the car, and I waited for him to round the hood.

When he cuffed my arm and escorted me through the front door, all my hopes disintegrated. The inside was as inviting as a James Wan set, and to my utter horror, the man welcoming us could've been Jigsaw himself.

They led me down a flight of stairs where padded walls, floors, and ceilings with no window in sight sucked the air out of my lungs.

For two weeks, I was strapped to *the chair*. It reminded me of a dentist's office the first time Marshall escorted me into the room—though those usually didn't have restraints.

Every day, Marshall stood in the same corner, watching. My father rarely left the plantation unless a business deal required his presence, yet there he was, observing, as the man whose name I learned was Doctor Lakatos made me comply.

I was still in the sweats I wore the night Marshall kidnapped me from my bed. The smell of my piss dried into the cotton gagged me on more than one occasion. Saliva would pool in my mouth, and all I wanted was to spit. Anything but swallow the rancidness coating my tongue. I refused to give Marshall or Lakatos the satisfaction, though.

Since they didn't give me much food, I didn't have to worry about shitting my pants, at least. But the first thing I did whenever I got locked up for the night was strip. I'd curl up naked on top of the cot and count the cushioned tiles of my padded cell— there was no other word for it. The room was near freezing. Goose bumps would roll in waves up and down my shivering flesh. Freezing was better than enduring that smell one more minute. Every so often, a rush of heat would warm my insides— all I had to do was envision my father in the chair.

On day four—at least that was the day I thought we were at— my ankles and wrists were locked by leather restraints once again. A similar belt was across my chest, holding me immobile as I watched the man insert a needle into my arm. *Again.* He connected the daily IV filled with clear liquid. I had no idea what it was, but it wasn't to keep me hydrated. Satisfied with the placement, he reached for one of many syringes he had prepared on a metal tray. My muscles involuntarily tensed, and he clucked his tongue. "You need to relax, or it will hurt." He rarely spoke to me directly.

I wanted to laugh in his face, but the red haze in my vision was fast morphing into an obscuring fog. Shadows flitted across the walls, making my heart beat in my throat. The urge to fight against my hold was overpowering. I knew, though, that it was of no use. There was no escape, even if I was able to get out of the binds. A shadow was moving closer, whispers filling my ears. My pulse was thrashing so fast I couldn't breathe. All I could do was squeeze my eyes shut.

It's not real. It's not real. It's not real.

With my lids blacking out the hallucinations, I waited for the next step—the headphones. But when they didn't come, I slowly blinked, focusing on my tormentor and ignoring the shadow that whispered obscenities into my ear.

"Trust me, kid, you'll feel better when we're done. No more worries. No remorse."

The way the words had flown from his mouth, the smile held no sympathy. I was a test subject. Something to...take apart and piece back together. *Fixed*, as he called it during a chat with Marshall. They thought I had passed out.

"A few years ago, I treated a little girl, you know. *She* also didn't want to forget, but in the end, she understood that it was better for her. For everyone. Even for a six-year-old, she was smart. Why don't you stop resisting? We'll be done much quicker. And it will be a lot less painful for you."

At the mention of the girl, a flicker of interest appeared on Marshall's face, but I knew better than to inquire what this was about. Understanding of the inevitable crept through my veins. I wasn't leaving this place unless I was...*fixed*. As if a lever inside of me was slowly pulled down, my coiled muscles relaxed one by one. I held Marshall's impassive stare as numbness settled into every cell of my body. With the numbness came the void. The void drove the shadows away. They didn't have anything to latch on to. No fear, no...Ethan.

We never spoke about what happened at the house. The dreams stopped, and whenever I was on a job, that was all it was —an assignment. A task to check off.

Until the night I had my first dream in seven years.

I JOLTED awake in the passenger seat.

What the fuck was that?

The pounding in my ears drowned out my brother's voice. I turned slowly in his direction, the motion taking effort. My mind was stuck. What just happened? It couldn't have been a dream. Nightmare. I wasn't capable of dreaming. I blinked, making sure what I saw was there. Corbin's gaze flew between me and the road. We were going at least forty over the limit on a deserted stretch of highway. The speed never scared me. If anyone could handle a car at that velocity, it was Cor. What had me gasping for air were the images that played out in front of me when I had been...asleep.

But I can't dream.

"ETHAN!" His shout was audible, yet it sounded like I was underwater.

I faced forward again, unable to respond to my brother. The thundering rhythm in my chest resembled the time I had to run thirty minutes in a full sprint—for training purposes. Something collided with my cheek. Agony exploded across my face. My head snapped to the left, where Corbin still sat with his hand raised, flexing and unflexing the fist that was not keeping the car steady.

"What the fuck, asshole?" My fingers balled up.

If I retaliated right now, we'd be dead.

"WHAT THE FUCK IS WRONG WITH YOU?" I didn't remember my brother ever being this unsettled.

An image of green eyes flittered through my mind, and I leaned back against the headrest, forcing the bile back down my throat. "I don't know what you mean."

Corbin stomped on the brake, making his Mustang fishtail as we came to a screeching halt in the middle of the road. I got thrown forward, the seat belt biting into my shoulder, and I braced myself against the dash.

I counted to three before swiveling toward my brother. I was about to lay into him for his stunt but then narrowed my eyes. Corbin's eyes were wide, his nostrils flared. I scanned his posture. He was holding himself eerily still. The only thing moving was the rapid rise and fall of his chest.

"Cor?" My throat hurt. Why did my throat hurt?

"You screamed."

What?

"What the fuck are you talking about?" I peered out the windshield—anywhere but his face.

"You screamed," he repeated. His tone was low, detached.

Fuck.

I couldn't speak. I screamed out loud. That hadn't happened since...

I'm in Poppy's living room. Her head is slumped forward at an unnatural angle. She is still in the chair we tied her to. Corbin had held her down while I put the zip ties in place. Crimson pools on the white tarp covering the stained beige carpet. I scan the room. Where are Corbin and Jenn? They should be here.

In the background, "HOT DEMON B!TCHES NEAR U !!!" by CORPSE and Night Lovell plays on a barely audible volume, yet I can make out every word of the lyrics. My pulse accelerates. Cor and I never play music; that's T's kink. This is not what happened.

Where are they?

Movement in my peripheral vision catches my attention, and I pivot on my heels. Poppy rolls her shoulders back. How the fuck is she moving? Jenn slit her throat. She is dead.

Poppy's head slowly lolls to one side, then to the other. More blood gushes from the wound, reaching from one ear to the other.

A whimper reaches my ears, and after taking in my surroundings once more, I realize it came from my mouth. I clench my jaw to swallow any involuntary sound. My lungs feel like a knife slicing through them. I can't breathe as I watch Poppy jerkily sit up straight. Her bones crack, mending what we broke. The sound is too loud, like it's amplified, and I sway in place, balling my hands.

Her blonde hair is caked with dried blood from the head wound I gave her when I forced my way in.

Nothing makes sense.

The background noise switches to "Vendetta" by UNSECRET and Krigarè. The moment the chorus starts, Poppy's head snaps up, and her eyes fly open.

NO!

Something materializes in my closed fist, and I lift my hand into my line of sight. No, no, no. Uncurling my fingers, something sticky drips from the edge of my palm. I choke on a gag, forcing the vomit back down.

The black orbs in her skull peer at me as she tilts her head. An unnatural sneer forms on Poppy's face. "What's wrong, Ethan? Take a look. I dare you. Everything you touch will die." She cackles at the last word, and I finally peer down.

A guttural scream bursts from my lungs as I stare at a pair of dark-

green eyes sitting in my palm. Poppy's eyes were brown. There is only one person with eyes the color of moss. My gaze flies back to the chair, and instead of Poppy, I find...Jules.

NOOOOOOOO!

"I HAD A DREAM."

Corbin's mouth opened and closed several times before finally stating the obvious. "You don't dream."

I couldn't look at him. "I know."

My brother was at a loss for words. A car zoomed by, honking and reminding us that we were in the middle of a highway.

A growl erupted in his throat. He glanced at me before putting the Mustang in drive and hitting the gas pedal, the roar of the engine causing a deafening sound.

We drove for several miles before he spoke again. "Father can't know."

I snorted. "No shit, asshole."

Corbin had no clue what happened during the two weeks I was gone. The fact that I stopped dreaming after my return and never refused an assignment was self-explanatory.

He side-eyed me but remained mute. After the seventh time, I frowned at him. "What?"

My brother wasn't the touchy-feely type. Neither of us was. There was no room for weakness in our line of work. Feelings were a weakness. It might as well have been branded into our flesh as many times as I heard the sentence growing up.

"Do you want to talk about it?"

In truth, he probably had no desire to listen to the details of my sudden instability. It compromised him the same way as it did me.

"Nah, I'm good." I plastered a smirk on my face that made

my cheeks hurt. "Probably a one-time thing." I added a shoulder shrug to convince myself as much as him.

A crease formed between his brows, but his eyes didn't stray from the road.

The five of us could read each other without visual connection.

Corbin cataloged my words, my posture...everything without ever making eye contact.

Eventually, he nodded his head. "OK."

AN HOUR LATER, we switched off. Cor folded his arms across his chest and closed his eyes. He didn't bother with headphones. My brother didn't allow for distractions—nothing that could potentially compromise him. For the first time since we were thrown together and became family, I felt sorry for him.

With him resting (I knew better than to think he was asleep), I let my mind wander.

What was that? Why now? Was it because Jules had become a distraction? Because she made me...feel?

Jules had pulled me in from the moment I laid eyes on her. Her flaming red hair reminded me of the depiction of a phoenix.

Growing up, I didn't read traditional children's books. I vaguely recalled two kids, a pail of water, and a chick named Maggy or Mary with a goat. Or was it a sheep? But that was while I was in the orphanage. Marshall's library didn't contain any of that. Instead, it was stocked with ancient texts, history of all sorts, but Greek mythology was his main fascination. One text specifically captured my attention from the moment I was able to decipher the words. It talked about how a phoenix had prayed to Apollo, the god of light, for strength when it felt old age upon itself. Apollo rewarded him with rebirth through fire in its full youth. I always associated the story with myself, how Marshall gave me a new life.

Until Jules.

"LET'S GO SEE SAVANNA," Corbin drawled after we unloaded our cargo and handed it to the local cleaner. He would confirm everything and eliminate any traces we may have missed. Not that we ever missed anything. Marshall had trained us better than that.

The thought of double-teaming Sav should have gotten me hard in seconds. She never said no to us and always gave us a good time. She was my go-to when Jenn wasn't around to let off some steam. Today, though, all I did was stare at my brother.

The rest of the drive, I repeated the same two sentences over and over in my head: *It was a dream. It wasn't real.* Yet, the taut feeling in my midsection wouldn't go away. I had to see for myself. Make sure Jules was safe—as safe as she could ever be with me.

Corbin's brows rose, and a sneer crept across his face. "Don't, E."

He knew what I was about to do. What I needed. *Who* I wanted. He had every right to be livid with me. I was playing a dangerous game.

My pulse slowed as acceptance settled in. Slowly, I turned and headed for my SUV.

"ETHAN!" Corbin barked.

I didn't stop.

CHAPTER FIVE

ETHAN

TWO TAPS AGAINST MY WINDOW SNAP ME OUT OF THE LOOP playing in front of my mind's eye.

I can still feel the weight of Jules's legs wrapped around my hips, rubbing her heat against my dick. I pictured her lips so many times. Though, nothing compared to the reality of feeling her mouth on mine, her tongue... I lean my head against the headrest.

I'm fucked.

Turning sideways, I meet my brother's gaze. An emotion I rarely find on his face has replaced his earlier anger: worry.

Prickling slithers across my scalp. Unbuckling, I push the door open, forcing Corbin back. I remove my P320 Nitron Compact from its magnet under the dash and put it in its sheath on the back of my jeans.

We are never to be without our weapons, but the chance of Jules discovering the gun on me was too risky. I disobeyed two of our cardinal orders tonight.

"Did you fuck her?" His question isn't laced with the anger I expected.

I square off with him. "No."

He jerks his head in a nod and pivots, stalking through the door to the house. His lack of...response(?), action(?), beating my face in(?) for defying the rules we've been brainwashed to follow makes the walls of the garage inch closer.

I head into the kitchen and grab several cans of Jenn's iced coffee drinks. This will be a sleepless night. I can't risk another dream until my crackling nerves have settled down.

If Jenn were here, I would seek her out. She'd ensure I wouldn't alert the property of my *in*sanity slipping. But she and T aren't expected back until morning.

"You did good, son." Marshall squeezes my shoulders as we're lined up in his office.

It's eleven a.m., and I lock my jaw to stifle the yawn that fights its way out. T and Jenn got back around six and now stand to my right with their hands folded behind their backs. Corbin positioned himself to my left with Paycen at his other side, mirroring the stance. Taking in the lack of expression on my little brother sends pinpricking shudders down my spine. No one at his age should be this...cold.

T has already delivered his report, what he was able to find out during his quick trip up north. This assignment will take several more visits over the next months. I'm not privy to the details of this mission, and my brother isn't going to tell.

The vibration of Jenn's toes tapping against the floor travels across the hardwood and itches the soles of my feet. Scanning the air around her, I narrow my eyes. She's unusually twitchy.

Marshall steps in front of Corbin. "Was the package delivered?"

Package.

The scene of my nightmare flitters across my vision, and I flinch. Thankfully, my slip escapes Marshall, but in my peripheral vision, Jenn tilts her head as if listening to my thoughts. Her eyes remain forward, appearing unbothered to the untrained observer. Sometimes, I wish we weren't all so in tune with each other. Or maybe our bond is this strong because we also share an...intimate connection. Or she's just a girl. Girls have a sixth sense for shit like that.

"Yes, sir. She took receipt of the package. The message was delivered," Corbin states, impassive.

Our father nods approvingly. "Excellent. Let's hope she has learned from her mentor's lapse in judgment."

He strides across the room and lowers himself into the leather chair behind his desk. Interlacing his hands on top, he pins us down one by one. "You five are here to set an example."

Where the hell is he going with this?

"It is imperative that you are always vigilant. If you notice anyone"—his gaze settles on me—"and I mean anyone, disobeying *The Order*, you are to immediately report back to me. Understood?"

My heartbeat slows as I hold Marshall's stare.

Does he know I went to see Jules?

"Yes, sir," all five of us respond in unison. We've been through this drill more times than I've taken a shit in my twenty-two years of life.

He dips his chin. We know better than to move before being dismissed, but the need to leave sends tremors through my legs.

"Jenn, I'd like a word."

My sister stops breathing, and T stiffens on her other side. I shift a fraction, my arm pressing against Jenn's, and she slashes her lips.

"The rest of you can go. Paycen, I got you the set of scalpels you wanted. Go play." At the wordplay, a wave of nausea rolls through me. "Boys, a new shipment arrived while you were gone. Make sure everything gets sighted properly and inventoried into the armory."

This is our cue. I throw my sister a curious look, but she refuses to meet my gaze.

I DON'T SEE Jenn for the rest of the day. T, Cor, and I spend most of it on the range at the back of the property before cleaning and inventorying the various rifles.

When Jenn is still absent at dinner, concern begins to eat its way through my core.

I meet T's eyes across the table, but he shakes his head imperceptibly.

What the fuck?

I force down the rest of the meal, not tasting a bite but also refusing to draw Marshall's attention. The moment we're excused, I race after my brother through the house. He's halfway to his twin's room when I catch up enough to wrap my fingers around his bicep. Latching on, I whirl him around.

"What is going on? Where is J?" I whisper-shout at him. The muscles in my neck strain as I quickly peer over my shoulder.

A mask of fury and concern settles on his features, and he tilts his head in the direction of our bedrooms. "Let's go."

I release my hold and trail him. With every step, my body grows tauter. Reaching our destination, T raps his knuckles against the door once before pushing his way inside.

The room is shrouded in darkness, the blackout curtains drawn. I blink, adjusting to the lack of light. I find Jenn curled on top of her comforter, knees pulled to her chest, one arm wrapped around her shins, the other clutching something to her chest.

My mouth goes dry, and I'm by her side in two strides, kneeling in front of the mattress. Her gaze is void of anything; she stares right through me. Theo toes his shoes off by the heel before padding around the bed and climbing behind his twin. His arm comes around her, and her eyes flutter closed. I watch as she bites her lower lip, but she can't keep it from trembling.

Unlacing my boots, I position myself on Jenn's front. Her eyes spring open as the mattress dips, and a lone tear rolls down her blotchy cheek. She's been crying. My sister doesn't cry.

A weight settles in my stomach, and I swipe the moisture away with my thumb. Letting my fingers rest on her neck, I caress her jaw as we wait for her to speak.

"Marshall sent Kroy to the Institute," she whispers.

Oh, fuck no.

The Institute is *The Order's* facility outside of New York, where the ones that don't conform to the rules are sent. The Institute will make you. Break you. *Train* you.

I didn't learn about the place until after returning from Lakatos. It was the only question Corbin asked me before we pretended my two-week *vacay* ever happened. "Did he take you to the Institute?"

My blank stare was the answer he needed. If I thought what the memory doctor did to me was bad, I was proven wrong when Marshall brought us to the facility a few years ago. It was a lesson, as he called it, to ensure his children wouldn't make the same mistakes others had.

THEO, Corbin, and I rotate staying with Jenn.

The loss of Kroy cut her deep. Where she and I are bound by family (and lust), Jenn and Kroy have—*had* a different connection. The only male outside of her siblings she allowed to see *her*. He wasn't like the rest of us, though—another orphan. Yet

Marshall hadn't taken him in as he did with me. He was just one of many executioners living on the property until he was permanently sent out into the world to do our father's bidding.

Jenn refused to tell us what made Marshall take such a drastic measure. In all my years here, I had never heard of anyone actually being sent to the Institute. The visit and threat are enough to force compliance.

Between taking care of Jenn and going through the motions, I haven't been able to see Jules. Every time her name touches my mind, a tingling sensation spreads from my lips to my groin.

It's T's time with his sister, and I'm leaning against the headboard of my bed. One leg hangs off the mattress, my foot resting lightly on the floor, while my ankle of the other is crossed over my knee. Next to me on the bed lays my Wild Bill. My thumb strokes back and forth over the bit. I sharpened the blade earlier, and a small cut begins to split the pad of my finger, yet I don't feel anything. I watch the red droplets staining the comforter. Nothing.

After dinner, Corbin pulled us aside. We needed to find a way to snap Jenn out of her catatonic state, or Marshall would send her next. It had been days. Our father was growing impatient.

I reach over to the nightstand and pick up my phone. I haven't allowed myself to look up Jules Arrow. She goes to the local high school—a senior. But that's where I drew the line. I stare at my screen—a random picture from the gallery that came with the device. Our phones are for communication only. We switch devices and numbers regularly. If Marshall ever found personal photos on them, he'd put us in *the pen* for a week—if we're lucky. The pen is what everyone calls the converted cattle pens, a.k.a. my father's personal torture chambers, on the property. Marshall's rules are commands. He is *The Davis Order*.

I unlock the phone and tap on the browser icon. Hesitating

one more second, I navigate to Instagram. Everyone has social media, right? (Besides my family.) Typing her name in the search bar, a rush of adrenaline surges through me. The possibility of seeing her face other than in my memory is a whole new rush—*if* her profile is public.

A string of usernames loads on the screen, but I recognize hers immediately. The buzzing sensation has me sitting up straight. I click on the name, and all I can do is stare as desire takes hold of every fiber in my body. In her profile picture, her fiery waves cover half of her face. She peers down at the camera with her lips pursed. An itch to feel her soft locks causes the fingers of my free hand to tremble. Beginning to scroll, I pause at the first set. It's a group of photos taken on the same day. Tapping on the first, it shows Jules and her friend Della. I've observed them enough at the diner to know they're close. Their arms are slung over each other's shoulders, laughing and flipping the camera off. The caption reads, *Party time, bitches!!!* My gaze lowers to the time stamp: today. An hour ago, to be precise. I swipe my thumb upward, and the next photo is a selfie. Jules has a sultry look on her face, and her dark eye makeup stands in stark contrast to how she dresses to serve food. Blood rushes to my cock. The third photo, though, evokes a different reaction. I have no idea who took it. Della, maybe? My girl hangs over a soon-to-be-dead guy's shoulder in a football jersey. His hands are on her ass and thigh, and her arms hug his waist. Reading underneath the photo, I have my confirmation that Della had something to do with this. The question is why, though?

"Since J doesn't want to take him back, he takes what he 'believes' is his.
XOXO"

I SCAN all three pictures for where they could be. I don't know anyone in town and definitely don't get invited to random parties. But as luck (or Della) might have it, the one with the fuckwad in it has a location tagged.

Bingo.

Pushing off the mattress, I swipe my keys from my desk.

Believes what's his. Right.

If he so much as lays another finger on my girl, I will break all twenty-seven—scratch that, fifty-four bones in his hands one by one. I could even venture to his feet. A hammer is such an effective option to shatter toes. Slicing them off with a rusty, dull knife would then increase the chance of sepsis. By the time I cross through the gates of the plantation ten minutes later, my mind has conjured up several more alternatives to drive my point home that Jules is mine.

Exiting the property requires a several-mile trek through the swamp. Anyone accidentally driving onto our land would never suspect what lies at the end of the two-mile driveway.

I pass the parking lot for the lake. The bonfires along the small beach illuminate the sand in circular halos. I picture clashing my fist into the football player's teeth before throwing Jules over my shoulder and dragging her out of there. Her existence has unhinged my life, causing me to consider exposure for the sheer satisfaction of claiming what's mine.

I slow the Bronco and swerve over to the pullout lining the road. Opening the door, I glide my fingers over the cool metal of my Nitron, ensuring it's in place before locking the Bronco. Once again, I disobey our never-be-unarmed rule. But what's a group of high schoolers going to do? Or, more importantly, what will I do if I find the douche's hands still on my girl?

My girl. That's the second time the term has entered my mind tonight.

The walk doesn't take more than a few minutes, and I

approach the scene from a group of trees. My pulse steadily pumps blood through my veins, my earlier thirst for inflicting pain giving way to what I was trained to do: observe before striking. Remaining in the shadows, I scan the area.

The bass from "No Good" by Morten shakes the sand, and I watch every girl's tits bounce in their skimpy bikinis as they jump up and down. Some still wear shorts, but I see no shirts on any of them. The guys have a similar lack of clothing. I spot shorts and swim trunks but nothing up top. Despite the late hour, it makes sense. The current heat wave keeps the temperature above eighty, even at night. Droplets of sweat begin to form on my temple, and I regret not changing into shorts before rushing out. My tee clings to my chest already.

I let my gaze wander further over the dancers and decide that I don't have a choice but to go closer if I want any chance of finding Jules. I remain outside of the glow of the pyres, making sure to stay in the dark. I don't think any of these kids have ever seen a Davis up close, and my presence would certainly be a reason to gossip.

Suddenly, someone materializes at my side, and I instinctively reach behind me, remembering too late that I left my gun in the car.

"You got my message."

Huh?

I stare down at Della Greystone. I'm rarely speechless, but this five-foot-*maybe*-three-inch girl just caught me off guard. Besides my siblings, no one manages to sneak up on me. But maybe I shouldn't be surprised.

When she raises a brow at my arm lingering at my lower back, I let my hand drop back to my side.

Finally finding my words, I cock my head. "Care to explain?"

The little blonde props her fists on her hips and puffs her chest out. The girl has guts. I like it.

"Well, since you up and left for nine days after basically assaulting my best friend at work, then you showed back up out of the blue and dry-humped her before pulling a Houdini again, it was time to smoke you out."

The groove between my brows deepens.

She throws her arms up. "Oh, come on, Davis. I watched you at the diner. While you may have your *sister*"—she makes air quotes around the word—"between your legs, you only have eyes for J."

She pokes me against the chest. Seriously pokes me. The last person to touch me uninvited lost his finger, yet I stand here in the middle of a high school beach party and let this chick berate me.

I fold my arms, parting my lips, but she cuts me off.

"You have Jules bent all out of shape. Until two weeks ago, her sole focus was to leave this place behind. Now, whenever the door opens, you'd think she got tasered the way she jerks toward the sound. Not to mention her disappointment when she realizes it's not you."

Jules has been waiting? For me?

Della catches her breath, and I take it as my opportunity to finally get a word in. "So, you orchestrated the groping, hoping I would find out about it?" I still can't believe her words. "You remember what I do for a living, right?"

She tilts her chin up. "Meh. I didn't expect you to show up here, maybe at the diner at some point this week, but—"

A squeal interrupts her, and we both turn in the direction of the commotion. Jules is running from the same—now also shirtless—asshole that had her earlier. I recognize him now. Ty Morello. She's laughing, liquid sloshing over the rim of her red Solo cup. He catches up and wraps his arm around her, pinning her immobile.

I inhale a coarse breath, the air filling my lungs with needles.

"Ty is her ex," Della's voice absently registers.

My head slowly moves back to her, and my brows pull up.

"They never fit," she explains with her eyes still on the two. "Ty is a Ren, through and through. He wants to stay local and settle as soon as he takes over his dad's shop after college. For as long as I've known her, Jules's goal has been to get as far away as possible." Della sighs, facing me. "He still has hopes, though."

Hopes I will squash like the kneecap of job number forty-seven.

Relaxing my jaw, I let the corners of my mouth quirk up. "And what do you want me to do?"

She chews on her lip for a moment before saying, "Make her happy."

We pivot in synchrony and watch as Jules swats at *Ty*. They talk, but she sidesteps his attempt when he tries to draw her back in. She shakes her head, the playful mood gone. The ex argues something, and I expect Jules to get upset. Instead, she places a hand on his shoulder and speaks calmly until he hangs his head. I want to feel sorry for the guy, but I don't.

Jules swivels in the sand and walks toward the edge of the lake, away from everyone.

A small hand gives me a shove. "There is your chance, Davis."

The command is masked behind her genuine smile, and I can't be upset about being tricked into coming here. I was outsmarted.

I dip my chin and make my way toward the water, careful never to step into the glow of the light.

CHAPTER SIX

JULES

MY FEET DIP INTO THE PISS-WARM WATER. NOT EVEN THE lake is refreshing with these sauna temperatures. Droplets of sweat run down my spine.

It took every ounce of self-control not to lash out at Ty. What the hell was he thinking? The last thirty minutes play on a loop in my mind. I crack my thumb with my curled fingers, the ache briefly stopping the twitch in my muscles. He won't give up. I get it; we've known each other all our lives. If I had any interest in staying in this godforsaken town, we'd be the perfect match. Our families have been friends forever. We had fun. And I played along earlier, but I can only handle—

"Going for a swim?"

I whirl around, spilling the rest of my beer in the process. My jaw drops as I take in what has to be a hallucination. I peer down at my now empty cup and back up. My heart hammers in my throat, my thrashing pulse mingling with euphoria and panic.

Did someone spike my drink?

Ethan chuckles. I glance down once more, taking stock. I feel fine, maybe a bit tipsy, but not...drugged. And I'm not tripping.

I've been craving his nearness since I left him standing behind the diner. His kiss had burned itself into my brain. Ethan strides forward, and my eyes track his biceps moving under his black shirt. My teeth sink into my bottom lip as I watch his throat bob.

"Don't do that." His hand finds its way into my hair, and his fingers thread into the waves. He angles my head, forcing me to shift my focus. His demand is clear.

"Don't do what?" I challenge. A different kind of intoxication quickly replaces the buzz from the few beers.

Ethan narrows his eyes. "Don't play games with me, Little Phoenix."

The way his voice lowers possesses my body to squirm. Heat shoots to my core, and I rub my thighs together. The motion doesn't escape him, conjuring a devilish smirk to his lips. I fight the urge to close the distance. Ethan Davis is the most dangerous drug of all. He makes me feel things no one should be capable of. Emotions I shouldn't want to feel. It gives him the power to keep me here, abandoning the plan that has kept me going for years.

He releases my hair, and I miss the slight sting instantly. His hand cups my cheek, his gaze cataloging everything like this is the last time he'll see me.

"I shouldn't be here."

All the air gets sucked out of my lungs, and I recoil.

How dare he do this again.

Ethan reaches for me, but I shrug out of his grasp. My knees threaten to buckle, and I scan our surroundings. For what? I'm not sure. He catches my retreat, latching on to my upper arms. His grip is ironclad. A voice in the back of my head whispers,

There is no escape from Ethan Davis—not if he doesn't want you to leave.

The thought should scare me. It doesn't.

When I don't fight, he loosens his hold. His palms glide up until they settle on either side of my neck, the path searing into my flesh, permanently burning the sensation into my brain.

"I didn't mean it that way." He lowers his forehead to mine. I cuff his wrists with my fingers, unable to control my body's need to touch him. We stand hidden in the shadows, covered by the blanket of night. I breathe in his exhale, and the flutter in my stomach expands through every limb.

Music and voices from the party travel through the air. I hear my name. *Ty.* He is looking for me. Fucking shit. Ethan's spine stiffens, and his entire demeanor morphs into something new. His gentleness is gone, and icy fear fills my chest. Not for me, but for my ex. I swallow over the sudden dizziness.

Ethan's breath speeds up, sending warmth across my skin. Dropping one hand, I touch it to the side of his face. "Let's go."

His eyes dart over to my group of friends. He doesn't hear me.

"Ethan."

Ethan's shoulders draw back, and I feel the tips of his fingers press into my flesh. He's zeroed in on his target. I follow his line of sight. Ty walks at the edge of the group, searching our classmates for me. I need to do something. Taking his chin between my thumb and forefinger, I force Ethan's attention back to me.

I let my thumb caress his sharp cheekbone. "Ethan. Baby, look at me."

His focus finally shifts, and when his caramels connect with mine, recognition flashes through them.

"Let's go," I repeat before pressing a featherlight kiss against his jaw. It's the first time I notice that he hasn't shaved. My heart stutters. Something happened. That's why he stayed away again. The realization hits me like a freight train.

Ethan and I have formed a connection that makes no sense given the little interaction we share. Yet, it's there.

Fire flares in the depths of his eyes, and I lean in once more, unable to restrain myself. The kiss instantly changes to a feverish level. I part my lips, and Ethan takes my invitation. Our tongues move in sync, and he draws me closer. Intertwining my arms behind his neck, I let myself fall—metaphorically speaking. Ethan has taken hold of my soul, and the knowledge settles that there will be no one else like him. Ever.

He pulls back, inviting a fraction of space between us. A whimper of protest rasps my throat, light-headedness making it hard to concentrate. Ethan shakes his head, and the way he drinks me in sends my pulse into a frenzy. This is the real Ethan, not the unattainable version he shows the world. *My Ethan.*

His hands drop, and he reaches behind me. Freeing my tank top from where I secured it through the belt loop of my shorts, he arches a brow. I scowl, not understanding. His eyes flick toward the party, and possessiveness flares in their depths.

Oh.

If this were anyone else, I would sucker punch him in the nose for such Neanderthal behavior, but my pussy has a different opinion on the matter. *We* relish the knowledge that Ethan craves us in a way that urges him to violence. Danger and desire run alongside each other.

Despite hating the feel of the cotton on my sticky skin, I pull the fabric over my head. Ethan nods approvingly and interlaces our hands. Without another word, he leads me away from the party and through a small group of trees. Fluttering whispers urge me to ask where we're going. There is nothing but swamp out here. One wrong step and you end up in a sinkhole or, worse, get your leg snapped off by one of the predators.

Which predator is worse, though?

Ethan squeezes my fingers as if sensing my conflict. "My car is right through here."

Oh.

Sure enough, just a few more steps and his Bronco comes into view. Familiarity numbs the mistrust toward the Davis family that has been ingrained into me for as long as I can remember. Tightness in my chest gives way to weightlessness, and I watch Ethan unlock the car. Opening the door, a jolt shoots through me when I let him help me climb in.

"Jeez, what's the lift of this thing?" I joke, not wanting him to see the whiplash of emotion I don't understand myself.

A boyish grin spreads across his face that radiates nothing but pride. "She has a four-inch lift with thirty-five-inch tires."

His excitement for such a simple thing is contagious. I lean back out and capture his mouth one more time. "Let's go."

Ethan cocks a brow but doesn't object. He throws the door shut, and I jump at the explosive noise. When he gets in on the driver's side, he apologizes, "It's warped. It won't close any other way."

The Bronco roars to life. Literally. The sound of the engine is deafening, and the vibration sends tingling from my feet all the way to my head.

"Where are we going?"

Ethan peers over before focusing back on the narrow road. When he doesn't speak, unease begins to simmer and replaces the excitement. Have I made a mistake? Has lust overshadowed the danger I've put myself in?

"Ethan?" I don't like the quiver in my voice.

His left hand takes over the steering wheel, and his right settles on my exposed thigh. "I want to show you something."

"Where?"

He doesn't answer at first, and I'm about to repeat myself. "Not far, maybe ten more minutes."

My racing heartbeat slows. Ten minutes. A map of the area forms in my mind, and I go over all the possible spots within that radius of the lake. There is nothing but swamp and more swamp. Even getting back into town is farther.

Exhilaration to be alone with Ethan and panic that he brought me out here to kill me spin circles in my head. There is a reason no one in town ever sees them. They don't associate with locals. Ethan is different, though. He isn't like Corbin. Is he? I should've let Della know I left. How long would it take her to start looking for—

Ethan jerks the wheel and pulls off the road. What the—? I lean forward in my seat, my internal hysteria forgotten. The headlights illuminate a narrow dirt path, and we pass several "private property" and "do not enter" signs. Where the fuck are we? He drives another minute or two before stopping the SUV and putting it into park. He kills the lights, and I suck in a breath. In front of us is a small lake I had no idea existed. The moon turns the tranquil water into a silver mirror.

"What is this place?" I breathe in awe.

Water around here is so murky it sucks in all the light, not reflecting it back. On the far end, a group of fireflies hovers. It's...magical.

Ethan exits and rounds the hood. He watches me, and with each step, the seed of doubt that attempted to plant itself into my mind evaporates. The hum in my chest expands until every fiber of my body is buzzing.

Opening my door, he holds out a hand. The instant I place my palm in his, an electric current rushes through me. Every-thing is right again.

My feet hit the ground, and Ethan winds an arm around my midsection. Pulling me close, he captures my mouth with his.

The kiss is a promise of what's to come, and the hair on my arms stands. Lingering with his lips against mine, his free hand reaches behind the passenger seat and reveals a tattered blanket. Releasing me, he clasps my hand, and I follow him to the edge of the lake. I'm convinced he can hear the drumming of my heart in the quiet of the night.

"Make sure to follow in my footsteps."

"Okay," I whisper. Speaking at a normal volume feels wrong.

I watch him shake out the blanket, and he motions for me to sit. A phone materializes from his back pocket, and Ethan taps on the screen. A random song fills the air, and he positions himself behind me, winding his arms around my stomach. His hands find their way under the hem of my shirt, caressing my skin. With every new swipe of his calloused fingers, shivers run like waves up and down my spine.

Resting his chin on my shoulder, he explains, "The pond is artificially made. The bottom is lined, which is why there is no moss and shit on the surface."

"And shit?" I can't help but giggle at his choice of words. Sometimes I forget that he is just a few years older, because of how he carries himself—with the weight of the world on him.

Ethan chuckles. "Yeah, swimming in mud sucks big hairy monkey balls."

"So poetic," I cackle. Craning my neck, I want to see his face when I ask, "Why would you swim in mud?"

Placing a kiss against my neck, he draws me closer to his chest, yet it's not close enough. Goose bumps prick on my exposed flesh.

"We're on the far end of my father's plantation. He had the lake built a few years back for us to train."

"Train?" *Wha*— A groove forms between my brows.

"You are the first person who doesn't live here to set foot on this land. If my father finds out...there will be consequences."

Consequences? I blink rapidly.

"I come here when I need to think. When I want to be alone." He remains still for a moment. "It's...peaceful."

"And it's not peaceful at home?" Why am I asking this?

Ethan snorts but doesn't grace me with a reply. "You won't find my brothers and sister here unless we do drills. Swim, dive, navigate through water."

The line on my forehead begins to pucker it's so deep.

Ethan keeps talking, more to himself than to me. "There are certain tactics you can't practice in a pool. But the swamp is too risky. We have several alligators on the property. One of them, Frank, likes to move around. I swear he does it on purpose to fuck with Marshall. He doesn't come here, though."

I'm fascinated by his words. Then it sinks in. I am on Marshall Davis's property. Holy shit. My father is going to kill me if he finds out.

He won't find out.

I swallow over my impending doom at home and ask, "Why do you have to train in water?"

"All kinds of circumstances. We never know what situation we'll be put in."

"You talk like you're in the military."

A sad smile forms on his lips. "Something like that."

Our eyes meet, and I understand I won't get anything else from him. He has already revealed more than anyone else has ever been privy to.

My throat closes. Ethan trusts me.

I shift between his legs so my shoulder leans against his chest. Lifting my hand, I trail the side of his face with the tips of my fingers. "Thank you for showing me this place."

A softness overtakes his features. "You make me feel things I never thought I was capable of."

Heaviness weighs on my chest. "That's...sad."

"Let's not talk about me anymore." His face inches closer, but he doesn't bridge the gap.

"Okay," I murmur, leaning in farther. I sense his lips without making the connection. The flutter behind my ribs becomes painful with anticipation. We've kissed before, but this is different. He's given me a part of himself no one else has ever seen.

"What am I going to do with you, Little Phoenix?" He tilts his head ever so slightly, brushing our lips together.

"Whatever you want," my reply comes out like a moan.

CHAPTER SEVEN

ETHAN

WHATEVER YOU WANT. JESUS FUCK.

My control snaps. I crash my mouth to hers. Jules parts her lips, and our tongues collide headlong into a ravishing dance of sensory overload. She shifts to her knees, and her fingers dive into my hair, tugging the strands. Tension strains in my jeans. I can't stop the rumble of approval filling in my chest.

Gripping the backs of her thighs, I guide her to straddle my lap. She complies without hesitation, rolling her hips forward, and I groan as the friction amplifies the heat between us, urging my need for her to a new level.

Squeezing the soft flesh underneath her ass, I trail around to her front, only allowing the tips of my fingers to connect with her skin, the lightness of my touch resulting in a protesting whimper.

I invert my hand. The slight drag of my short nails slowly strokes up the inside of her leg until finding their destination at the seam of her panties. Or bikini bottoms. Whatever still covers her pussy under her barely existent shorts. Where her minimal clothing nearly sent me into a rage earlier—the thought of her dipshit ex touching her—it now allows me the access I've craved since I first had her body pressed against mine in the hallway of the diner.

I hook my fingers into the fabric, stretching it aside, and cup her with the other. Jules moans, desire flashing in her eyes, like throwing gasoline in an already blazing inferno. She thrusts against my palm, and the moment her hips roll back, I sink two fingers into her heat.

"Fuck. So wet, Little Phoenix." What I wouldn't give right now to replace my fingers with my cock.

"Oh, my god, yes. More." Her whimper cuts off with the feverish fight of our mouths.

The pounding behind my ribs intensifies at her command. My erection throbs, demanding to be inside of her. Instead of taking what I want, I give her what she asked for. I thrust a third finger between her folds, and Jules cries out.

"The Saint and The Sinner" by AViVA fills the air as Jules coats my hand with her arousal. I continue to pump in and out while pressing the heel of my hand against her sensitive spot. Her movements become frantic, and I withdraw. Flipping her over, I cage her between my forearms.

"I thought I was supposed to do what *I* want with you." I smirk as I flick my tongue along her jaw to her ear. "The question is, what do I want?" I let my tone drop to the level I've noticed she likes.

Jules trembles.

I continue, "I don't do gentle. Never learned how, Little Phoenix. I don't want to ruin you." I thrust my hips forward, and she whimpers.

Suddenly, she lifts her chin and surprises me. Tilting her head ever so slightly, she says, "I'm already ruined. I want you to be the one to break me."

My heart stutters in my chest, and I'm momentarily frozen in place. She is already ruined? What the fuck does that mean?

Then Jules touches her fingers to either side of my face. "Stop thinking, Ethan. The past and future don't matter. We're here, you and me."

"Waking Up" by MJ Cole and Freya Ridings plays in the background. I search her face for answers, but she shakes her head imperceptibly.

The past and future don't matter.

Sitting back on my haunches, I reach behind and pull my shirt over my head. Letting it drop beside us, I quirk a brow. She wants to be in charge, then let's see what she's got.

Her body is an invitation unto itself. Her parted legs rest on either side of me. Her shirt has ridden up, exposing the underside of her bikini top and her red hair fans over the blanket. She sinks her teeth into her bottom lip, and I groan. Propping herself on her elbows, Jules studies my body.

"Strip, Davis."

I bark out a laugh, but the exhilaration of her telling me what to do has my fingers reaching for the button of my jeans.

"Actually..."

I halt and watch as she climbs to her knees. I shift to mirror her position. What is she going to do?

Jules pops the button and pulls the zipper down. My heart hammers in my chest as she reaches inside my jeans and pulls me free. The pressure of my cock finally unrestrained is both exhilarating and heady at the same time. It is almost too much. I hiss through my teeth and have to bite the inside of my cheek. Her small hand strokes my shaft, moving up and down in a rhythm that feels like the limits of my body are already pushed beyond its capacity and will. When she reaches the tip, her thumb swipes around the head, rubbing my precum into the movement.

Hypersensitive to her touch, I groan, and Jules peers up innocently. Before I comprehend what's happening, she drops down, propping herself on the hand that's not gripping me. Without breaking eye contact, she takes me in her mouth, and my eyes flutter back.

"Oh fuck." My hand finds its way into her hair, wrapping a thick strand around my palm until I have a tight hold. Her saliva coats my length, the warmth of her mouth a sensation like no other. I guide her forward and back, forcing her to take me all the way. Her eyes widen as I hit the back of her throat, but she doesn't let up. Instead, she sucks faster while pumping and twisting her hand on my dick in a frenzied corkscrew motion.

"Yesss, just like that, Little Phoenix." She presses her tongue against the underside of my cock and moves her hand to my balls, massaging them with expert motion.

As overwhelming as the temptation, I use my hold on her hair to pull away. Coming now, like this, is not how I want this moment to end.

She settles on her heels and wipes her mouth with her thumb. "What's the matter, baby?"

Her sultry tone mocks me. I narrow my eyes, contemplating what to do. *To* her. I didn't exaggerate; I have no clue how to do vanilla. My first time was with one of Marshall's many mistresses when I barely knew the use of my dick for anything other than taking a leak. She taught me what she liked, and not knowing that there was any other way, I complied. A few years later, Jenn took her place. Claiming Jenn, no one else on the plantation was allowed to touch her. And while I never loved my sister that way, I would do anything to protect my family. We quickly figured out that we complemented each other in our preferences until...I saw Jules.

From the moment I laid eyes on her, I've wanted every inch of me inside her cunt. At first, it was purely physical, but then I watched closer. There was more than the shell of a goddess. The moment I had her in my arms, there was no turning back.

I reach for her tank top and pull it over her head. A pathetic excuse of a bikini top shields her tits. I've seen pasties cover more. I reach out, hooking my fingers under the fabric and exposing her pebbled nipples. Saliva pools in my mouth.

"Like what you see?" She pulls her bottom lip between her teeth.

"Very." I stroke myself with one hand. "Take your shorts off."

"You didn't say please."

The corner of my mouth twitches. I never had to use that word to get my dick wet. I lean forward until I'm propped over her. I lower my head and suck her nipple into my mouth.

Rolling it between my tongue, Jules moans. "Oh, my—"

I bite down, and she cries out. Her eyes fly to mine, but she doesn't push me away. My Little Phoenix likes pain. The realization makes me want to find out what else she enjoys. I climb her body and lick the seam of her mouth before saying, "I don't say please."

She quirks a brow. "One day you will, Ethan Davis."

As much as I want her to take charge, my body vibrates with the need to be inside of her. I tear her shorts and bikini bottoms off in one motion. She parts her legs wider, exposing her dripping pussy to me. I lick my lips, unable to stop staring.

She's bare. Not shaved, but waxed or lasered. (I recognize the difference, thanks to my years with Jenn.)

Smelling Jules's arousal, there is no going slow. I grip her bent legs behind the knees and tug. Her upper body flops down, and before she can protest, I'm on top. I drive inside her heat with all my length, making her scream in pleasure.

Her walls tighten around me, and I let my head fall to the

crook of her neck. Jules clutches her hands to the sides of my rib cage while I thrust in and out. "Fuck, baby, you feel so good."

"Oh my god."

Her nails claw my back, leaving marks I want to tattoo on my skin as a permanent reminder of tonight. My need for her shoots through every cell of my body, overwhelming any rationality. I can't help but bite down on the spot between her neck and shoulder. A coppery taste explodes on my tongue.

Her loud moan is followed by, "Oh, god, yesss." A burn signals how her nails just broke skin. "Harder."

Jules pants underneath me, and I can't believe what's happening. Her legs wrap around my hips, inviting me to explore a new angle. I won't last much longer. My abs lock as my balls tighten, and tension shoots up my shaft, playing a tortuous game of tug-of-war with my body. Her hips move in sync with mine, meeting my every thrust. Swiping over the teeth marks on her skin with my tongue, I lean up to see her face. The moment our eyes connect, she captures my mouth in a frantic kiss. Her walls clamp down on me, and—

A guttural groan builds in my chest as stars explode behind my lids. I hold my body utterly still as she continues to milk my cock, and I spill inside of her.

In the back of my head, a voice chastises me about my carelessness, but I can't give two shits about that right now. Coming down from a high I've never experienced before, I collapse. Our rapid breathing is the only audible sound. I push up far enough not to crush her under my weight. Scanning her features, I need to confirm that she's not regretting this. Us.

She gazes out at the water. The wait for her to meet my eyes feels like an eternity when, in reality, it can't be more than a few seconds. She finally turns her head, an undecipherable expression causing my stomach to drop.

"What are you thinking?" My forehead wrinkles.

She blinks slowly. My chest tightens at the dullness in her green depths.

Her expression morphs in front of me. "I'm thinking..."—she pauses dramatically—"this was pretty decent." She smirks and winks.

While I have the urge to call bullshit on the shift in demeanor, I selfishly refuse to ruin the moment. My dick is still buried between her folds, fluttering echoes of tension and softening still pulsing down my shaft, and I just had one of the (if not *the*) best fucks of my life.

I pull out and roll to my side. Propping my head up, I rest the palm of my free hand on her cheek. "I could be convinced for a repeat," I drawl with an extra shot of boredom. Two can play that game.

We stare at each other for a long moment before a wicked grin creeps over her face, and I can't help but match her expression.

There is my girl.

Her fingers find my jaw. "What happened?"

Her thumb swipes back and forth across the stubble on my chin, sending tingles down my spine. She's perceptive, and while I can't tell her that my sister's boyfriend was sent to hell, literally, I settle for a half-truth. "Jenn got some bad news."

Jules reaches for my neck, pulling me to her. Our lips brush in a feathery caress.

"She is lucky to have you," she murmurs as our mouths part. There is no malice in her words. Jules is completely genuine, and I feel an ache behind my rib cage. The indestructible wall I've built around my heart has just experienced the first step to its destruction.

BUZZING JOLTS ME AWAKE.

What the fuck?

A breeze brushes across my arms and chest. Something is pinning me down. *Someone.* A body I will forever recognize after last night. I blink once, twice. The dark blanket of night is giving way to a hue of pink on the horizon. It's somewhere around six in the morning.

The buzzing continues, and Jules stirs.

"Hey. Time to wake up, Little Phoenix." I place a kiss on her forehead.

She jerks into an upright position. Her eyes dart around, then she settles on me. She's wearing my shirt, her coppery hair in a tangled mess. Her eyes bulge when she meets my gaze, and she jumps to all fours, patting the blanket.

"Oh shit, oh shit, oh shit." Her hands frantically search for something. "Fuck, fuck, fuck. Where is my phone?"

I sit up and scan our makeshift bed. The blanket I always keep in the back of the Bronco is bunched in several spots. I let my palm glide over the fabric and find the desired object hidden under one of the edges. Handing it over, she nearly rips it from my grasp.

"My father is going to kill me. Fuck." She crisscrosses her legs, swiping at the screen. A heavy sigh deflates her chest, and her hands drop to her lap.

I cock a brow as she peers sideways at me and holds out the device.

Della: Texted your parents. Pretended to be you. Said your phone fell into the water, and you're spending the night. Where the fuck did you run off to?

Della: CALL ME! (Just so I know Davis didn't kill you.)

Kill. Just wonderful.

I stare at her, carefully keeping my features neutral, and Jules grins sheepishly.

"Were you in on your friend's little scheme last night?" I distract my thoughts from Della. Not that I care, but I don't like to be manipulated.

When she frowns, I shake my head. "You might wanna change your Instagram password."

Her eyes narrow before she starts tapping away on her phone. I can see when she finds what I was referring to.

"That little bitch!" Jules puts her palm to her forehead. She peers at me. "I didn't know."

Before I can respond, another round of buzzing interrupts us. I find my phone in the grass a few feet away. How the hell it ended up there is beyond me.

Corbin's number flashes across the screen. "Hello."

The same rule Marshall has about pictures applies to contacts. Our phones are just shells.

"Where the fuck are you?" my brother barks, and I have to pull the device away from my ear.

"At the pond." I'm not lying. He could easily check my location by tracking the Bronco or my phone.

"Why the hell are you at the pond?" he asks, puzzled, then shifts gears. "Whatever. You need to come back. Marshall sent Theo back north, I'm on shift, and Jenn is freaking out."

Fuck.

"OK, uh, give me thirty. Forty-five tops." It only takes fifteen minutes to get back to the house from here, but I have to drop Jules off.

There is a pause on the other end before he hisses, "I hope it was worth it."

CHAPTER EIGHT

JULES

The drive is quiet. The only sound is the Bronco's engine.

I watch bald cypresses and willows zoom by, yet, not seeing them. The rising sun bathes the passing landscape in a rosy light. I've lived here my entire life, but this morning feels different.

Ethan's shirt hangs loose on my frame. Where the fabric touches, my skin tingles in a soft caress. He had pulled a different one from his trunk, and I swallowed my relief. The worn fabric smells like him. I don't want to give it back. It is just a shirt, but at the same time, it isn't. He is the unattainable Ethan Davis.

I had pulled my shorts over my bare ass, ignoring my bikini, which is now balled somewhere in the blanket in the back seat.

Without averting his eyes from the road, Ethan's hand reaches over, palm up. I stare at his offering before interlacing our fingers. His gaze darts over, and a soft smile tugs on his mouth. His mouth. A memory of his kisses and— I reach for the spot between my neck and shoulder with my free hand. My heart instantly beats faster at the dull ache under my fingertips. I trace the raised marks where he branded me with his teeth. When he had clamped down on the soft flesh between my shoulder and neck, the nerve endings all over my body had fired in a sensory overload. The slicing pain nearly sent me over the edge.

The knowledge of him claiming me as his has my stomach in knots. Do I want to be his? He is a Davis. I am...not. Yet, the answer is as easy as it is impossible: yes.

Ethan didn't interrogate me on my slip, but his expression had promised that it was not the last time we would speak of it. *I'm already ruined.* He had no idea what my words meant. I wasn't broken in the way he assumed. Until the day he brings it up, that part of my life is of no importance. It had never been for me to live. To be me.

I sit up straight. "Pull over." I point at the upcoming bend. The diner and our house are behind the turn.

His brows shoot up, and I explain, "Dad will be in the kitchen, prepping. I can get to the house through the trees and sneak in."

Understanding settles on his face, followed by confusion. "You don't want your father to see me?"

I purse my lips. "Do you?"

When he doesn't reply, I know I've got him.

The Bronco rolls to a stop, and I reach for the door handle. I have no clue what to say. Lingering with my fingers around the plastic, Ethan tugs on my hand that's still connected to his.

My gaze flicks between our joined hands and his face.

How did I forget that?

Oh yeah, I was stuck in the memory of his teeth on my skin, delivering pain and pleasure in a way I would always associate with Ethan. I had sex with Ethan Davis. And not just once. I taste the words on my tongue. I should regret this. We don't have a future; I won't delude myself. At the same time, nothing has ever felt so...right.

We went three more rounds after the first, using protection those times—not that one time wouldn't be enough to change everything forever. After the last time, we collapsed on the blanket, which was not long before we got woken up by my phone.

As if on cue, my eyes burn from the lack of sleep. I need caffeine.

"Jules." I focus on Ethan. I've gotten used to my nickname, and hearing my given name out of his mouth sounds wrong. Like he's inviting distance between us.

Ethan leans over the middle console. His fingers dive into my hair, and he pulls me close. Swiping his nose to mine, he places a brief kiss on my mouth. "I'll come see you."

I search for deceit in his words, an indication that this meant nothing to him.

"Okay." Unable to stop myself, I frame his face. Ethan groans as my lips close on his.

"If you don't get out now, we'll both be in trouble soon."

I grin, not breaking the connection. Ethan nips on my bottom lip before drawing back. "Go, Little Phoenix."

While I give him my best pout, I can't stop the buzzing excitement from breaking through. I climb out of the Bronco and slam the door shut. Ethan smirks at my proud expression that I managed to best his SUV before he pulls out into the road.

I watch his taillights disappear around the bend before dashing through the trees.

AFTER ETHAN DROPS ME OFF, the day is a blur. Not because I am busy but because I can barely keep my eyes open. I need to catch up on schoolwork, so taking a nap is not an option.

Sitting at my desk, I go over the same math problem for the umpteenth time. A nagging voice in the back of my head distracts me with whispers that when I leave for college, the likelihood of seeing Ethan again will be in the negative.

Am I considering giving up my dream after one night of sex? Granted, it was the best sex I've ever had, but my dream has been my number one priority since I realized there was more than Renneton. That I didn't want this to be my future.

A knock behind me jolts me out of my thoughts, and I swivel in my chair. My eyes bulge at the last person I ever expected to see in my house. *My home.*

I pick my jaw up off the floor as I continue to gape. "Uh, hi?"

"Hi." Jenn leans against the frame. Her feet are crossed at the ankles, her arms folded over her chest. She's dressed in black jean shorts, a loose-fitting black crop top that hangs off one shoulder, and combat boots. Across her hips sits a black leather belt, and I slant my head. It's an odd accessory for the outfit.

Jenn follows my gaze and straightens. She turns sideways and wiggles her ass, which allows me to identify the belt for what it's not—a fashion accessory. On her backside are two small sheaths. Gray, T-shaped handles stick out of each.

Jenn reaches behind her, pulling one of the objects out. Her fore- and middle finger curl around the handle on either side of the triangle-shaped blade.

"It's a push dagger," she explains, presenting it with the normality of friends showing each other their new pair of shoes.

Friends. I didn't think Jenn and I fell into that category. She's always friendly at the diner, and she's Ethan's...sister. But we've never hung out. Is she a friend?

Holding it up, the blade glints in the light, and I'm suddenly wide awake. She turns her wrist so I can see it from every angle, and my fingers tingle.

Fascinated, I stand and place one foot in front of the other. I blink, unable to avert my eyes. "May I?" My mouth has gone dry. I'm aware of everything in the room—the rays of the sun illuminating a spot on my carpet, tiny dust particles hovering in the air, the ticking of my old-fashioned alarm clock across the room.

"Sure." Jenn shrugs and holds the dagger out to me. I watch my fingers wrap around the handle in slow motion. As soon as I make contact, an electric current surges up my arm. I tighten my hold, feeling the rough texture.

Why does it feel like it belongs here? In my *hand.*

"It's beautiful," I breathe with my gaze locked on the object.

A chuckle reaches my ears. "They sure are." After a pause, she adds, "They were a gift from Ethan. He gave them to me for my sixteenth birthday. Haven't been without them since."

At Ethan's name, I'm finally able to focus on her. Stepping aside, I gesture for her to come in. Jenn smiles and strides over to my bed. Plopping down, she pulls her legs up in a cross-legged position as if we've done this hundreds of times.

Friends?

Then something clicks. "Uh, why are you here?" Isn't she supposed to be with Ethan?

"I needed a change of scenery." She holds her hand out, palm up, and I realize I'm still holding the dagger. Quickly, I relinquish it to its owner, missing the feeling instantly.

Jenn tucks it back into the belt before facing me. "You're why my brother didn't come home last night."

My spine stiffens at her statement. I don't detect an accusation in her tone, but her choice of words has me on edge. I'm not sure what to say. Instead, my hand flies to my neck. After showering this morning, I chose an old plaid shirt. I had cut the sleeves off once upon a time. The high collar and a lot of concealer managed to hide most of last night's evidence.

Jenn zeroes in on my neck, and the corner of her mouth quirks. "He's different with you."

Now, I'm really confused. "Why are you telling me this?"

Jenn pats the spot beside her. I shift from one foot to the other, staring at my comforter where her hand lingers. After a moment of hesitation, I accept her invitation.

"I don't remember a time when Ethan wasn't part of my family," she begins, then stops herself, chewing on her bottom lip.

Seeing Jenn like this is an odd sight. She almost seems vulnerable.

"I don't have girlfriends," she continues, speaking toward her lap. "It's always just been my brothers and me. There are girls on the plantation, but they are just after one thing."

"Oh?" My brows arch.

Jenn peers up. "You can probably guess what that is."

I mull over her suggestion and cringe.

She nods. "My brothers. Or father. Anyone who has a say and a dick."

I rub my thumb over the inside of my wrist, forcing my hands to rest in my lap. "Should you be telling me this?" There is a reason no one knows anything about the Davis family.

Jenn chuckles. "Definitely not. But you got involved the second my brother claimed you."

Claimed?

"He has never cared for a female. It's always been just him and me. He gave me the ability to choose my...partner." The way she enunciates *partner* sends a wave of sorrow through me. After a moment, she adds, "And I deterred any of the whores trying to ride his dick."

My eyes narrow at her choice of words. She talks like Ethan, which I guess shouldn't surprise me if the guys are all she's ever been around.

"It's my time to keep him safe."

Her words hit me like a slap to the face. What is she saying? "Are you warning me off?" I ask, somewhat in disbelief.

Jenn blinks, a sad smile on her face. "No. But you need to understand that once you're in, there is no getting out. You still have a chance." Her hand lifts and the tips of her fingers touch the spot on my neck.

She smirks. "He's never done that with me."

"Excuse me?" I reel back.

Shaking her head, she takes my hand. "Jules, I know you've heard the rumors. Everyone has." She winks.

I wait for jealousy to set in. She basically admitted that she's been sleeping with her adopted brother—the same guy who has turned my world upside down for weeks. But there is...nothing.

It's always been just him and me. He gave me the ability to choose. I deterred any of the whores trying to ride his dick.

"You don't love him," I state.

"Not in the way you're insinuating. We live in a different world. Ethan...he never belonged, but he doesn't have a choice. We helped each other. I would do anything for him."

My chest tightens at the way she speaks about...their relationship.

"I lost my boyfriend the other day."

Her words suck the air from my lungs, and my hand flies to my mouth.

"He didn't die, but he might as well have. Death would've been more merciful."

Fear begins to seep through my veins like slow-moving venom. "That's why Ethan stayed with you."

Jenn nods, her gaze trained on a spot on the carpet.

I narrow my eyes. "Didn't Ethan go back because your other brothers were busy?"

Her lips press in a thin line. "Yes, but Father made him work with Paycen. It was his way of forcing me out of my room. The guys have been guarding my door day and night."

"Why would your father have a problem with you mourning your boyfriend?"

The Davis riddles get increasingly unsolvable, and my father's warnings to stay away from them rush to the forefront.

Jenn remains quiet for so long I assume she won't answer. Then, she whispers, "Because Father sent Kroy away."

Her trust in me is humbling and terrifying all the same. Della has been my best friend since we were toddlers, but Jenn trusting me causes my throat to close.

I reach over and squeeze her hand. "You have one girlfriend now."

Jenn tenses. Shifting, she pulls her phone out of her back pocket. "Hey, T."

Her eyes meet mine as she listens. "No, I had to get out for a bit." The voice—her twin—on the other end speaks, but I can't make out the words. "I'm fine. I went to see Jules."

This time, there is silence. She pulls the phone away and peers at the screen before lifting it back to her ear. "Hello?"

Theo speaks again, agitation bleeding into his modulation.

"Stop stressing. If anyone checks, I'm at the diner." Pause. "Do you know when you'll be back?" She listens. "Ugh, I wanna know what's so important about this job. What the fuck is in Westbridge, Virginia?" She snorts at something T says. "Okay. I'll talk to you later."

After she hangs up, Jenn faces me head-on. "Do you care for my brother?"

Taken aback by her bluntness, I fumble. "Uh, I... We... I don't really know him."

"You don't have to know someone to care about them. You learn things over time," Jenn says matter-of-factly.

Drawing in a deep breath, I confess what I wasn't willing to admit to myself. "I do."

"Good." She hollows her cheeks before continuing. "All I'm asking of you is to trust him. Ethan will never betray you." She pauses. "Purposefully. But he will disappear for long stretches— all of us will. I would offer to keep you company, but most of the time, I am with one of them." Scanning my face, she adds, "I will make sure he comes back to you."

My body drains of its warmth at her words.

If she senses my unease, she doesn't show it. Instead, she surprises me once more. "Ethan and I haven't been together since the day he walked through the door of your diner for the first time. You are special, and that makes you special to me."

All I manage is a stiff nod.

Jenn stands, and I follow suit. Before she walks out the door, she turns one more time. The sadness in her eyes sends shards of glass through my lungs.

"I hope I'm wrong."

And with that, she leaves me standing in the middle of my room with more questions than before.

CHAPTER NINE

ETHAN

"YOU DID WHAT?" MY VOICE GOES THREE OCTAVES higher as I drop my pool cue. It clatters to the hardwood floor next to where it feels like my jaw is. Jenn uncaps her ChapStick and applies the translucent goo with careful precision before smacking her lips together and flashing me a grin. You can't even see the shit on her mouth. My fingers curl and uncurl as I count to ten, fighting against the urge to choke her.

"I went to see your girlfriend," she states calmly, perching on the arm of the couch.

"M-my..." I splutter and start choking on my spit. Gray swirls materialize in my vision, and I suck in small gulps of air. Just a few hours ago, I taught my little brother where to slice into a body without hitting any arteries, but Jenn *visiting* Jules sends me into a near panic attack.

"What did you expect?" Corbin drawls as he pockets the five ball.

We're in the game room. We often congregate here at the

end of the day to relax and have a few drinks. It's the only time we can pretend our lives are not led by death and destruction. Though, we have to take our thirteen-year-old brother out of the picture to fake such a fairy tale. Paycen leans against the pool table beside Cor with a beer in hand. At least he's not into the hard stuff tonight. Sometimes, I contemplate taking the booze from him, but then he'd probably slit my throat in my sleep.

Paycen Davis is not your average teenager.

As soon as I got home this morning, Marshall called me into his office and declared I was to work with my little brother today. Apparently, one of the guards fell asleep on his shift, and instead of reporting it, Paycen took matters into his own hands. The guard is alive but *unusable* for the foreseeable future. Instead of disciplining his son, Marshall needed him to learn more efficient methods to punish someone for their disobedience. Methods that would not incapacitate the subject and require reconstructive surgery.

There was no point in arguing with my father. While his logic was equivalent to asking Frank to stop hunting on the property, the man possessed even less compassion than our resident alligator.

I didn't realize that Jenn had left until she pulled into the garage in one of our less flashy vehicles. With too many witnesses around, I just made eye contact to ensure that she was okay. This was the first time she had been out of her room since we got the news about Kroy.

"I had to get out. I have no friends besides you assholes, and I needed space." Jenn throws her hands up.

How did she turn this around on us all of a sudden?

"And that means you have to befriend Jules?" I take one step toward her, my hands balled at my sides.

Paycen slams his bottle on the edge of the pool table, and I stop in my tracks. He slants his head, his gaze emotionless. His actions speak more than any words ever could.

"I'm not going to hurt her, *brother*," I bark. Besides our father, the four of us are the only ones who get away with raising our voice at Paycen. Not that our family connection automatically implies we're spared his insanity. Paycen has come after us, but so far, our size advantage has kept us alive. Once he reaches his full height (and weight), no one will walk away alive unless he chooses it.

My little brother lifts his beer back to his mouth. Murder averted—for now.

Not giving him my back, I shift my focus. "What did you say to her?" I relax my shoulders.

"I told her about..."—Jenn draws in a breath—"Kroy."

My brows sit somewhere near my hairline. I flick my eyes to Corbin. His face contorting with fury, the white of his knuckles in stark contrast to the ebony of his custom cue. It's my turn to defuse the situation.

I cross the distance and pull Jenn into my arms. She hugs me back, shuddering in my hold.

Lowering my head, my cheek brushes hers. "I assume you didn't tell her the truth?"

"No." Jenn recoils, grasping my shirt between her fingers. She levels me with a crease between her brows. "E, something was...off."

What the fuck does that mean?

With whom? Jules? Jenn?

I regard my sister carefully, not allowing my voice to give away the adrenaline surging through my veins. "How so?"

Jenn lets go and drops onto the couch behind her. She rolls her lips under, gliding her gaze over Paycen and Corbin and finally settling on me. "I basically told her that we've been fucking for years. It didn't faze her."

"You told her— Jesus fuck, Jennifer." My fingers rake through my hair.

"She didn't care, E," Jenn cries. "Listen to my words. Every other girl would go nuts with jealousy. She didn't even touch on the subject. And she's seen us for months at the diner. I'm always with you."

"Maybe she's into Jenn, too." Paycen's monotone statement silences everyone.

The three of us stare at him with equal expressions of confusion and shock. He rarely speaks voluntarily.

Taking another sip of his beer, he regards me with disinterest. He picks up his cue and focuses on the abandoned game— like it never happened.

I swipe my palms on my jean-covered legs and drop down beside Jenn. Leaning my head against the back of the couch, I tilt it in her direction. "What am I supposed to do now?"

She pats my leg, mashing her lips together. "Don't get caught." My lungs constrict as she regards me with sadness. She whispers, "You know Father's rules about Rens."

"That's exactly what I'm worried about," I admit. I've been selfish. Jules has woken a part of me I thought had died in my padded cell so many years ago.

"Maybe Paycen is right. She could want me, not you." Jenn flutters her lashes in my direction. "She really liked my daggers."

I laugh, despite the hollow void that's gripping my chest. Draping an arm around her, I place a kiss on the crown of her head. "Nah, she likes my dick more than your daggers." I bow my gaze to her tits.

"Aaand that's my cue." Corbin throws the game and marches out without a backward glance. Paycen watches the empty doorway before placing his cue into the floor stand in the corner. With his hands in the pockets of his jeans, he strides after his big brother—like we don't exist.

When it's just Jenn and me, she swivels in her seat, pulling one leg onto the cushion. "I like her, E. I don't want her to get caught in the cross fire."

I like her, too.

"I'll walk away before I let that happen." I surprise myself with the conviction in my statement. I silently repeat it, letting the words melt across my tongue and swallow. A calm settles in my core.

I'd walk away to protect her. Even if it kills me.

Let's hope it never comes to that.

IT'S PAST MIDNIGHT.

My earlier acceptance has slowly evaporated like the steam from my shower. With only my gray sweats on, I lean against the headboard and stare at the wall across from me. I'm not used to...feeling. *Worry.*

As the water pelts on my skin, darkening the tattoos that have covered my arms nearly half my life, Jenn's words began to play on repeat in my head: *I don't want her to get caught in the cross fire.*

My gaze trails the inked pictures across my body, remembering each event that triggered me to add to the map that was my life. While they appear random to the oblivious observer, they all symbolize...something. A place. A person. A kill.

Not averting my eyes from a small nail in the wall, I wonder what used to hang there. I never bothered with decorations. My fingers find the newest addition of red and black on the inside of my upper arm. I saw our on-property tattooist the other night after Jenn cried herself to sleep yet again. A corn poppy. But instead of its usual center, I made him ink an eyeball—with a brown iris. My dream attempted to manipulate the event. This way, there is no mistake about who died (or didn't die) that night.

The thought of Jules being harmed because of me makes bile rise in my throat. I should walk away before we're too deep. There is no reason for our paths ever to cross again. It was only one night. I'm the one who made us go back to the diner. We don't ever go into town. It would be easy to avoid her. The mere consideration, though...of never touching my fingers to her soft porcelain skin... tears open a chasm of despair inside of me.

I tap on the screen of my phone. 12:47. Opening a new text window, I key in the number I memorized weeks ago. It wasn't hard to find it. I didn't even have to involve Corbin and his computer skills.

Renneton is small, the civilians unexpectant of anything bad happening here—let alone the devil living among them. The local high school has their students' contacts listed. Anyone with sinister intent could pick and choose freely from the crops. Thank fuck Marshall doesn't harvest locally.

Me: I heard you had a visitor, Little Phoenix.

I don't expect her to respond, but when the three dots appear while I'm still re-reading the message I shouldn't have sent, my breath catches.

Jules: Ethan?

My thumbs hover over the digital keyboard. What should I answer? Yes? Fuck, I'm in my early twenties and have no clue how to interact with a human. Or a girl.

Me: Is anyone else using that name for you? Who do I have to kill?

Someone take my phone. Why did I just write that?

My palm hits my forehead. Might as well spell it out. *Hey, Jules, loved fucking you senseless last night. Oh, by the way, I murder people for the roof over my head.*

Her reply pops up. Occupied with my internal chastisement, I missed her typing.

Jules: Why do I get the feeling that isn't just an empty threat?

Well, fuck me sideways.

Staring at the ceiling, I wait for the clawing behind my ribs to stop.

Delete the number. Don't respond. Walk away.

I can't.

Me: JK

Jules: Riiight.

Me: Seriously.

I can dismember a body without a second thought, yet this exchange makes my stomach roll.

Jules: Relax. I'm just messing with you.

Is she?

I find the nail again. This small object is embedded in my wall, and I have no idea how it got there. Identical to how one redheaded girl etched herself into my...soul. Vibration alerts me to another text.

Jules: You there?

I need to change the subject. What do normal people talk about? What would her ex say? The case crackles under my vise grip. How can I have anything with her when I'm incapable of holding a nonviolent conversation? Inhaling and holding my breath, I type.

Me: Why are you awake?

Jules: I was studying for a test. I tried earlier but fell asleep. Someone kept me up last night.

My dick twitches under the cotton, and the air leaves me with a whoosh. My mouth pulls up at the corner. That's a topic I can work with. My pulse accelerates for a new reason.

Me: Oh, what a coincidence. Same here.

Jules: Haha
Me: What are you doing tomorrow after school?
Jules: Working.
Me: I'll see you after.

The three dots dance and disappear several times before her reply appears.

Jules: I can't leave in the middle of the night.
Me: Let that be my concern.

When she doesn't respond, I exit the text and delete the message string. They're still on the server, but unless Marshall has a reason, he never checks there—and Corbin won't rat me out.

I fling the phone carelessly onto the mattress and slump down on the pillow. Folding my arms behind my head, I close my eyes, listening to the steady rhythm of my heart.

I can do normal. For Jules, I'll find a way.

I WAKE UP LATE. The upside of this life is that we don't live by a schedule—unless on a job.

With T still gone and no new assignment on the horizon, the four of us train. Jenn challenges me to a hand-to-hand—something I never say no to. We're in the former sunroom. When it became apparent that the property needed more than one gym, Marshall had this part of the house remodeled.

Surrounded by weight benches and cardio equipment, Jenn and I face off in the cage. Paycen lounges in the corner, and Corbin strides over to the sound system. He plays around on his phone, and suddenly, "Bodies" by Drowning Pool thunders through the speakers in the ceiling. The volume doesn't faze me; we're used to Cor setting the mood. And he's been in a shit mood, which explains his choice of music.

I cock my head as Jenn reaches behind her back, pulling out

the push daggers I gave her a few years ago. I needed her to have a weapon she could carry concealed. The blades are only a little over two-point-five inches long with an overall length of four inches. She can easily keep them in her boots when she isn't wearing the custom belt.

With her arms hanging at her sides, one blade in each hand, she waits for my first move. I twirl my WK Contingency in my palm, contemplating my strategy when a thud alerts me to another opponent in the ring. My head jerks to the side, and my mind halts in its tracks. Paycen has joined the party. I'm suddenly hyperaware of the thirty-foot diameter surrounding us. While not real, in my peripheral vision, the six-foot fence enclosing us grows in height.

He fists his tactical Bowie knife. I cock a brow. *Really?* It has a saw-edge spine and a total length of twelve inches.

"Are you planning on gutting me, little brother?" I tilt my head, the excitement of the challenge swirling with the knowledge that Paycen has no sense for healthy competition. It's kill or be killed—surviving his only mission.

We rarely see any expression on his face, but when he graces us with one, it's even more apparent what a danger he will be one day—to the world and women.

The corner of his mouth tilts upward, and Jenn sucks in a breath.

"Scared, big brother?" I almost miss the dare, too captivated by the smile and amusement in his tone.

Shaking my head, I flick my gaze to Jenn, who chews on her bottom lip. She also doesn't know how to take this surprising change in circumstances.

I lift one shoulder dismissively. "Let's have some fun."

Leaning down, I pull my second Contingency out of my boot. I didn't plan on using both, but with three blades against me, I need all the help I can get.

As soon as I straighten, Paycen lunges. I manage to block his attack at the last second, a sneer turning his mouth to a manic grimace.

I'm surprised he waited until I was upright. What's he up to?

I signal to Jenn to go ahead, and she readies her stance. Averting Paycen for the second time, I strike back. He curves his body out of my reach. Retreating with a jump, he lands in a crouch with his fingers propping him against the vinyl floor cover.

Jenn uses that moment to attack. The downside of her push daggers is that she has to be in close contact to inflict damage, which is why she puts herself in a fighting stance, dancing on the balls of her feet. When I mimic her position, she shifts her weight on her back foot and executes a push kick with the front. My breath is already coming in spurts, thanks to Paycen, and I'm speeding through my options. Both my hands are holding on to a blade. I can't block her without also stabbing her. Making a split-second decision, I take her heel to the stomach. No matter how seriously we take our training and sparring, I put Jenn's safety first.

With the guys, that's a different game. Which immediately changes when Paycen surges forward again.

The match doesn't last ten minutes, but when Corbin cuts "Reaper" by Glaceo and RIELL midsong, the three of us are panting, unable to draw in a full breath. My shirt hangs in ribbons off my torso, and something warm trickles down the side of my abs. Peering down, I narrow my eyes. Fuck, that'll need stitches. Paycen sports a similar wound on his leg, and Jenn has a bruise on her cheek. While I draw the line at cutting my sister open for funsies, I have no issue using my fists—or elbow, in today's case. We all learned how to take a punch before we could ride a bike. I would rather her train and fight me than any of the randoms on the property.

Slow clapping from the far end of the room causes us to turn. Marshall and Carolyn stand at the door. My brows arch at the sight of his wife. Jenn and Theo's mother isn't your warm and fuzzy parental figure. She cares for the twins, but in a very different way. She tolerates Corbin and me and ignores Paycen, which is probably for the best.

As soon as Paycen spots her, he grabs his blade and scales the fenced wall. He disappears through another exit before Carolyn climbs the three steps to the cage.

Marshall stops outside, interlacing his hands casually behind his back.

"Jennifer." She clucks her tongue. She scrutinizes the swelling on Jenn's cheek, then scans me. "Did you do that, or was it—?"

"We were training, Moth—" Jenn starts, but Carolyn silences her with a look.

"I'm waiting." Her gaze bores into me.

"It was me," I say, squaring my shoulders. I would confess even if it had been Paycen. Carolyn just waits for a reason to put him down.

She crosses the distance, and before I can react, she backhands me across the face. "If you have to hit her, do it somewhere no one sees it."

Slanting my mouth, I shutter my eyes for the briefest of moments to reel in my temper. My fingers tighten around the wasp handle of my blade, and I nod. "Yes, Carolyn."

"Bruises on her face show weakness."

Opposed to hidden bruises.

"I will not tolerate you drawing attention to this family, do you understand?" She levels each of us with a glare, and we respond in unison.

"Yes, ma'am."

The woman is as deranged as her husband.

"Jenn, get an ice pack and then put some concealer on." She

waves at her daughter's face. "You are not to leave the property until the swelling is down. I will inform your brother that you will not join him in Westbridge."

Jenn's shoulders slump, but she doesn't object. Instead, she sheaths her daggers, walks over, and places a kiss on Carolyn's cheek. "Yes, Mother." She stops in front of Marshall and repeats the same gesture before exiting.

Marshall's eyes drop to the small stain of crimson that started pooling on the mat. "Get this cleaned up. Then I want you both to get ready." He flicks his gaze between Corbin and me. "We're expecting visitors, and you'll be there."

Fucking shit.

So much for seeing Jules.

CHAPTER TEN

JULES

OF COURSE, ETHAN DIDN'T SHOW UP. WHAT DID I EXPECT?

His text Sunday night surprised the shit out of me. Sitting in the middle of my mattress, surrounded by my textbooks, notepad, and laptop, the sentences had long begun blurring together. My eyes glossed over the message sliding in at the top of my computer screen. When the two words registered, I almost fell off my bed. *Little Phoenix*. Where did he get my number? Not that I cared. Ethan messaged *me*. The playful banter was so him, yet it wasn't. Using a phone for something mundane, like texting a girl in the middle of the night, wasn't a regular occurrence for Ethan Davis. I knew that. And his jealous side sent all kinds of signals to my body, flooding my senses with memories of the pond. Why was it such a turn-on to envision Ethan wrapping his hands around Ty's throat to claim what's his? Was I? Ethan's? Jenn said he was different with me. But that didn't mean he wanted a relationship. Did I want a relationship?

Fuck, what was wrong with me?

The same thoughts had been running laps in my mind since I switched off the light at two a.m., accepting Ethan wouldn't come.

Tuesday morning, Della immediately sensed that something was off. Not only did the dark circles under my eyes resemble the time in kindergarten when she and I used purple and blue markers to give each other a makeover, but my shit mood was also a dead giveaway. I'm not your all-time bubbly, happy type, but I am generally not a bitch *(without reason.)* Della nagged and assaulted me with missile-like, balled-up notes through our first two periods until I finally admitted what happened—or didn't happen.

Walking to our next class, she drapes her arm over my shoulder. "He'll come."

"And how do you know that?" I rub my right eye, unable to stop the damn itch. It's been three nights in a row with less than five hours. I need sleep.

"Let's just say I have it on good authority." She winks.

I attempt to question her about her hijacking my Instagram, but she switches the topic and ignores me after that. This is so unlike my friend.

I massage my temple with my fingers in a circular motion. Not only do my eyes sting like a mother, but the dull ache behind my forehead hasn't let up since last night. It's getting irritating.

"Whatever, Del." I dig out from under her arm and quicken my pace. I don't want to be here. I don't want to be anywhere in this godforsaken town. But in order to leave, I have to graduate.

"Jules," Della calls after me.

I wave without turning and veer into the classroom.

The rest of the day, I avoid my best friend and ex-boyfriend with equal effort. Renneton is so small that there are only two classes for the seniors, and we share most of them.

Ty borders on harassing me, demanding to know where I disappeared to on Saturday.

Della strikes up meaningless conversations at every chance. When she realizes that the most she is going to get out of me is a dismissive grunt, she finally gives up.

Guilt wraps its way along my rib cage. She's my best friend, but I need space to sort through the turmoil of contradicting emotions.

I contemplate texting Ethan before heading to the diner, but pride makes me delete the words.

WORK WAS the distraction I needed. We were busy till closing, and my mind was blissfully blank the entire time.

After my shift, I take a quick shower. My lashes feel like they're attached to a five-pound weight, but I don't have a choice. My Spanish essay is due tomorrow. Where I am an *A* student in any class that consists of numbers, equations, and logic, languages are the bane of my existence.

Sitting at my desk, "Another Level" by Oh The Larceny blares through my earbuds. I study the best with deafening music blocking out the world and let's be honest, I need it to stay awake.

I lightly tap my fingers against the keyboard, formulating the next sentence in my head, when suddenly, fingers wrap around my throat from behind. My heart pauses for several beats, and time slows. My eyes fly around my desk, but besides my text-book and laptop, there is nothing I can use as a weapon. Reality snaps back into place like a rubber band. My pulse thrashes in my ears as I throw my arms up to strike my attacker. I can't get hold of anything. Anyone. It's like the hand is not attached to a body. I can't breathe, and a steady burn builds in my lungs. One of my headphones gets plucked out of my ear, and as soon as the owner of the voice registers in my oxygen-deprived brain, my body goes slack.

"Tsk, tsk, Little Phoenix. You should never lose sight of your surroundings. What if someone broke into your room?"

My head falls back, and this time, I make contact with Ethan's stomach.

"Usually, people don't attack me in my bedroom." The words scratch my throat.

His fingers massage my neck, chasing the ache away, and I tilt my head up. A black hoodie covers his head and throws a shadow over his handsome face. He looks deliciously dangerous, and I crook my finger at him.

He smirks and bends down, placing a kiss on my lips. "We need to change that. I can't have you vulnerable."

I pull my other earbud out and place them into their case. Pushing to my feet, I pivot until my front is to his.

"What are you planning on doing about that?" I purr, and my hands settle on his chest. The drumming behind his ribs vibrates against my palm. Interlacing my fingers behind his neck, I rise to my tiptoes. My lips flutter over his. There is barely any pressure behind the kiss, but enough for him to understand what I want.

The devilish smirk that has captivated me from the moment I laid eyes on him appears. Ethan brushes his mouth to mine, and I automatically part my lips. He nips at my invitation, and I moan as he tangles our tongues together in a delicious fight for dominance. His fingers glide under my loose tank top, and where his calloused tips stroke my skin, his touches burn themselves into every cell. I tighten my hold and draw closer, but Ethan winces, folding into his side.

I recoil, my eyes flying over his body. "What's wrong?"

He gives me a crooked grin. "My brother and sister got the best of me."

What?

His torso is angled sideways like he's suppressing pain. Scowling, I clasp his hoodie and lift the hem. A massive bandage covers half his side.

"What the fuck?" I cry, my eyes flying between his face and his wound. "Did someone stab you?"

He nods curtly, and I rear back.

My stomach knots and the pressure pushes itself up to the back of my throat. Is he messing with me? Ethan reaches out, but I hold my palms up toward him. "No!" I shake my head as I try to make sense of it.

Ethan tries again. This time I let him touch me. His arms wrap around my shoulders, and I lean my forehead against his collarbone, breathing through my nose.

"It's long but shallow. Nothing to worry about." Ethan kisses my temple. "I like you worrying about me." His last words are spoken with an amused chuckle.

I wrap my arms gingerly around him, not putting any pressure on the side with the bandage. We stand like this, and my nerves settle. Sensing that I've regained my control, he withdraws and forces me to loosen my hold.

Ethan intertwines our fingers and leads me over to my bed. He drops onto the mattress and lounges against the pillows, relaxing one hand behind his head. I stand with my shins against the frame, catching up to what has transpired in the last five minutes. This guy, who spins my world off its axis, broke into my bedroom, choked me, tongue-fucked me, then revealed that one of his siblings stabbed him, and now he lies on my bed like this is where he belongs.

My tongue swipes against the corner of my mouth as I drink him in.

He does belong here.

Ethan's eyes flare, tracking every move as I gingerly climb over him to the center of the mattress. Curling into his side, he lifts his arm and tugs me closer. He leans his cheek against the crown of my head and sighs contently. I don't think he even realizes he did it.

I rest my hand over his pec, drawing figure eights on the black fabric. "Why would your siblings stab you?" I need to know the answer as much as I don't.

Ethan draws in a deep breath. "We were sparring. It's part of our training. Paycen got carried away."

My head jerks up at the mention of his little brother. "Isn't he, like, fourteen?"

"Thirteen, actually." He frowns at the wall opposite us. "You wouldn't know it, though. He... I shouldn't tell you any of this." Ethan closes his eyes and massages the bridge of his nose with his thumb and forefinger.

I touch my palm to his jaw, letting my fingers caress his smooth skin. He shaved. A hum travels from the pads of my fingers to my heart. "It's okay. You don't have to say anything. But know that I will never betray your trust."

Ethan angles his head to meet my gaze. "It's not that I don't want to. It's what this knowledge can do to you."

I place a swift kiss on the underside of his chin, allowing the warmth to spread from my heart through every part of my body. His words intend to push me away. Intentionally or to keep me safe, it doesn't matter. "Then teach me to protect myself."

A smile tugs at the corner of his mouth as quickly as it's gone. "It's a date."

He lifts his head off the pillow, signaling what he wants, and I seal our pact with a kiss.

Settling back, I let my gaze flit across my room. A room that used to represent me. With Ethan, I question everything that's...me.

I haven't known him for long. He's been coming to the diner for a few months, but it wasn't until recently that we exchanged words. *And more.* At the same time, I can't deny the connection I felt the moment our gazes collided. Something ignited and set me aflame from the inside out. He gave me something I didn't know I was craving. I thought I had it all figured out, but then Ethan breathed new life into me with his kisses and touches. I became his phoenix—rising from the ashes of an existence I had outgrown years ago.

My eyes settle on the green vase on my dresser. It holds a rather unconventional *flower.* Della always argues that it's a weed, but she can say what she wants. Beauty lies in the eye of the beholder. I keep my eyes trained on the spikes surrounding the bloom as I speak. "I love thistles."

Ethan shifts, probably following my line of sight.

I collect my thoughts. "When I was seven, I saw a field of thistles. It was one of the few vacations we took when I was little. Their purple heads were the most beautiful thing I had ever seen. Then, I tripped over a log, and..." I chuckle. "You can imagine how it ended."

"Did you get hurt?" His hold on me tightens, and the concern bleeding into his question warms my heart.

"Not terribly. I think it was more the shock that something so beautiful could be so...harsh. Its sharp prickles cover its leaves and stem to protect her from herbivores, you know?" I smile at myself. "I've been fascinated with the different species ever since and even managed to grow some that you normally wouldn't find in this region," I say with pride.

We lie quietly as his fingers stroke up and down my exposed arm. My eyes remain across the room as my mind slowly empties.

My lids begin to droop when he murmurs, "Full of beauty and passion. Laced in the desire to survive. You've pricked my heart."

My heart stumbles. Pressing my lips together, I blink a few times to chase my cloudy vision away. A flutter builds in my core and expands like wildfire. I shift until I'm propped on my elbow, scanning every inch of his gorgeous face. The corners of his eyes crinkle, and he gives his lopsided smirk I love so much. Love? No, it can't be. It took months before I even considered the L-word with Ty. But what I feel for Ethan makes the affection I once had for my ex seem like a speck of dust in a mushroom cloud of emotion.

"Who are you, Ethan Davis?" I whisper, scared to use my normal voice.

He lifts his head, angling it toward me before bridging the distance. Before our lips connect, he says, "I'm yours, my Little Phoenix."

WHEN MY ALARM sounds the next day, Ethan is gone.

Turning the obnoxious sound off, I let myself fall back onto the bed. Rolling over, I press my nose into the pillows. Ethan's lingering scent overpowers my senses, and I squeeze my eyes shut as butterflies take flight in my stomach.

Nothing happened last night. Not with his guts playing peek-aboo with the outside of his body. I exaggerate his injury in my head, but who the hell trains with real knives? I can't wrap my mind around the fact that Paycen did this. Despite being enveloped in my comforter, an icy shudder runs down my spine. Are the rumors about the youngest Davis true after all?

Still chasing the mystery of the Davis family dynamic down the rabbit hole, a knock forces me to reemerge. "Come in."

My door swings inward, and Dad appears in the gap. He smirks when he takes in my morning bird's nest. I inherited my hair color (and texture) from him and our Irish ancestors. Thank you very much. Not. Where he simply crops it close to his scalp, I spent all of middle school figuring out how to control the red mane. Mom was of no help as she has spaghetti-straight brown hair. She never had to use a product—or six—to make herself presentable, which was almost resent-worthy.

"Just checking that you're awake after your night of studying." My forehead wrinkles and Dad continues, "I saw your light still on when I walked over around two."

A flush creeps up my neck, and I quickly swing my legs out from under the comforter, so the most he sees of me is my profile. I busy myself unplugging my phone from its charger on my nightstand when his words sink in. "Why were you at the diner in the middle of the night?"

He doesn't answer and instead flicks the thistle with his fingers. "Don't be late for school."

I stare at my empty doorway. What the hell was that?

OF COURSE, I didn't have my essay ready when Mr. Warner collected them during class. I didn't bother making up an excuse. I simply informed my teacher that I had fallen asleep. Which I did—with a boy in my bed. Man. Drifting into peaceful oblivion next to Ethan is worth the *F*.

I have a few months left to make up for it.

Della and I walk toward the parking lot. She picked me up this morning, and we now veer toward her matte-black MINI convertible. She meticulously designed it the entire year leading up to her sixteenth birthday—complete with custom cherry-red leather seats and black-and-red eighteen-inch rims.

Scanning the lot on autopilot, a certain SUV catches my attention. My feet stop moving, much to the oblivion of my best friend.

When she realizes she's alone on the walkway, she turns with furrowed brows. "What are you looking—?" She zeroes in on the two figures in the green Bronco. "Oh. Why is Corbin here?"

Corbin?

The hairs at the nape of my neck stand, and instead of questioning why she is on a first-name basis with the oldest biological Davis, I throw a glance behind me. Fucking shit. Ty and half the football team are congregating at the main entrance, staring in our direction. As our eyes meet, my ex starts forward. Straight for me. *Oh, crap.* Still facing him, my feet move of their own volition. Backward. I don't make it three steps before I run into a wall. No, not a wall. Two arms come around my midsection, and despite the unavoidable altercation, I melt into Ethan's embrace.

"What did I tell you about losing sight of your surroundings, baby?" he greets me, his breath fanning over my cheek before he bites down on the shell of my ear. The sting sends waves of pleasure to my core, and I murmur my approval.

A shadow casts on the walk, and I don't have to look to know that Ethan has been joined by his brother. Ty's eyes widen for a fraction of a second, but he remains on track until he is maybe ten feet away.

Della takes a position on my other side.

"Jules." Ty's eyes narrow as they glide over the human wall surrounding me. "What's this?" The words contort his mouth to a sneer I've never seen on his face before.

The possessive attitude over something—me—that he lost months ago triggers me to melt into Ethan. Not to seek his protection. No. The flames of *my* phoenix slither through my veins, burning away the old Jules. Lifting my arms, I intertwine them behind his neck. Ethan's fingers start roaming my abdomen, and Ty follows the movement, nostrils flaring.

"What exactly are you referring to, Morello?" Ethan answers for me. His pinkie dives under the waistband of my shorts, and I slam my lips together to not moan in front of everyone. He's taunting Ty. And I let him. I want him to.

"Jules," Ty barks.

Warren, his best friend and teammate, appears next to him.

While Warren wants to show support, his tight shoulders betray him.

"Ty," I sigh. "What do you want?"

"What do I want?" His face reddens. "What are you doing with them?" The disgust he throws into the last word propels me forward.

Ethan doesn't stop me.

My arms hang loosely by my sides, the steady thudding of my heart propelling me forward. Where other girls would prop their fists on their hips or fold their arms across their chest to appear confident, I don't put on a show of false bravado. I stride toward my ex until I'm a foot away. Slanting my head, I drop my eyes to Ty's rapidly rising and falling chest.

Lacing my fingers in front of me, I slowly raise my gaze until I meet Ty's. "I don't owe you an explanation, nor do you have the right to demand answers from me."

In my peripheral vision, more and more students pause and stare. They're expecting a scene. The Davis brothers in town are one thing, but them being here...for me...facing off against the school's golden boy... They want a front-row seat.

I don't wait for his answer. Instead, I pivot on my heels and meet my boyfriend's amused gaze. Boyfriend? Does Ethan fall into that category? I put one foot in front of the other while my thrashing pulse suddenly floods my senses. Not because this whole situation could've ended very badly if Ethan—or worse, Corbin—would've gotten involved, but because suddenly my girlish heart wants a label.

I stop in front of Ethan, and he cocks a brow. "Ready, Little Phoenix?"

Ready for what?

"Yup."

He gives me room, and as soon as we're parallel, his arm slings over my shoulder. Corbin falls in line beside his brother, and Della follows on my other side. Students scramble off the walkway as we approach the Bronco.

Out of earshot, I tilt my head up. "Why *are* you here?"

His palm cups the side of my head and places a kiss on my temple. "We have a date, remember?"

A date?

"Then teach me to protect myself."

"It's a date."

Oh!

CHAPTER ELEVEN

ETHAN

CORBIN IS PISSED. NOT ONLY DID I DRAG HIM TO RENNETON High, of all places, but we almost got into it with Jules's dipshit of an ex. Explaining the murder of Ty Morello to Marshall would've been a doozy, especially with the town's entire teen population watching with popcorn and 3D glasses. Rens crave the scandal as much as T *the hunt*.

I navigate the Bronco down the dirt path leading toward the pond. What remained hidden from Jules the night I brought her here was the fork in the road. Instead of veering left, I take the other way. Jules leans forward between the seats, and I peer at her before concentrating on avoiding the potholes you could bury bodies in. Another deterrent for rogue trespassers. The path is shit, and not many would risk their suspension to satisfy their curiosity.

In the rearview mirror, I watch Della, with her arms crossed, staring out the side window. She doesn't show interest in where we're going. Cor's fists flexed when she climbed in after Jules, but he mashed his lips and remained mute. So, I didn't object, either. We'd have to take her back to her car.

We round the last curve, and I bring the SUV to a halt at the edge of the clearing—another man-made area on the property. We don't always train in the sunroom, preferring the outdoors every once in a while—especially when the house gets too crowded.

Marshall had the one-acre area filled in a few years ago. It's surrounded by swamp and trees on all sides, which gives us complete seclusion. Not that we need it on the plantation.

Jumping out, I move the seat for the girls to follow. Cor remains with his ass planted—his way of declaring his disapproval of my idea.

"Grab the blanket," I tell them as I start walking.

Della's hiss close behind me catches me by surprise. "When I said to make her happy, I didn't mean to risk her life, Davis."

I stay on track. With my back to her, she can't see my shock.

After several more steps, I halt. Della stops at my side, pursing her lips. She was the one luring me to the party, sending me after her BFF. Now this... She's correct. I should be more careful, but there are only so many options to be alone with Jules. With this one sentence, she injects a new dose of paranoia into my veins. I let my gaze glide over the trees, scanning for any indication that we're not alone. Of course, no one is here. There is only one access road. I take slow breaths, calming the buzz inside of me.

Before I can interrogate her on her contradicting cues, Jules appears with the blanket in hand. I take it from her and shake it out on the ground.

Della drops on her ass, straightens her legs, and props her upper body up on her elbows. Angling her head skyward, she's fucking sunbathing—acting like it's nothing new to drive onto Davis' property and *hang out.*

Jules frowns. Before she can ask questions, I clasp her hand and lead her farther into the clearing. I don't need her best friend listening.

Jules follows without hesitation, which pleases me as much as I want to yell at her to run. Far away. I curse inwardly. Della is right. But maybe, just for a little while, I can be happy. If I have to leave her to keep her safe, it's a price I'm willing to pay.

Out of earshot, I pivot Jules to face me. "I got you a present."

Her brows shoot up. "You did?"

I rub the back of my neck with my palm. The only female I've ever given a gift to before is my sister. "Jenn mentioned how much you...liked her daggers." The green in Jules's eyes flashes. I made the right decision. "Unfortunately, they're custom, and I can't get more anytime soon. I have something else, though."

She follows my movement as I crouch down and lift my pant leg. My Contingency is sheathed at my ankle, the main reason I wear long pants in this unbearable heat.

While no one around here would dare question the Davis family, one of Marshall's rules is to conceal our weapons around civilians at all times.

When I raise it to Jules's line of sight, her mouth forms an O. I'd hoped she would like it. It is my favorite blade and the first custom knife I purchased, yet her reaction catches me off guard. Her tongue swipes across her bottom lip. She leans closer on the balls of her feet, transfixed by my offering.

Her eyes flick up before she tilts her head and scans my offering more. "You're giving me this?"

I clear my throat, an unfamiliar emotion strangling me. "Uh, if you want it?"

She peers up and holds my gaze. Her beautiful face morphs from surprise to utter joy and... My heart thuds out of sync, and I want to grip my chest. What is that?

Jules squeals and launches herself at me. Her mouth slams

onto mine, and she's lucky I drop the blade before she impales it in her thigh. The kiss ends as fast as it started, and she stares at me with her legs wrapped around my midsection and her arms interlocked behind my head. I'm hyperaware of where our bodies are connected.

"If I want it? Are you nuts? Of course I want it." She untangles herself, steps back, and rubs her hands together. "Okay, teach me."

My mind races to catch up with what just happened, and I find myself peering in the direction of the Bronco. Corbin has joined Della, towering over her. Her mouth moves rapidly as she peers up at him. They're locked in some type of standoff.

What the fuck?

I draw in a deep breath. Whatever.

Focusing back on my girl, her excitement is contagious. Buzzing zips through my veins, and I let my mouth curve up. This will be fun. My goal is to work on defense first. With her eagerness to learn, it won't take long before we move on to offense.

I pick up the knife from where it sticks—handle up—in the dirt, and I square my stance. Jules mimics me, and I nod approvingly.

"A few things you need to understand when it comes to knife attacks." I transition to a fighting position with the left foot forward while grabbing her behind the neck with my left hand. I'm careful not to apply too much pressure. *Yet.* Once we train, I won't go easy. Blood rushes to my cock at the mental picture of us sparring, pinning her to the ground. Overpowering her to force the phoenix to take over. No one learns from being coddled—one of the few lessons I appreciate my father giving me.

I continue, "Seventy-one percent of all knife attacks are executed by grabbing the victim by the neck or the front of their clothing." Adjusting my grip, I angle my head toward my feet. "The dominant leg is forward."

Lifting my gaze, I wait for her to meet my eyes. "The hand holding the knife will be low, by his...*or her* side before stabbing it into the intended victim's stomach." I simulate the strike in slow motion, stopping before the tip connects with her body. "We'll be working on this attack first."

I let go of Jules and retreat.

"If someone attacks you with a knife, the person is out to kill. Even a simple mugging...statistically, the average number of stab wounds is twenty-six."

Jules's eyes bulge, but I don't stop. I was never educated in English language arts or social studies. Our lessons focused on the subjects we'd need to survive. To kill.

"The assailant doesn't just threaten and slash you once before disappearing with your wallet. Someone who uses a blade of any kind is out for one thing. But..." I place my palms on her shoulders and put my forehead to hers, needing the contact as a flash of my nightmare flitters to the forefront. "If you can get your attacker off balance, it doesn't matter how strong you are. You will have the upper hand."

I slant my head toward my brother and Jules's best friend without actually looking in that direction. "Corbin can bench-press twice his body weight, but in a one on one, Paycen beats him every single time."

Jules sucks in a breath. "How?"

I straighten and twirl the Contingency between my fingers, its wasp handle rough against my palm. "Under stress, your cognitive ability to rationalize and analyze a situation drops. Getting attacked—knife or any other weapon—is a life-or-death situation. The *ultimate* stress."

Jules peers between my hands and my face before huffing noncomically, "I'd say so."

I smirk. "What you"—I point the blade at her—"will use to your advantage is that your attacker is under the same amount of stress." A fact many people don't consider. "All your intentions, everything you thought you would do or learned in the past, will go out the window. Your brain's ability to think logically at that moment is 0.01%." I wait for the information to sink in.

Her gaze is trained to the upper left, and she gnaws on her bottom lip.

"You need to have years—and I mean twenty-plus—of training for your reactions to become second nature." I flatten my mouth as a vision of Jules lying in a pool of blood suddenly penetrates my thoughts.

Shaking my head, I say, "Statistics also show that your attacker won't change hands, even if you have his knife hand pinned. Why?" I pause for a beat. "Stress." I tap the side of my head. "So, what I want to do is work with you on not thinking."

A crease forms between her brows.

I curl my fingers around the handle. "The first thing you do is create a wall between you and the knife."

Jules purses her lips and is about to speak when I cut her off. "Let me finish."

Her mouth snaps shut.

I dip my chin. "When I say wall, I mean you use your forearm to block the strike. The attacker will continue to stab you because he won't realize for several seconds that he's not meeting his target. That is your time line to save your li—"

"E!" I'm about to show Jules how to form a block when Cor's shout interrupts me midsentence.

Jules and I turn toward my brother.

Scanning his face, I don't bother asking what he wants. I throw my arm over her shoulder, and she returns the embrace around my midsection. "We'll pick this back up next time."

Jules's eagerness and excitement lighten some of the weight on my chest.

Striding toward the others, I'm going over my schedule for the next few days when Corbin barks, "Get moving. You can continue your little lesson another day."

Della slugs his arm, and Jules rears back.

"What the hell?" Her mumbled shock gets drowned out by my brother.

"Do that again, Greystone, and I'll hit back."

Della slants her head, scanning Corbin up and down with disdain. "Don't make promises, *Davis*."

Irritation burns in my core. I should've come alone.

When we reach the Bronco, I unfasten the sheath from my ankle and hand it to Jules, together with the knife. She cradles it to her body, and warmth floods me.

This girl is perfect.

WE DROP Della and Jules off at the now-deserted school parking lot. I couldn't pull the seat forward fast enough before Della jumped out, storming to her MINI.

Jules follows a little slower, stopping at my side once her feet hit the pavement. Flicking my eyes to my brother, he's watching Della with an impassive stare. I know him, though. The tic in his jaw is a dead giveaway.

Jules grazes her finger along my neck and lets her hand drop to rest against my stomach. "Thank you for my gift." She peers at me through her lashes.

How can one female be this gorgeous?

"Don't thank me yet. You still have to learn how to use it." I grin, cupping her face.

Her fingers sink lower, and she hooks them into the pockets

of my jeans. Pulling me close, she rises on her tiptoes, and I wrap my arms around her smaller frame.

"Is this a promise?" She hovers her lips against mine.

Heat sparks in my core. "You can bet on it." My mouth settles against hers.

Before I can take the initiative, she swipes her tongue over the seam of my lips, seeking entrance. I groan at her taking charge. Applying pressure to her lower back, she arches and molds her tits against my chest. My cock strains against my zipper. What I wouldn't give to strip her naked right here and fuck her against the side of the Bronco. Screw who could see us.

Jules moans as she deepens the kiss, meshing our lips together.

"JULES!" Della yells, followed by laying on the horn like a lunatic.

Jesus Christ.

Jules doesn't let this deter her, though. Instead, she continues with her *assault.* My hands sink lower, cupping her ass. Her shorts have ridden up, displaying the swell of her cheeks. My molars grind together as a low growl builds in my chest. "We need to talk about your attire at school." I dig my nails into her flesh. "I don't like *my* ass being on display for everyone."

Jules cocks a brow. "Your ass?"

"Mine," I say, grazing my teeth along her jaw.

My girl whimpers as I pinch the sensitive skin under her ear between my teeth.

"What about you?" Her question is breathy.

Drawing back, she challenges me with her gaze. I drown in the green of her eyes. "I already told you that I'm yours, Little Phoenix."

A soft smile lifts the corner of her mouth, and I'm about to plant my lips back on hers when Della revs the engine.

"If you don't get in now, Davis can give you a ride home." Her tone has grown chilly, and Jules sighs.

"I better go."

"Okay."

She drops a swift kiss on my cheek before walking backward, playing with her new knife.

"I'll text you later," I call. I'm fucking whipped.

Jules salutes me with the sheathed blade before pivoting on her heels, racing toward her friend.

IT'S BEEN two weeks since I brought Jules to the clearing.

We've gone back a few times. With every visit, her ability to handle the blade improved exponentially, and I've caught myself envisioning how it would be if I could show her off to the world —my world. She'd be feared and worshiped equally.

Jules still has a long way to go with regular hand-to-hand, which is as much my fault as it is hers. Teaching her how to get out of a choke hold frequently got interrupted by Jules stopping the fight as I squeezed the air from her lungs. She'd reach back, grip me through my pants, and I would change my attack to plunging my fingers into her pussy until she screamed my name.

With the Contingency, though, she's a natural—to the point where she nicked my arm once. When her eyes widened and she profusely apologized, I simply tackled her to the ground and tore her shorts off her frame. We didn't continue the training that day either.

Theo finally came home last night, and Jenn suggested we celebrate their reunion at the diner. She wanted to see *her* friend —not that I objected.

Sitting in our usual booth, Theo peruses the menu. Jules doesn't ask me anymore what I want. My answer is always the same—her—and she, in return, brings me a burger with a whole pickle on the side. It's become our running joke. Even Cor started quirking his mouth, warming up to Jules.

Jenn lounges between my legs, spinning my paracord bracelet on my wrist while I rest my hand on her stomach.

"I'm fucking sick of lurking in the shadows in that town," Theo grumbles about his assignment as he flips the menu over.

"You should enroll in their high school," Jenn casually suggests.

Cor arches his brows and whips his eyes to me. I lift a shoulder. "Might be fun." I smirk. We've never attended a regular school. The only times we were not limited to online and homeschooling were when we visited specialized facilities to perfect our other abilities.

Theo scrunches his nose but then cocks his head. "Maybe I will. I'll be up there long enough."

Jenn rubs her palms together. "See, sometimes I have good ide—"

"Hi, Ethan," a way too sultry voice interrupts my sister, and Jenn's head jerks around.

The intruder flinches, but then she straightens her shoulders. The girl can't be older than Jenn or Jules.

I slant my head, waiting. This'll be interesting.

In my peripheral vision, Corbin leans back in his seat, cuffing his biceps. For once, an amused expression covers his face. No one has ever approached us openly in public.

Theo mimics Cor, but instead of folding his arms, he reaches under the table and places a black object on top of it. "How may we help you?"

The girl's overly lined eyes pop as she stares at my brother's CRKT RITUAL. Where I favor WK blades of any kind, Theo goes for the more unconventional ones.

"I, uh... I was wondering if Ethan—"

"If Ethan what, Ivy?"

Ivy peers over her shoulder at Jules, who stands behind her with our drinks. My girl's icy question reminds me of my little brother, and the hair on my forearm stands.

Our visitor's demure expression morphs to distaste without blinking an eye. "I was wondering if Ethan would want to have dinner wi—"

"No." Jules's features don't move at all. She holds the other girl's daring look, not giving Ivy what she clearly expects.

A flutter of excitement mingled with anticipation simmers in my gut, and I fight to keep my expression neutral.

"No?" Ivy scoffs, and two girls suddenly appear at her side, flanking their leader.

"No," Jules repeats herself, placing the cups of water on the table.

Jenn's shoulders begin to shake in silent laughter. Scanning my brothers, Cor is now fully invested, his eyes crinkling in the corners.

Theo meets my gaze. He hasn't been around Jules as much. He tilts his head: *What's she gonna do?*

I let my eyes flick to his blade in response. T frowns but then interlaces his hands behind his head, giving Jules open access. He's intrigued. And I know my girl. She has an addiction to blades like no other.

Ivy plants one palm on the tabletop and props the other against her jutted hip.

Cliché much?

Jenn gets comfortable, snuggling her back against my front to have a better view of the show. I should stop Jules, but at the same time, I'm too curious. There is nothing better than seeing her wield a sharp object. Except for being impaled by my—

Jenn elbows me in the ribs when she rubs against my hard-on. I drop my arm from the back of the booth and rest it above her collarbone, whispering in her ear, "This is not for you, sis."

She hums in approval, patting my leg. Jules's attention briefly shifts to us. My girl doesn't blink an eye at the position Jenn and I are in. Instead, she focuses back on Ivy.

"Go back to your table, Ivy," Jules orders calmly.

"I'm here to talk to—" Ivy's words end in a shriek.

Faster than any of us can comprehend, Jules picks up the RITUAL, flicks open the blade, and impales it into the tabletop between Ivy's middle and ring finger.

Slanting her head, she places her hand on top of the shaking girl's. "I said go. Back. To. Your. Table. Ethan is mine. Next time, I won't *miss*."

Theo whistles, and Corbin knocks his fist to the table. "Hear, hear."

Ivy jerks her fingers out from under Jules's and whirls on her heels, stomping out of the diner with less dignity than she thinks she has. Her two friends are rooted to the floor, staring wide-eyed at us one by one. Corbin bares his teeth, and one squeaks before dragging her friend out the door.

Jules extracts the blade, examining the table. Scrunching her mouth, she states, "Well, shit, Dad is so gonna dock my pay for this."

Corbin barks a laugh, and she has just gained a whole new respect from my family.

I shove at Jenn. "Let me out."

"Wha—" She peers behind her.

CHAPTER TWELVE

JULES

IT'S BEEN FOUR MONTHS SINCE I OFFICIALLY CLAIMED ETHAN Davis as mine. Graduation has come and gone, and the summer is in full sweat-running-down-my-ass-crack swing.

We never put a label on our relationship—I no longer need one. No title could define what we share.

The day I almost stabbed Ivy, Ethan ambushed me in the hallway. I was about to grab the rest of their drinks when he dragged me to the men's bathroom. An inferno of lust and desire flashed in his caramel gaze, igniting my insides until I burned like the phoenix he titled me. He showed me thoroughly that I was his as much as he was mine. He had to clamp his palm over my mouth, or the entire diner, including my parents, would've heard that as well.

Ethan would sneak into my room in the middle of the night. On the days I wasn't working, we met in the clearing. He was a phenomenal teacher—patient when I struggled, but at the same time, never treated me like a breakable doll. He pushed me to my limits, proving how much I had to learn. Ethan had a lifetime of experience, and I was determined to catch up. When he trained his blade in my direction, he became *a Davis*. He let me see the side of himself he hated, but for me to prepare for all possibilities, he became the person he was trying to protect me from.

I slowly understood why his family was so feared.

THE CLOSER ETHAN and I became, the more cagey Della acted. She remained at my side in school, flipped Ivy and the pom-pom squad the bird when they hissed insults in my direction, but something had shifted between us. I couldn't put my finger on it, and when I brought it up, she insisted that everything was fine. It wasn't.

One afternoon a couple of weeks ago, I mentioned it to Ethan. His gaze strayed from mine, staring over my shoulder at nothing. He was quiet for so long I thought he wasn't going to acknowledge my worry at all. When he finally returned to me, he was...not *my* Ethan.

"Cor probably fucked her, and now she hates him. He's not very subtle when it comes to dropping a lay."

What?

"I would know if Della had slept with your brother." I searched his eyes for the truth. The lie he just fed me was so far out there he couldn't possibly believe I'd buy it.

Della and I were best friends. I knew what flavor floss she preferred, why she basically threw up when serving cooked carrots to customers, and who her first was. There was nothing we didn't share.

Ethan slashed his lips and pulled me close until my cheek was nuzzled against his chest.

"What are you keeping from me?" My arms found their way around him. I was pissed. Livid.

Contradicting whispers filled my mind.

He's protecting you.

He doesn't trust you.

He doesn't keep things from you unless it's necessary.

He doesn't think you can handle it.

"I..." His hold tensed. "It's not my secret to tell, Little Phoenix." The tips of his fingers traveled up and down my spine.

I concentrated on breathing through my nose, the motion soothing my irritation. "Then, whose is it?" My voice echoed in my ear as I listened to the steady thud behind his ribs.

Ethan shifted, framing my face and angling my head so I had no choice but to look at him. "Please stop asking. You know I don't keep anything from you, but this is not my burden to bear. In time, you will understand." The plea in his gaze sliced at my heart.

I dropped the subject. For now.

THIRTEEN DAYS AGO, Ethan left for another assignment.

I listen to the pebbles crunching under my flip-flops as I walk from the diner to our house. Dad is closing. With every step, the grinding sound under my soles slows, and the distance to the back door becomes longer—another lonely night ahead.

I despise it when he leaves for a job. It's the only time I feel like your stereotypical, clingy *girlfriend*. Not that I'd act on the urge to text him hourly to make sure he is still alive. No, I'd rather let the fear of losing him fester and eat me from the inside out, my stomach slowly corroding with worry until I see with my own eyes that he is okay.

Him and Jenn hanging out in a booth with her literally on top:

inconsequential. Well, that is not completely true. It doesn't stir any negative sensations. I enjoy seeing them as a family. Their lives are driven by a power they can't fight. They serve a purpose to their father, but when they come to the diner, they are just *them.* The dynamic between Ethan and Jenn is no threat, even when she has confessed their past. I can read in their expressions that they have a different bond than Ethan and I. There is nothing romantic between them. My claim toward Ivy was merely a statement to her. She had assumed she was above everyone since kindergarten. It was time that someone put her in her place.

Usually, Ethan has an idea when he'd be back, but this time is different. It isn't a long-term gig like Theo's, but something has kept them away.

Jenn visited a few days after Ethan left and informed me that she'd join her twin until the others were back. I gathered over the last few months that she hated being on the plantation alone. I never dared ask where Paycen was in all of this. But then, what could a thirteen-year-old with no emotions be able to give her?

I toe my shoes off and fling them into the corner of the mudroom. Picking them up and dropping them in the designated shoe basket is one more task I don't feel like completing.

Grabbing a bottle of water from the fridge, I pad down the hall to my room.

The door is ajar, and I halt. I closed it this morning. We keep the bedroom doors shut. Always. A weird quirk my mother has. Reaching behind me, the sheath with my knife is tucked inside my shorts, my long tee hiding it from the customers—or my parents. The cotton of my white flowy tank tickles my skin as my fingers disappear under the material. The coarse texture of the wasp handle calms my erratic pulse.

It took some getting used to having the object pressing into my lower back. Ethan made me promise never to be without it, and I couldn't do long pants in this heat. I tried the first day. Dressing in loose linen joggers and fastening the sheath around my ankle, I almost passed out. I may have exaggerated a bit, but Ethan showed up with a different option the same night.

The heel of my hand presses into the wooden barrier. The only thing missing is a creaking sound as the door slowly swings inward.

With my bed situated across the room, my visitor comes into view. My chest squeezes. I blink. He's still there. The muscles in my arms and legs begin to coil, and the skin over my knuckles that clasp the handle burns.

"You can leave your little toy where it is, J." Ty doesn't move from his spot on the mattress. He lazily lounges with his back against the headboard and legs stretched in front with his ankles crossed. He lifts his arms, lacing them behind his head. His biceps stretch the sleeves of his tee. Did he bulk up?

Ty and I have been equally avoiding each other after the almost altercation. I assumed it was a mutual truce, that he accepted our time has passed.

A growl builds in my throat. *He's sitting on Ethan's pillow.*

My eyes fly over my room, searching for anything out of place. How long has he been here? How did he— "How did you get in here?"

Ty swings his legs off the mattress. He stands in a fluid motion that doesn't match the boy I grew up with. His hands clasp behind his back, and he strides toward me.

A crease forms between my brows at his posture.

Halting a few feet away, he cocks his head.

The hair at my nape prickles with unease, my shoulder blades so tense they could hold a pencil between them. I prepare myself. Something is off with him. My thumb braces against the sheath, ready to pull my blade out.

"Your mother let me in." His detached voice solidifies further that he is not the same.

"Why would she—?"

"I told her I came to apologize." Another step.

My eyes narrow. "Apologize for what?"

"Well, to be honest..." He suddenly turns ninety degrees and saunters over to my window. The sun has set, and our eyes connect in the glass. "I don't see the point in apologizing. My father still holds out hope to join our families."

What the ever-loving—

"I'm fully aware I have no chance against the false Davis."

"The false—" I gape.

"We all know that Ethan is not a pureblood. He will never have the same rights as—"

"What do you know about that?" I snap. He goaded me, and I fell into the trap. Mashing my lips together, I pull my blade from its confinement. I need to feel the 80CrV2 against the pad of my finger, the cool steel settling the firing nerve endings.

"J," Ty bristles. He pivots, leaning against the window frame. His arms cross over his front. "We might all be *Rens*, but do you really believe you're the only one that has the scoop of what's going on on the plantation?"

My breath stalls and my reply freezes in my chest.

"I'm here to make you an offer." He pushes off and makes his way back over. Dropping his gaze to the Contingency, the corner of his mouth lifts, but he doesn't comment on the knife. Instead, he shocks me to the core. "Come to college with me."

My brows shoot up, and my lips part, but no sound comes out.

"You got into Lakewood. Not as far as you wanted to run"— he chuckles—"but it'll allow us to start over. From this. Neither of us wants our parents' lives."

"But..." I have no idea how to respond. He's right. I got my acceptance letter months ago, but Ethan has changed things for me—my need to get out of Renneton. We haven't discussed what happens after the summer is over. I've been avoiding the topic, needing to figure it out myself before I let anyone else in on it.

But this? He's asking me to run away with him? My mind is reeling. "You always wanted to take over your dad's business." My parched tongue makes it hard to speak.

Ty stops in front of me, placing his palms on my shoulders. "My father's business won't get me anywhere. He may be content with his position, but I'm not. I want more. And if that means leaving Renneton...with you..." His fingers dig into my flesh. "Then let's do it. *We* can do it. Build our own—"

"I'm with Ethan." I recoil.

Ty's arms fall to his sides. "You won't be forever."

What?

"What is that supposed to mean?" my voice rises, yet I can barely hear it over the rushing in my ears. Is he threatening me? Threatening Ethan? My peripheral vision disappears. All I see is Ty. I can take him. I just need an opening. He wouldn't expect me to attack. Not here in my home, with my mother down the hall.

He shrugs a shoulder. "Just stating the obvious, J." A devious grin twists his features. "You are not a Davis and will never be part of their inner circle. Corbin might be able to snatch himself a piece of Ren ass, but Ethan would never get away with it. Not *you*."

Red stains my sight. "Stop fucking speaking in riddles. What does Corbin have to do with all of this? You haven't spoken to me in months, and then you show up in my bedroom in the middle of the night? What the fuck, Ty?"

He bares his teeth. "There is the fire you kept hidden when we were together. I knew it was somewhere in there. I just needed to find a way to...spark it." His expression resembles the first time Corbin dissected me under his obsidian stare.

I rear back. *Who is this guy?*

"I will never," I speak purposefully slow. "Ever." I position my left foot in front and distribute my weight. "Go anywhere with you."

A flush creeps up Ty's neck and tinges his cheeks. His gaze hardens, and I watch his chest rise and fall. Ty may have changed, but his tells are the same. He's always been one easy to blow. Never with me—until now—but he became the QB for a reason. He takes no prisoners in his pursuit of a goal. He wins. At all costs.

"Jules." His tone gentles. "What can Ethan give you besides a meaningless fuck? He will never—"

I lift my free hand, palm out. "No. You need to leave."

"Not without you agreeing to go with me."

Heat rushes through my body, burning my face. "Did you listen to me?" I seethe. I'm starting to not care if Mom hears us. What the fuck is wrong with him? "You and I are over. Why would I go anywhere with you? I don't love y—"

"But you love Ethan, huh?" He gets in my face, and instinctively, I raise my hand.

Ty's eyes grow wide, and his mouth opens. My gaze drops to where my blade is embedded in his side.

Oh shit.

I jerk the knife out before I can rationalize that this might have been the wrong move. Ty's hands clutch to the rapidly expanding stain on his shirt.

"Oh my god. Fuck. Shit." I frantically search for something to press against his wound.

His lips curl back. "Don't touch me."

"Ty, I'm sorry. You startled—" What am I even saying? I wanted to stab him. I just didn't expect it to happen. Ethan drilled into me from our first lesson to not think. I didn't think. Fuck.

"Shut your slutty mouth, Jules," Ty growls.

He shoves me with one hand while the other holds on to his stomach. I stumble, and my lower back slams into the knob of my dresser.

I yelp. Which impact causes the sound, I don't know—Ty's hand or the sharp ache in my kidney.

He rushes out the door, and I stare at the empty spot, three crimson droplets staining my carpet. My blade falls to the floor, and I sink to a crouch.

What have I done?

TIME HAS NO MEANING. I have no idea how long I sit there, but my legs ache when I finally manage to stand. I stumble to my bed, propping my arms against the mattress. I inhale and exhale through my nose, counting to eight every time. It's not working. I feel like someone has tied a noose around my heart. It hurts.

Breathe.

The vibration against my ass jolts me upright. Jesus fuck. My palm flies to my throat. What time is it? Did I miss calling Ethan? I was supposed to text after my shift. I reach for my phone in my back pocket. I have to clench the device between my fingers to prevent it from slipping.

Three tries later, I manage to answer the video call. "Hey."

The little picture in the corner shows my skin paler than usual and my hair disheveled.

"What's wrong?" A groove forms between Ethan's brows.

"I..." The words escape me. I don't even know what happened.

"You're scaring me, Little Phoenix." Ethan's tone has an

edge, and he scans the screen, searching for clues. Suddenly, his eyes widen. "Is that blood?"

Blood?

I peer down at myself, and sure enough, where Ty shoved me aside is a red handprint on my shirt and skin.

"What the fuck?" Corbin inquires in the background, and his face appears behind Ethan. His brows pinch and a shot of warmth shoots through me at his concern.

"I stabbed Ty," I whisper, the confession sounding surreal to my own ears.

There is silence, both men staring at me. Several beats go by.

"You stabbed your ex?" Ethan repeats incredulously as he exchanges a look with Corbin.

"He came to my house." The words begin to flow, and once the floodgate opens, I can't stop. By the time I finish, I'm out of breath, and their faces are contorted with rage.

Corbin snatches the device from his brother. "You need to stay away from Morello."

"What is going on? How does he know...whatever it is he knows. What the fuck *does* he know?" My voice rises with every word. I'm surprised Mom hasn't come in yet.

Corbin paces. Ethan's form flashes in the background every time he changes direction. Corbin gazes at the ceiling, hollowing his cheeks. I've never seen him anything less than stone cold. My insides knot at the sight. "Morello is not important. He's a loose end we'll tie up when we get back." He halts and looks past the screen. At Ethan? "We'll talk when we get ho—"

"Give me the fucking phone, asshole," Ethan barks and, after some jostling, appears in front of me. "Baby, do not go anywhere alone. I never trusted that fucker, but it seems he's more involved than we knew."

My eyes sting with frustration. "Involved in what?"

"Cor is right. Not over the phone. I'll explain everything

when I'm home. We finished today. We just have to clean up and then head back."

Not much scares me, but the unknown is the one thing that hunts me in the dark.

"How long?" It takes effort to form the question.

"Four days tops."

THE FOUR DAYS turn into six.

Della has been glued to my side. Before hanging up, Ethan ordered me to call and tell her. My eyes had flicked to Corbin in the background, and he approved.

One of these days, they will give me answers.

They came back two days ago, but apparently, Marshall had some big thing going on at the plantation, and Ethan couldn't leave. Of course, he didn't tell me what it was. His cryptic shit was slowly pushing me to my limits. I jumped at every sound. Any customer that wasn't a regular became suspicious.

During our last exchange, Ethan literally pleaded with me.

Ethan: Little Phoenix, I'm doing the best I can.

Me: Don't LP me, Davis. You have 24 hrs to give me answers.

Or what?

What was I going to do? March onto the plantation? Break up with him? Fuck.

Ethan: I'll be there.

CHAPTER THIRTEEN

ETHAN

IT'S BEEN GETTING INCREASINGLY HARDER TO KEEP MY composure. The last few days have been a parade of who has the bigger dick.

My plan was to drop my shit and head straight to Jules's. Instead, we arrived at a house packed with America's most wanted. Half a dozen of Marshall's business *acquaintances*—also known as keep your friends close but invite your enemies inside your home to maintain control of your territory—welcomed us. Anyone with some say was in attendance, and of course, we had to represent our father.

I envied Jenn and Theo, who were still away. Showing these people a shred of respect was like cutting off your foot with a dull, rusty blade—something you'd never voluntarily consider, but when your life depended on it, you did what it took to survive.

Given Corbin's role in the family, he was the only one allowed to witness the meetings. Paycen and I were stationed outside of the large dining room to ensure no one left or entered. One look at my little brother and anyone attempting to disobey my father's order quickly changed their mind.

"Wanna have some fun?" I inquired without making eye contact with Paycen. My feet ached like a mother, and I was bored out of my skull.

Peering at him in my peripheral vision, Paycen cocked his head.

"Let's play tic-tac-toe with the next fucker that tries to get past us." I grin to myself. The last asshole actually got so close to my face, attempting to appear threatening, that I could see his fucking tonsils.

Paycen snorted—a rare sound from him. My brother never declined to carve into something...or someone. But then, he stated quietly, "I don't feel like sleeping in *the pen*."

My stomach hardened, and my head jerked to the side. "What happened while we were gone?"

The mask of...emptiness he always wore slipped for the briefest of moments.

"Paycen." I fully faced him then, but he just stared ahead.

I took a step toward him when he said, "Father was in one of his moods."

Father or Carolyn was the real question here. It was at these moments that Paycen looked his actual age.

"Just let it go, E."

I scanned him up and down, noticing the bruises around his wrists. "Which pen?" I kept my tone low, refusing to let the sour taste coating my tongue seep into the question.

"The last," was all he replied.

My fingers twitched, and I wanted to pound the wall. I opened my mouth, but Paycen stopped me.

"Let it go." His gaze returned to its usual void.

I drew in a slow breath and repositioned myself on the other side of the double door.

I needed to see Jules. Needed her warmth and to feel something other than this...darkness.

I KNOCK at the doorframe once before entering Marshall's office. "You wanted to see me?"

Marshall's *guests* finally left this afternoon, and I was on my way to the garage when his second intercepted me. I don't recall the last time my father wanted to speak to me alone.

My father peers up from a stack of papers. "Yes."

It's past ten. I was supposed to be at Jules's two days ago, and she is furious—rightfully, though. I've been avoiding giving answers as to why I can't come.

I approach his desk and stand with my hands clasped behind my back. We don't sit unless invited.

"I got some unfortunate news." His focus is back on his papers.

Unfor—?

"You are familiar with Grant Arrow?" Marshall continues to scribble his notes.

My spine goes rigid. "I am. He owns the diner outside of town." My interlaced fingers crack.

Finally, my father places his pen down and graces me with his attention. "Grant Arrow is one of our Laundromats."

What the fuck?

I abandon my stance, my arms dropping to my sides. "How did I not know that?" I instantly regret my slip of control.

Laundromat is code for money laundering. Marshall has them all over the country, ensuring none of the business deals can be traced back to him.

"Now, why would I share this piece of information with you?

You are not the one taking over one day." He leans back in his chair, folding his arms. His lifeless eyes bore into me.

He knows. He fucking knows about Jules. Is this a test? Is Cor involved? I may not be the next in line in *The Davis Order*, but usually, we know Marshall's general business dealings. My rib cage shrinks, constricting my airflow.

I try to come up with the right words. "My apologies, Father. I assumed we didn't have local facilities." I draw my shoulders back, concealing the itch to dive over the barrier between us and wrap my fingers around his throat. In all the years, no matter what he did to me—to us—it never crossed my mind to execute revenge—until now.

"You assumed incorrect, *my son*." After a pause, he adds, "I put your brother on rectifying the issue."

Panic surges to the surface, snuffing out the burning rage under my skin. I fight the need to press my fist to my sternum. Putting my brother on a job solo means only one thing. Corbin has a special talent. One we don't use often. It's messy and draws attention to the scene.

I lock my knees, and every fiber in my body is stretched to the point of tearing. The seconds tick by, and I swear Marshall is making me wait on purpose, giving his other son more time to complete the task. A task I'm not needed for, which solidifies that this is a lesson.

"Grant has been stealing from me. *Us*."

Stealing?

"He's been withholding small amounts over the last several years, which now have added up to a rather significant sum. This is unacceptable."

I nod, not trusting my voice.

"We need to send a message to all the Laundromats. I do not tolerate disobedience, let alone theft."

Holding his gaze, I draw in a deep breath. "What do you need from me?"

Marshall narrows his eyes. He's waiting for me to slip. While Grant Arrow's actions are basically a guaranteed death sentence, acting all of a sudden is just an excuse. There is no way Marshall just found out.

"Assist with the cleanup. You know what to do. Jenn is not back, and Carolyn is busy. I want confirmation that all three bodies are there." He pins me down.

Three. A sheen of sweat forms on the back of my neck. *Three bodies.* A tremor rolls through me, nearly forcing my knees to give out. *Jules.*

I whirl and start running.

"ETHAN."

I don't stop.

I SPOT the black pyre when I'm still a mile away. The smoke is dulling the moon in the cloudless sky.

No, no, no.

I press my foot into the pedal, the howling of the engine drowning out the pounding of my heart. Black spots fade in and out over my vision, the pressure in my chest constricting the airflow to my lungs. My palms are clammy, slipping from the steering wheel and forcing me to grip the leather until my fingers ache. Refusing to slow down, I almost fly out of the last bend. The Bronco lifts on one side, and I regain control at the last second.

My brother would never do this to me.

Coming to a screeching halt, my heart stops. I can't move, staring at the carnage and destruction.

The parking lot is empty except for Cor's Mustang at the far end. It's hidden in the shadows, partially covered by a low-hanging willow.

Red-and-orange flames engulf the diner and house behind it. He torched everything. It won't take long, and nothing will be left.

Corbin is the *Firestarter*.

My mind screams at me to move, and the connection to my body snaps into place. My paused heartbeat jumps into action, thundering against my ribs. I throw the door open and make a run for the Arrows' small house. Jules wouldn't be in the diner anymore.

Out of nowhere, arms lock around me. My feet kick out. Attempting to break free, all I accomplish is making us nearly fall. Corbin roots me in place.

"JULES! JUUULES!" I struggle against his ironclad hold. I'm strong, but he is a tank. He has three inches and at least fifty pounds on me.

My cheeks tingle as tears stream down my face. Why? How can he do this? She wasn't part of this world. Our world. Bile rises as violent sobs rack my body. Emotions I've never experienced cripple me.

I scream until my voice gives out, ignoring the pain scratching the back of my throat. I lose all sense of time, watching as part of the roof collapses into the main dining area —onto the table we sat at so many times.

My stomach revolts and my body goes slack as the crackling of the fire mingles with the crashing sound of wood falling on wood. When I stop struggling and make no move to *interfere* again, Corbin releases me.

The realization that there is no life behind the charred walls severs my ability to fight. My gaze is trained on the house behind the diner. The once-cream exterior is marred with black, where the flames have already broken through the facade, escaping their confinement and fueling their purpose of destruction with fresh oxygen.

We don't have to worry about being caught. This stretch of the road is busy during the day, but once the sun sinks, no one travels through here.

I drop to my knees and let out one last hoarse scream as my fingers grip the earth underneath.

I've lost the one person that made life worth living.

Corbin's boots remain in my peripheral vision.

I don't move until the flames begin to die.

A hand lands between my shoulder blades, and I recognize her without looking. Jenn crouches and hooks her hand under my armpit. Tugging, she rights me. I don't resist. I can't. With one hand cuffing my bicep, she threads her other fingers with mine. A thousand needles prick my skin where she touches me, yet I'm unable to shrug her off. I have nothing left.

We don't need a cleaner. The fire did the job. No one will ever suspect foul play; Corbin is good like that. Marshall wanted me to see what he does to anyone who doesn't follow *The Order* —his orders. He killed two birds with one stone—Grant and me.

I let Jules in. I signed her death warrant.

Theo appears on my other side, and his hand clamps on my shoulder. A voice in the back of my head wonders where they came from, but as quickly as the question enters my mind, it's already gone. Jenn squeezes my fingers, but I can't give her what she wants. Our lives are tainted by evil. I tell myself that, without my involvement, Marshall might have only killed Jules's father to set an example.

With his phone pressed to his ear, Corbin blocks my view of the smoldering ruins. "It's done." Pause. "Yes, confirmed. We're back in thirty."

I cock my head, watching my brother as his eyes find mine. The grief that overwhelmed every cell in my body mere minutes ago is shadowed by a thick blanket of...nothing. My heart thuds in a steady rhythm.

It's all gone. She's gone.

I reach behind my back and pull my gun from its holster. Aiming it point blank at my brother's forehead, I wait for my fingers to tremble, signaling that I can still...feel. There is...nothing.

Corbin doesn't flinch. He has taken everything from me, and he knows it.

"Ethan," Jenn warns.

"He killed her." The words slice at my throat.

"He didn't have a choice," T reasons.

"He. Killed. Jules." I gnash my teeth, making it hard to speak.

"And if I hadn't, Father would've killed both of us. And then sent someone else to take out the Arrows," Corbin states, never breaking our connection. "It was the only option."

I press the barrel into his skull, the whitened skin around the indent visible even in the dark night. "You could've come to me." My tone wavers as my finger slips onto the trigger.

"Same outcome, brother." If Corbin feels any remorse, he doesn't show it.

Suddenly, his eyes flick to T. Too fast for me to react, Theo takes control of my gun, and Corbin flips me around into a choke hold.

With one arm in front of my throat and the other behind my head, my feet lose connection with the ground as he leans back. This is not a wrestling match. He's taking me out.

My lungs burn. I only have seconds. A voice in my head yells at me to fight back, but my vision is already blurry.

"Guys!" Jenn's cry is the last thing I hear before everything goes black.

PART TWO

How the phoenix rose from the ashes...
-Ethan

CHAPTER FOURTEEN

ETHAN

PRESENT

THE TIGHTNESS in my core has morphed and expanded to a bowline knot around my neck. My jeans have darkened where I continue to swipe my clammy palms. The itch to go closer has prevented me from unbuckling my seat belt since arriving two hours ago. I know better than to just walk in, no matter how much every cell of my body craves to be in her vicinity. I had accepted that I would never lay eyes on her again. All of that has changed.

My Bronco is tucked in the far corner of the gravel parking lot. Except for the spot next to me, they're all filled.

Rezoned.

The red-and-white neon sign is like a beacon in the foggy night. If I didn't know better, I'd swear the light is pulsing, taunting me that Jules is somewhere in there. Large, globe-like fixtures hang over each table lining the windows and illuminate the inside as much as the cars parked in front. Nearly every booth is occupied, and I watch the waitstaff buzzing back and forth.

No one with red hair, though.

JENN GAVE me all the information she had before she went radio silent.

ABOUT FOUR YEARS AGO, JJ Smith bought the old diner on Maple Avenue in Montson, Maine. It was purchased in cash, and the buyer, a.k.a. Jules, spent the next two years remodeling it. Jules lives on the second floor in a small two-bedroom and has no mode of transportation—under her name or JJ's.

WHILE I SUSPECTED that Jenn kept an eye on Jules, I never asked. I couldn't. Jules had lost everything because of my family. She deserved a life without a reminder of why she ended up here.

I attempted calling T, but he either ignored me or was with his twin. Which alternative was worse was up for debate.

My heart beats in my throat, a million insects crawling up my stomach walls at the possibility of getting my first glimpse of her in almost a decade. Does she look the same? Has she changed? Is her hair still long and the shade of red I love so much? How does she stay under the radar? Does someone help her? Is she *with* someone? At the last thought, the muscle in my jaw strains. I have no right to claim her, but at the same time, she will always be mine—my phoenix.

I pull my phone from the cup holder, swipe it open, and type out a message.

Me: Made it. Will be in touch.

Bax: Copy. Do not engage.

Me: Yes, sir.

He can insert the eye-roll emoji himself.

Bax: Call if you need backup.

Me: You have your hands full.

Bax: Call if you need backup.

I shake my head. This man has a split personality. Where he is soft as a Twinkie with his girl, he's as unbending as the steel on my Wild Bill axe when it comes to everyone else—especially work. Marcus Baxter, a.k.a. Bax, has been my boss and closest friend since I got hired by Altman Hotels and deposited into his team. We instantly connected, our souls—what was left of them—recognizing another occupant of the purgatory forged by our desecrated lives.

The head of the Altman security, George, plucked us damaged misfits off the street—or in my case, jail—and gave us a second (or third) chance. I lost count years ago. To this day, I have no clue how he found me. Or why he chose to give me a place in his ranks. Without G and Marcus, I would probably be dead. Instead, I work as personal security for one of the *(legally)* richest families in the US.

Marcus hadn't been raised by the devil, but he went through his own personal hell. It has never been a secret to any of them who I am—used to be—especially after we had to bring Jenn into the mix a few weeks ago to save Marcus's now girlfriend. Yet, Jules was the one topic I kept to myself. The one burden I refused to share.

We sat in our employer's home office with George on speakerphone when I revealed that part of my life. Closing my recollection with, "I have to make sure she's safe," none of them objected. They made me swear to remain in the dark until we devised a plan. First priority was to keep Jules alive. The rest...

That was four days ago.

EXITING BAX'S TEXT, Jenn's last communication appears underneath. I straighten my shoulders in an attempt to chase away the tightness. It's not working. I need to know that she's okay.

Returning to the home screen, I tap on the photo icon next. Only one small square appears—the only memory I've made sure to never lose, no matter how many times I've switched phones. Closing my eyes, I inhale an unsteady breath before rushing the oxygen from my lungs and pressing my thumb down.

Blinking, I stare at my twenty-two-year-old self with the only girl I've ever loved in my arms. Love. Yet, I never told her. My chest constricts, and I swallow over the needles in my throat as my eyes trail over the freckles on her nose and cheeks.

For the first year after her *death*, I spent hours counting the tiny brown spots. Her fiery hair partially obscures her face as Jules laughs up at me. The day replays in front of my mind's eye every time I allow myself to look at my last physical memory of her.

WE JUST FINISHED TRAINING. Jules is a natural, but whenever it would come down to it, she'd hesitate. Dripping sweat from every pore, I stripped out of my shirt an hour ago. I'm beside the Bronco's open passenger side, sheathing my new knife as I peer over at her.

She does the same with the Contingency. Whenever I watch her handle the blade, my lungs expand. She treats the knife like it's her most precious possession.

Her gaze meets mine, and her eyes roam my body. Her tongue swipes over the corner of her mouth, and my cock instantly swells.

"See something you like, Little Phoenix?" I laugh as I fling the blade onto the seat.

Jules arches a brow and saunters over. Placing her knife next to mine, she drops to her knees without a word. Her swift fingers unbutton my cargo shorts, and they pool at my feet before I can blink. Her palm wraps around my shaft, and she strokes me once, twice before wrapping her lips around me.

Eyes rolling back, my hand shoots out, steadying myself against the frame. "Fuck, baby."

She doesn't let up until I forcefully extract my dick from her mouth. I pull her up by the hands. "Since when are you in charge?" I joke.

I'll follow her command any day. There is no bigger turn-on for me than when Jules shows me what she wants.

Sinking her teeth into her bottom lip, I know what my girl craves. I flip her around and let my hand glide from the base of her spine to between her shoulder blades, where I apply pressure. She props herself on the floorboard of the Bronco—thank fuck the car is raised the way it is— as I pull her shorts down her ass.

"Burn" by 2WEI and Edda Hayes comes from the portable speakers we always use when we're training, and I wrap her long ponytail around my fist. Pumping my cock once, I align myself with her pussy and thrust forward.

Her moan drowns out the song for a second, and I'm lost in the sensation.

Later, we're sitting in the back seat, Jules curled in the crook of my arm, when she reaches forward and swipes my phone from the middle console. I don't stop her from snapping the photo.

ANOTHER ONE of Marshall's rules I broke.

I click the side button and place the phone face down on my thigh. The people in the picture don't exist anymore.

I lean against the headrest and watch as the diner slowly empties. Employees busy themselves cleaning the tables, mopping the floors, and one by one, the lights in the diner turn off.

My rib cage shrinks.

Maybe she isn't here.

I lock my jaw to stifle a yawn. I want to stay, but after spending the last ninety-six hours driving across the country, my body is shutting down. The dull throbbing behind my eyes has grown into a pounding headache. I only stopped twice to get a few hours of shut-eye and consumed an unnatural amount of caffeine the rest of the time—which has finally left my system.

My lids droop. The Bronco is the only car left in the lot. I can't sleep here. For one, I don't want Jules to find me like this or, worse, someone to call the cops. If I get arrested, I can't protect her. The only option I have is to trust that she'll be alright for one more day while I gather my strength.

Pulling up a map of the area, I locate a motel less than a mile away. Based on the rates, I suspect my car is more luxurious, but it'll have to do. No one will suspect me in that shithole. Marshall or anyone working for him wouldn't be caught dead setting foot there.

ONE WEEK IN MAINE, and still no word from Jenn.

Today's parking spot of choice is across the street from the diner in the lot of the local hardware store—one of those original places that supplied the area before being put out of business by ACE and Home Depot. The place has seen better days. The windows are so dirty you can barely make out the display, and the hedge separating the lot from the street is overgrown.

For my purpose, it is the perfect setup, but I doubt it would attract many customers this way.

I still have to be careful, though. The Bronco is not the most inconspicuous vehicle. I changed its color since Jules last saw it, but that doesn't mean anything. I'll have to find a rental for a while if this drags out. I assumed Marshall would send someone to finish the job immediately.

During my check-ins, Bax and I came up with a plan—how to handle the situation without drawing attention. If I had my way, Jules would never know what was going on and continue her life as is. She deserves peace after everything my family did to hers—and her. But if I take out one of Marshall's men, Jules wouldn't be safe here. He would just send more and make her death more painful for resisting.

I'll have to reveal myself to her eventually.

Concentrating has become a physical challenge. I can't sleep for more than a couple of hours at a time without jolting awake. While I don't dream, my mind makes up for it during the day. Between visions of my sister being in *the pen*, and my girlfri—*ex*-girlfriend being executed, my focus is shit.

T's line got disconnected, which technically isn't surprising. He never keeps the same number for more than a few weeks, but I would've expected him to let me know. The chance that Marshall doesn't believe whatever story Jenn dished him steadily rises.

I've almost reached the point of desperation to contact Corbin or even Paycen—assuming the communication protocol is the same.

AFTER MY SIXTEEN-HOUR COMA, I swept the surrounding streets. A beat-up station wagon behind the diner caught my attention, but when running the plates, it came back under

Marvin Fisher. Through Bax, and with the help of our employer, I learned that it belonged to the previous owner of Rezoned. My best guess is Jules kept it under the guy's name to dilute her footprint. *Smart girl.* Yet, in the entire seven days, I have not laid eyes on her. The second floor of the diner is lit up at night, but I haven't seen so much as a shadow behind the blinds.

Am I in the right spot? I mean, JJ Smith is not the most unique name, and a quick Google search proved that theory.

Having the seat pushed all the way back, my knee is propped against the steering wheel. I'm flicking through Spotify in an attempt to find some music that does not somehow remind me of what a shit show my life is. I swear the radio playlists are all fucking with me when "Poem of a Killer" by WE ARE FURY and Elijah Cruise is suggested.

A shadow falls over my lap a second before the driver's side door rips open and I have a knife to my throat.

My heart halts before thrashing violently against its confinement. I don't have to see her. I lift my hands in surrender, phone between my thumb and forefinger as the damn song continues to play. "Little Phoenix."

The tip of the blade punctures my skin. Adrenaline has taken over, and all I feel is warmth trickling down my neck.

"You lost the right to call me that when you tried to kill me," she seethes near my ear.

Hearing her voice for the first time in so long, no matter how angry she is, my nerves fire. "I never—"

She applies more pressure, and this time, a biting pain shoots from the nick up and down the entire side of my body.

"Fuck!" I curse and drop my phone. The clatter distracts her enough for me to wrap my fingers around her dainty wrist. I swing my leg out and gather the needed momentum to push both of us out of the car. With both soles on the ground, I tighten my hold and twist until her hand is pinned behind her back.

A yelp escapes her throat, but she doesn't cry out.

I wrap my free arm around her neck, the crook of my elbow aligned with her throat, and hold her immobile.

I'd only have to make one small adjustment, and I would be doing the dirty work for my father.

The counter was automatic. When the realization hits, I shove Jules away as if she burned me. She might as well have with how my body is ablaze from the brief contact of her skin against mine.

She stumbles but catches herself before eating it.

Whirling around, she positions herself in a fighting stance, both arms up. The glint catches my eyes, and I recognize the blade that once was mine.

"What are you doing here, Ethan?" Some of her anger has drained, and suddenly, she looks exhausted.

"You're in danger." My profound reply evokes a response I don't expect.

Jules's eyes widen before she doubles at the waist and... laughs. A hysterical, nonsensical cackle.

Have I pushed her over the edge? My mouth opens and closes, but no words form.

Swiping underneath her eye, she straightens and levels with me. "Good one, Davis." She points the tip in my direction. "Now go fuck yourself." The amusement gives way to a new level of pissed.

She pivots and is about to march across the street when I take a step toward her. "Jules."

Jerking around, Jules's hand shoots out. Her fingers curl into my hoodie as she aligns the blade under my chin. "First off, you do not touch me. Ever. Again. Second, I don't need you. I can

take care of myself. Go back to LA and leave me the fuck alone."
She shoves at me, and I let her.

Her words are like a bucket of icy water emptied over my
head.

How does she—?

With those parting words, she does a one-eighty and marches
across the street. Halfway to the diner, she sheaths the Contingency in the back of her jeans and pulls a phone out of her back
pocket. I can't see what she does until she lifts it to her ear.

Who the fuck is she calling?

CHAPTER FIFTEEN

JULES

"You better be dying."

"Fuck off." My pulse throbs in my neck. "Ethan is here. Why the fuck is Ethan in Montson?" I clench my phone harder to ensure my trembling fingers don't drop it.

My feet pound up the stairs to the diner. I feel him everywhere. My skin tingles—no *crawls* where he touched me. A sensation my body equally welcomes and revolts against. The nearness to him stalled my breath. And when his strong fingers wrapped around my wrist... Fuck. I refuse to let him have this kind of power. Never again. Flinging the door open, I aim straight for the back.

We're not busy, and Cody leans against the bar, chatting with Lina, who's refilling napkin dispensers. He calls out, but I ignore him, focusing on my soles connecting with the steps that lead to my apartment.

"Marshall has a new hit out on you."

My feet root to the wood as my stomach drops. I reach for

the railing, the stairwell having turned into a barrel of fun—without the fun.

"Why didn't you warn me?" My question is barely a whisper as I fight the bile back down.

That night begins to flash in front of my eyes.

I SHRINK INTO THE SHADOWS. The same trees I always walked through when Ethan would drop me off are now my only shelter.

I watch my home...and parents...engulfed in flames, eating away everything that made up my life. Instinct wants to cry for help, but even my hazy mind comprehends that no one will come. I'm alone.

My lungs burn from the smoke and earlier screams, inhaling the soot without a care for my health.

The heat instantly dries any new tears escaping my stinging eyes. No matter how I strain my ears, there are no pleas for rescue. My family is gone. They killed them before turning them to ashes.

The last memory of my mother will forever be carved into my brain.

Something woke me up. I don't remember what. I don't care either. My room was filled with smoke. The house was on fire. I had to get to my parents.

I dropped to my knees and crawled into the hall.

Stay below the smoke.

I pulled on the loose fabric of my sleep tank, holding it over my mouth and nose. The rasp in the back of my throat intensified, and I coughed into the material. It felt like an eternity until I reached my parents' bedroom. They were both still in bed. Why haven't they woken up?

"Mom," I choked on the word.

My vision blurred, the air so thick it became hard to see the hand in front of my face. When I tried to shake her awake, she didn't respond. I screamed for her to open her eyes. We needed to get out of here. Attempting to pull her from her bed, I slipped and busted my elbow against the edge of the bed frame. Pain exploded in the back of my mind. I *couldn't stop. I needed to keep going. If I could just get her out— Then, I noticed that her eyes were open, staring at nothing.*

No, no, no.

Something covered my face and...

Next thing I remember is coming to on the dirt-covered ground behind our property, where I watched my boyfriend holding his sister's hand as they watched me burn.

"NOTHING WILL HAPPEN TO YOU."

The nonchalant answer is the push I need for my feet to operate again. My throat aches from my shallow breathing. "How did he find me? You promised that I could stop moving."

I have to pack. Give up the first home I've had in years. Clouds fill my vision, and I bite my cheek to stifle a sob.

"Crying will not help you."

As much as I want to reply with a snarky remark, I can't. My focus is on not breaking down. Emotions I haven't experienced in so long surge to the forefront, clashing against the wall I built around myself over the years. Brick by brick, it begins to crumble, and there's nothing I can do.

"Fuck, Jules. This was not part of our arrangement." A sigh travels through the earpiece.

"I-I'm sorry." For what, I don't know. I just have the urge to apologize.

"I'm on my way."

The line disconnects before I can reply. I stand in the middle of my living room, staring at the lone chair next to the tattered table I picked up at a garage sale. Everything I had went downstairs, leaving my living arrangements with the bare minimum.

FOR THE NEXT FEW DAYS, my patience is tested.

The urge to pack the duffel that held my life since I was nineteen crawls under my skin, making me jump at every unfamiliar sound. I used to be afraid all the time, looking over my shoulder every step of the way. The longest I had settled until *Rezoned* was two months, and even then, I wouldn't sleep in the same location for more than a couple of nights.

Montson is my home. The phoenix in me wants to flip Marshall Davis the bird. He ruined my life once. He burned me, and I clawed my way out of the ashes. I refuse to lose everything again.

Ethan doesn't bother moving the Bronco. He simply parks in the far corner of the lot, his monstrosity becoming a permanent fixture outside. He doesn't come near. He only leaves after we close for the night, and by the time I unlock the front door, he's already back.

Where does he sleep?

Cody intercepts me on my way from the office to the front to close for the day. "Jules."

Fuck, shit, fuck.

I pivot on my heels and plaster a smile on my face. "Yeah?"

"What's going on?" He dries his hands on the dish towel that's always tucked in his front pocket.

"What do you mean?" I feign ignorance, and he gives me *the look*.

Cody is a few years older. He was living out of his car when I met him. I had just taken over Rezoned and had no clue what to do next. What did I know about renovating a building? I offered him a roof over his head if he helped me remodel the place, did some of the heavy lifting. One evening, I walked in on him whipping up a feast on the stove that was older than the two of us combined. It was, by far, the best meal I had had in years. Since my father... I had burst into tears midbite and offered him a job.

He stayed in my spare bedroom until he had enough saved

for his own place. He's been a good friend—the only person I let close—and while he'd like there to be more, I can't. I haven't been able to open my heart to anyone since...

My shoulders slump. "I got some news I didn't expect." I force lightness into my tone. "It'll blow over in no time."

Who am I trying to convince? It won't be over until Marshall successfully eliminates the last living Arrow.

Cody studies me, filtering the true meaning of my words. "Does this *news* have anything to do with the guy that's been camping outside for the last week and a half?"

He noticed Ethan. And not just the last few days. Cody's smart, which is why it's such a mystery to me how he ended up on the street. Neither of us has ever volunteered our past to the other.

"Partially. But he's just the byproduct of the news." I deserve an award for vagueness.

"I don't like this, JJ." His shoulders slump, and my heart sinks. I take a step toward him, and he spreads his arms. His presence has been my comfort for so long; I hate shutting him out. My arms wrap around his midsection, and I squeeze. A childish gesture that always broke any tension between us. I would pretend to crush his ribs, and in return, he'd tickle me. We'd end up laughing on the floor in a mock fight. He was like the big brother I never had.

His chuckle cuts off, and his entire posture stiffens.

The hair on the nape of my neck rises, and I sense him. I close my eyes and inhale Cody's scent of shower gel and kitchen. It doesn't help.

Ethan still has the same effect on me after all these years—after everything he did.

I untangle myself from Cody and put my back to his front. Facing my past, a fluttery sensation spreads through every limb.

Of its own volition, my hand moves to where I have the Contingency in the back of my jeans.

Ethan fills up the mouth of the hallway, hoodie covering half his face, thumbs hooked in his pockets. His chiseled features have only gotten more handsome with age. His caramel eyes haunted my nightmares for so long, jolting me awake to find my cheeks wet with the tears of my past. His tongue swipes at his bottom lip, and my heart rate picks up, pumping heat I don't want to feel through my body. A hand comes to the small of my back, and Ethan's eyes narrow. His nostrils flare as he slants his head. I'm familiar with the cues, and sure enough, his brow arches in a challenge.

"What are you going to do, Little Phoenix?"

His inaudible taunt echoes in my mind.

I peer over my shoulder. Cody is rigid. He matches Ethan in height, maybe even build, but without the same training, Ethan will obliterate him in minutes.

Angling my body, I let go of my blade and place my palm in the middle of his chest. Cody's gaze flicks to mine, and a low growl reverberates through the narrow hallway.

Something stirs deep in my core, battling the knowledge of him being the reason I lost everything.

I let my fingers splay, absorbing the thuds of Cody's heart with my palm. Once I have my friend's attention, I nod. "It's okay. You head home, and I'll call you after I take care of this." I keep my tone purposefully low, so only Cody hears me.

After the visceral sensation Ethan ignited, I want him to experience how it is to lose control of a situation, paralyzing your physical ability to be in charge. He commands his surroundings, but with this one touch, I take that from him. And cataloging the signals, his shift in stance, he is still as possessive as before. I don't need a visual connection to read him—some things never change.

Cody glances behind me one more time. He wants to argue but then bobs his head. I sigh inwardly. *Thank God.* He disappears back to the kitchen. It doesn't take long before he reemerges with his messenger bag slung across his body.

He pecks my cheek like every night when he leaves, but this time, I tense. I don't know what I expect to happen, but when Cody's body disappears through the back door, *alive*, a whoosh of air escapes me.

CHAPTER SIXTEEN

JULES

WARM BREATH FANS OVER MY NECK, AND I JUMP.

Jesus fuck.

Ethan bridged the distance between us without a sound. His chest touches my back, the fabric of his hoodie mingling with my thin cotton tank top. I curl and uncurl my fingers into fists, fighting the dizziness overtaking my senses at his nearness.

Rationality hurls accusations at me as my core throbs with the need to feel him between my legs—just one more time.

"You need to leave!" It wouldn't have surprised me if my command had ended with a moan. It didn't, though. Thank God.

"No."

I take a step forward and whirl around. The separation severs my inability to think. Reality snaps into place, the drive to hurt the man I once loved with every fiber of my being becoming my singular thought.

Ethan's posture is casual, and at the same time, murderous confidence bleeds from every pore. With his legs slightly wider than his shoulders, his arms hang loosely by his sides. I know this stance, having seen it in action whenever his siblings joined us, and our training morphed into them fucking around in the clearing.

If he thinks I don't notice the familiar outline of his Nitro under his hoodie, he's freaking delusional. He forgets I know his body better than he does.

Knew—you knew him better.

Suddenly, my hatred for his betrayal is overshadowed by new images. Ethan with other women over the past ten years begins to play like bad porn, overlaying my vision with a green haze. I slowly inhale and exhale through my nose, suppressing the unwanted emotional onslaught to nothing but a simmer. How is this happening? With every second he holds my gaze, white-hot rage seeps like slow-moving lava through every cell of my body. Loathing for him invading my life. Fury at my body's betrayal, like the man in front of me didn't attempt to burn me alive. My fingers tingle with the need to wrap themselves around his throat.

While riding his cock, a voice cackles in the back of my mind.

Ten years. Ten fucking years, and he is more gorgeous than ever. But that's all he is—a pretty shell hiding a blackened soul of destruction.

I slowly reach behind me, wrapping my fingers around the wasp handle of my knife—the knife he gave me so long ago.

"Don't do it." He cocks his head.

He was the one who drilled into me never to be unprotected. Little did I know back then that he was talking about himself. I've carried this blade with me every step of the way. I slowly pull my mouth into a grin that displays anything but amusement. "Or what, Ethan?"

"I'll have to take it from you."

This fucker.

A crunching sound reverberates in my ears as my molars grind onto each other. He can try.

I pull the blade from its sheath and shift my body—not the stance he taught me, though. Ethan's eyes narrow, a crease forming between his brows. My posture mimics his a second ago —feet hip width, arms by my sides. I roll my shoulders back, the muscles in my arms coiling as I wait.

He expects me to be reckless. Attack first. I won't. I analyze his body language. He's steady, but confusion mingles with confidence. He recognizes my tactic but can't place it. Yet. Lifting my chin, the corner of my lips turns up.

Suddenly, Ethan lunges. He hasn't drawn his own blade, but I know he has one. He prefers the sharp edge of steel over a firearm. Marshall had two number-one rules: always be armed and never let your opponent see your weapons. Over the few months we were together, he had told me a lot of *The Davis Order* rules, probably assuming I was too dense to remember.

Ethan aims for my unarmed hand. My adrenaline soars, and as if in slow motion, his intent projects in front of me—I've trained for this moment. The final confrontation. If you incapacitate the free hand and inflict enough pain, your opponent will disarm themselves.

I step out of his reach, bring my back against the wall, and shoot out my foot. A straight teep kick to his side. Ethan staggers for the briefest of moments. Not long enough. Eyes wide, he latches on to my ankle and twists. My lungs burn, and I suck in a breath. Exhaling all my air, I use his momentum on my leg to propel my body around until my hands are on the floor. Bracing myself, I distribute my weight evenly between the heel of my palm and my fingers, gripping the hardwood. Both legs in the air, he still holds on to one when the heel of my free foot comes around and connects with his head.

Most men (or women) wouldn't be able to withstand such a blow, but Ethan is not just anyone. He is a Davis.

He drops my foot, and I whirl around, crouching as I wait for his next attack. Never letting him out of my sight, I find my Contingency where I dropped it next to me on the floor. Ethan shakes his head and stares, exhaling a sharp breath. He knows. But instead of asking the question that burns his tongue, he withdraws until he is pressed against the opposite side of the hall. Neither of us speaks. Sweat trickles down my spine, my shirt clinging to my body.

I have no idea how long we stand like this, but restlessness slowly vibrates like a low hum through my limbs. I want this to end, one way or another.

Standing, my question comes in spurts. "Why are you here?"

"To protect you." His answer is swift and serves like a blow to the gut.

"Liar," I hiss. My rage threatens to overpower my rational thinking. I need to calm my pulse. However, this will end. He won't win this time.

"I never lied to you, Little Phoenix. I may not have told you in detail what jobs my father had me do, but you and I..."—he points between us, sincerity bleeding from every word—"we were always real. The realest thing in my li—"

He doesn't get to finish the sentence. The thrashing in my ears drowns out his words. With a guttural scream, I launch myself at him. All I can think of is taking his life the same way he snuffed out my parents'.

My impulsiveness is the opening he needs, though.

Before I can comprehend what's happening, my back is to his front, and I have my own knife angled under my chin. His fingers cover mine. A quick flick of his wrist and I'll slit my own throat.

The heat of his body radiates against my naked shoulders, his rapid breathing fanning over my neck.

His nose nudges the shell of my ear, and I fight the shudder that runs down my spine. "Drop the knife, Little Phoenix."

Hearing the name he used to whisper while he made love to me causes my eyes to sting. "I hate you." The rasp in my voice betrays me, which makes me loathe him even more. I fell for his lies.

"And I never stopped lo—" He stops midsentence. His grip on my armed hand turns to a vise, the cracking of my fingers the only sound in the empty diner. I wince but swallow the cry.

"Drop it." His arm that's wrapped around my midsection begins to move. His thumb strokes up and down while his fingers splay over the fabric of my shirt.

In the back of the diner, "Back from the Dead" by Besomorph, AViVA and Neoni comes over the speakers.

How ironic.

When I don't comply, his hold on me tightens. I feel the firmness of his dick pressing against my ass. His arm tenses, and while I'm the one that has the blade in my hand, he guides it effortlessly away from under my chin. He's as strong as ever. I'm about to sigh in relief when the cold edge slides down the side of my neck. My pulse buzzes under the rough scrape of the blade. Anticipating. Craving the rush only Ethan ever gave me. He doesn't break the skin but makes sure to leave a mark.

I'm hyperaware of my lack of clothing. I had already stripped out of my work shirt since I was just quickly going to lock up. My tank top is the only barrier between us.

In one swift move, the tip of the knife slips under the strap. He doesn't have to put any tension behind it. I've kept it sharp. The thin piece of fabric tears, and the material drops free.

My rapid breathing accelerates into a treacherous pant as the cool air from the AC hits my half-exposed breast.

The muscle in his arm tenses, and I do the same, pathetically attempting to stop him from moving the blade to the other side. We both know where this is leading. A sliver of me has been aching for him from the moment I saw his car in my parking lot, but that small piece is buried under a decade of anger and hatred.

"Get fucked, Davis," I bite out the insult and rub my thighs together at the same time. With a flick of his wrist, he severs the other strap and bares my chest to the empty hallway. A deep-rooted knowledge I suppressed with my need for revenge for so long suddenly surges to the forefront of my mind, nearly making my legs buckle: *He would never hurt you.*

Maybe not, but I will be damned if I make it easy for him.

My nipples harden to diamond points, and a low moan escapes my lips. I loosen my grip on the knife, and Ethan lets it clatter to the ground.

His now free palm covers my breast while his other holds me pressed to his hard torso. My head leans against his shoulder, fitting perfectly into the crook of his neck.

Like nothing has changed.

He rolls my nipple between his thumb and forefinger before pinching it hard. The sting shoots a wave of pleasure to my pussy.

Ethan's lips lower to the side of my face, where he nips on my skin. "Are you still mine, Little Phoenix?"

"No." My breathy tone says the opposite of the word.

"I don't believe you." His teeth sink into my neck, and my eyes roll back.

"Fuck." I find Ethan's thighs and dig my nails into the denim.

His tongue licks over the sore spot. His nose trails the cord of my neck until his mouth aligns with my ear. "I thought you died that night." He places a soft kiss underneath my ear, and my heart falters.

He's lying.

Ethan slowly loosens his hold, and I take that as my chance. Pushing off his thighs, I sprint toward the opening leading to the diner. I don't expect to escape him. I just need to get closer to the gun taped under the counter.

Arms wrap around me before I get anywhere near my ticket to freedom—away from him. He lifts me effortlessly, pinning my arms to my sides.

A high-pitched scream of frustration accompanies my thrashing. "You're a fucking liar! You killed my parents!"

All his effort is concentrated on restraining me. When my heel connects with his shin, Ethan groans.

Once you have a point of weakness, you go after it.

See, I paid attention, asshole.

I attempt another kick, but Ethan surprises me. His arms disappear, and I drop to the wooden floor like a wet rag. Agony shoots from my tailbone up my spine. The vertebrae in my neck shudder on impact, and I suppress the cry threatening to burst out. Instead, I recall the first lesson my *new* trainer gave me: *Pain is not real. If you don't let it in, it can't distract you from your goal. Your goal is to kill. Survive. Nothing else.*

I flip over into a runner's start, prepared to attack again when Ethan is already in front of me. His large hand wraps around my throat, and he lifts me like I weigh nothing. My only connection to the ground is the very tips of my toes. His fingers bite into either side of my neck, cutting off my oxygen expertly.

"STOP IT!" He gets in my face, our noses almost touching. Lowering his voice, he continues, "I had nothing to do with your parents. I had no idea what was happening until Marshall threw the kill order in my face."

My hands clutch at his wrist in a pathetic attempt for him to release me. He nods at my submission and eases his grip, allowing my feet to support me again. I gasp, drawing oxygen back into my lungs. As soon as his fingers fully release me, I massage my throat gingerly.

My top is completely bunched around my waist, my tits on full display, but I don't bother covering myself. Ethan's eyes glide over my breasts, and his nostrils flare when he sees the tattoo.

Two years after I *escaped*, I had saved up enough to get my permanent reminder that I would always rise from the ashes—no matter what life throws at me. The black-and-red-shaded phoenix covers most of my right rib cage. One wing curves around the underside of my breast while the other expands under my shoulder blade. Its fiery tail winds down my side, disappearing in my shorts. It took four sessions to complete the piece.

"Little Phoenix," he breathes my name.

The two words puncture my heart. My chest constricts, and I take a step toward him. "You didn't know?"

His shoulders slump, and he swallows. "No."

For the first time in a decade, the man I gave my heart to stands in front of me. A sob bubbles up my throat, and I throw myself at him.

CHAPTER SEVENTEEN

ETHAN

I catch Jules under her ass at the same time her mouth collides with mine. *Home.* A sense of peace slows my drumming heartbeat as I feel the tears running down her cheeks. All I can think of is that I want to take away her hurt. Every agonizing second she has had to endure over the last ten years—at the hands of my family or anyone else.

My hood has long fallen off my head. With her arms resting on my shoulders, her fingers dive into my cropped hair. Her nails scrape against my scalp as she rolls her hips forward. Lips parting, I groan at the blissful sting. She takes the invitation, her tongue slipping into my mouth. The instant her tongue meets mine, my nerve endings shoot into overdrive.

I walk us to the nearest booth and deposit her on the edge of the table. Despite being directly in front of one of the windows, we're only visible to the outside if someone looks closely. The glass is slightly mirrored, and the lights in the diner were already muted when I walked in.

During my time watching her, she always closed the diner at nine p.m. sharp. Not a minute earlier or later. Tonight, when she didn't show up by 9:02, I had to confirm that she was OK. She kept the back entrance locked from the outside, but someone could've always forced their way in. B and E weren't rocket science. The images of the dream that shocked me to the core a decade ago flashed in my mind, and I was out of the Bronco before any conscious thought could stop me. I had no intention for it to come to...*this*. But now that I have her in my arms, I refuse to let her go.

Jules grips the hem of my hoodie, and I automatically surrender to her. She pulls the fabric over my head and throws it somewhere behind us. I arch a brow, and her eyes crinkle.

I trail my forefinger from her wrist along her arm and over her collarbone until I meet the red line I left on her delicate throat earlier. I trace the mark with my nail, adding to the soreness, and she shudders. She always liked when I claimed her body in ways anybody could see.

I continue my exploration down the valley of her breasts, circling each nipple once before making my way to the hem of her shorts. I tilt my head. "Lie back."

Her teeth sink into her bottom lip, but she follows my command.

Good girl.

Jules reclines on her elbows, watching me through her lashes.

I shake my head. "Nuh-uh. All the way."

She draws in a shaky breath of excitement, but she obeys. When she's flat on the tabletop, I reach down to my boot. Extracting my Contingency, I raise it to her line of sight. It's almost identical to the one I gave her so many years ago. The only difference is the crimson custom wasp handle—a reminder of my phoenix. I was explicit when commissioning the blade and its twin shortly after I took the position with Altman Hotels. I didn't care how much it would cost me.

Jules grips the edge of the table above her head. Her tits rise and fall as my blade slips under the remains of her top. With one swipe, the material parts.

My cock strains against my jeans. If I'm not inside her soon, I'll lose my mind. I glide the tip of the blade from her navel to the hem of her shorts. Jules whimpers and her hips buck.

"Careful, baby," I chuckle. "I don't want to hurt you."

Her head slants slightly. "What if I want you to?"

Jesus Christ.

"Don't tempt me, Little Phoenix." But she doesn't have to say anything else. The tip of my blade disappears under her shorts, and the tearing sound mingles with her moan.

Her legs fall apart, displaying her glistening pussy. No panties. While I appreciate it for what I have planned for her, the ugly monster of jealousy rears deep inside. She was alone with Cody Mantz in here. I know who Cody is. *And was.*

I made it my mission to learn everything about Jules's one male employee while my ass was glued to the driver's seat of the Bronco. All it took was to send a text with his name to my employers. The two owners of the Altman Hotels have a similar talent to Cor when it comes to computers—digging up anything there is about a person.

He kissed her. Does he do that every night before leaving? Have they done more than that?

Mine, a menacing growl demands to claim what has always been mine.

I couldn't care less if Kitchen Guy is of any importance to her—a boyfriend or just a cock to pass the time with. Jules fucking Arrow is mine, and she will soon scream my name again to prove it.

I stab my knife into the tabletop, less than an inch from

Jules's waist. She sucks in a breath but doesn't move otherwise. Unbuttoning my jeans, I let them fall down my legs. I run my tongue along the front of my teeth and circle my finger in the air. "Flip, Little Phoenix."

Her nostrils flare, though she doesn't object. Can she sense that this is how I need her right now? That we both need this moment? The connection we shared snaps back into place like it was never singed away, and I'm grounded for the first time in a decade.

I help her up, but the instant her feet connect with the floor, I grab her by the hips and spin her around. Without warning, my palm settles between her shoulder blades, and I push her into the wooden surface. Rising to her toes, her lower back arches, offering her ass and pussy up for me.

A groan builds in my chest. "So ready."

She wiggles under my hold. Instead of removing my hand, I splay my fingers. "Stop moving." I don't have to put any pressure behind it. I use the tone that can make a grown man piss themselves. My girl, though, mewls as she stills. With her cheek to the table, she peers back, wetting her lips.

I dig the tips of my fingers into her muscles, curling them so my nails bite her flesh. I smile to myself. Her willingness to concede (*to me*) stands in opposition to her fiery personality. A trust that warms my chest as much as it strokes my ego.

Saliva pools in my mouth. I press my tongue to the roof while gripping my length. Slowly stroking myself, I ignore my cock's protests. I can't deny her or myself a taste.

I sink to my knees and take hold of the sides of her hips, angling her ass to give me better access. Her arousal invades my nose, and my dick twitches.

Soon.

I swipe my tongue along her folds, plunging it into her heat.

"Oh fuck. Yes." Jules pushes her pussy in my face.

"Shhh," I mumble as I take another deep lick. "Let me eat."

Jules shifts, wrapping her fingers around the edge of the table on either side. "I need you now, Ethan." Her demand is nothing but a breathy moan. "Fuck me so hard it erases the lies from the last ten years."

"Mhmmm." I follow her slit all the way to her third hole. "I think"—digging my fingers into her skin, I angle my head—"I can"—I sink my teeth into her ass, and she yelps—"do that," I finish and rise to my feet.

God, how I've missed her. Us.

I drink her body in. The way she holds on to the table, waiting for me to eliminate the past and bring us to the present. My fingers wrap around my cock, pumping up and down. I line myself up with her opening, and she whimpers.

I withdraw at the last moment. "Are you still mine, Little Phoenix?" Her lips part, but I beat her to it. "Think carefully about your reply." I swipe the tip of my cock along her ass crack, stopping at the entrance she didn't anticipate.

Her teeth sink into her bottom lip, and she nudges back at me.

Well fuck.

"What if I say no?" she teases.

"I guess you have to find out." I feather my fingers down her spine. Leaving her skin, she shivers. Then I let my palm crack on her cheek, and she shrieks. "*Are* you still mine?"

She glowers over her shoulder. "No."

That little devil.

I slant my head. While she deserves a good ass pounding for that, I'm not the kind of man that would force that on her.

So, I adjust, and without another warning, I thrust deep into her. Jules cries out, her knuckles turning white as I pump in and out of her wet cunt.

"Let's try this again, baby. Who do you belong to?" I grind out as I drive forward.

"You!" Jules screams. "Oh god, yes. Always you." She pants. "Harder."

I wrap her red strands around my fist and tug, forcing her to arch up. Her eyes flutter closed, and her moans grow louder. Watching her come apart under me, my dick sliding in and out, is a sight I never thought I'd see again.

I pull, making her prop herself up on the tabletop as I fuck her raw. She's still on her toes, attempting to match my height, but I gladly squat if it means feeling her heat surrounding me. Trailing around to her front, my fingers circle her clit.

Releasing her hair, I shift to cup her tit while continuing to massage her sensitive spot.

Jules tilts her head, exposing the column of her neck. An invitation I can't, nor do I want to, decline. Pinching her nipple between my fingers, I lean forward and sink my teeth into the soft part between her ear and shoulder.

"More," she groans. "Make it hurt."

I've never refused her. A coppery taste fills my mouth, and Jules moans. Her walls tense around me. I trail my tongue over the spot, kissing and nibbling on the mark I left as I speed up my pace, chasing the high with her.

She removes one hand from the tabletop and reaches around my neck, guiding me back to where I had already branded her.

"Mark me, Ethan. Make me yours again."

Right before my lips connect with her skin, I halt. "You were always mine. There was never anyone else for me."

Not emotionally. And then, I add a second mark to the first.

Surprising me, Jules lets go of my neck and reaches down between her legs. She grabs hard on my balls and begins to pull toward herself in a stroking motion.

Holy fucking shit.

Her palm glides along my shaft as I thrust in and out, the buildup so sudden I'm not prepared. My eyes roll back, and my knees nearly buckle. I empty inside of her with a groan. "Fuuuck."

I hold her, not sure who is keeping whom upright at this point. Sweat trickles down the nape of my neck. Blinking, I find her looking back. Unspoken emotions pass between us, and I capture her lips in a gentle kiss, contradicting everything I just did to her.

JULES NESTLES between my legs on the bench seat. The cool glass against my overheated back feels good. Her cheek rests against my chest, and she circles the tattoo I got the year after her *death*.

"Full of beauty and passion. Laced in the desire to survive. You've pricked my heart." She whispers the words that filled my mind the first night she revealed her favorite flower to me— three lines in my own handwriting under a red thistle framed by a circle.

I place my finger under her chin and tilt her head up. "Knowing I could never see you again, it was my way of keeping you with me."

She searches my eyes. "You had no idea I was alive."

I inhale a shaky breath. "Not for the first year."

She opens her mouth, but I cut her off, voicing what's been burning my chest for the last thirtyish minutes. "Why do you fight like my brother?"

"Because I've been training her." The voice comes from the hallway, and we jerk to a sitting position as Paycen steps out of the dark.

What. The. Fuck?

My eyes flip between Jules and my little brother, who lounges against the side of the counter like he's been here a hundred times.

Jules covers her tits, and realization slams into me. "Turn the fuck around."

Paycen tilts his head, the corner of his mouth twitching. He remains mute and, instead, walks back the way he came.

Jules slides out of the booth, avoiding my gaze. I want to grab her by the arms and demand answers. Why is my brother here? In Montson, Maine. How the fuck did this happen? And more importantly, how long has this been going on? My pulse speeds up with every new unanswered question.

Since I destroyed her clothes, she grabs my hoodie. I pull my jeans over my legs and slip into my boots. I don't bother sheathing my blade.

Clasping Jules's hand, I fist my knife and aim for the stairs.

CHAPTER EIGHTEEN

ETHAN

PAYCEN STANDS IN THE MIDDLE OF THE ROOM WITH HIS BACK to us.

Jules untangles her fingers from mine and beelines through the only other door, but not before throwing a glance at my little brother.

This is fucking surreal.

I position myself with my back to the wall next to the entrance. Cuffing my biceps, my knife presses into my naked arm. The skin over my knuckles begins to burn, forcing me to loosen my grip.

I've only seen Paycen one other time in his adult life. He's the most dangerous out of all of us. I had predicted it when he was a pubescent teen, and it has been confirmed since. Paycen Davis is more of a moving corpse than a human being. He could put the fear of Satan—or Marshall Davis, or whoever he represented at the moment—into the most dangerous men without lifting a finger. There is something in his silver-blue eyes (or the lack thereof) that tells you without words that he'll die before surrendering. He is dubbed *Coldblood* for a reason.

Jules reemerges in oversized sweats and a new tank top. My gaze drops to her tits. The muscle in my jaw tics when I notice that she's not wearing anything underneath. *Again.* My brother is of no concern in that way. At the same time, any dick getting a front-row seat to what's mine triggers a murderous craze I've never experienced with anyone else.

Peering at me briefly, Jules walks over to Paycen. She wraps her arms around his midsection, and my eyes bulge. When he lifts one hand to pat Jules on the back, I all but choke on my saliva.

Am I in some alternate universe?

This guy never let anyone touch him unless he was gravely injured. Even then, we usually had to tranq him to give him the required medical attention. Even Jenn has never hugged our little brother.

Jules steps back, the fabric of his black, long-sleeve Henley still pinched between her fingers. She peers up at him, and something passes between them. The familiarity makes my stomach roll.

Paycen matches my height, and while my girl is not short by any means, he towers over her.

"Sit." She spreads her arms, gesturing at a sofa that has seen better days and a single chair. The chair and table threaten to collapse if you so much as breathe near them. The downstairs is the complete opposite with its sleek design. An unnatural rage burns my throat for how she's been living.

Paycen accepts her invitation and lowers himself without a care in the world. He doesn't worry that I'll attack him. He's incapable of fear—or any genuine emotion.

Jenn once told me that she found him drunk out of his mind when he was around sixteen. He was lying in the dirt near *the pen.*

He couldn't stand, and she had to drag him to his room. He's been *drinking* long before he should've even had caffeine, but to this day, no one knows what triggered his attempt to poison himself with booze. He had slurred that he'd rather die than give anyone what they wanted. It was the only time he showed any type of vulnerability.

Jules drops onto the sofa cushion, and a cloud of dust puffs up.

Jesus.

Grinding my teeth, I slowly make my way over and sink down next to her. My thigh grazes hers, and the familiar current of calm Jules's nearness has given me since the first day spreads through my coiled muscles. I relax, and she leans into my side.

To my surprise, Paycen is the first to speak. "Looks like I'm no longer needed." He puts his palms on his thighs as if to push off.

Jules scowls. "If you get out of that chair right now, Pace, I will cut your pretty ears off." She crosses her arms.

Pace? Pretty ears?

Now I'm convinced I fell asleep in the Bronco.

Paycen mimics her, except he looks intimidating in doing so. "I don't follow your orders, Jules."

She jackknifes up and marches to him. "Maybe not." She pokes him against the forehead. "But"—*poke*—"you"—*poke* —"care"—*poke*—"for me." *Poke, poke.*

"Do that again, and I will snap your finger off." There is no emotion in his words, no anger or annoyance.

"No, you won't." She props her fists on her hips. "I'm your only friend."

"Friend?" I can't stop myself. Utter disbelief in this exchange has me gaping.

Both turn toward me as if they forgot I was even there. Jules's hands drop and hang loosely by her sides.

I prop my ankle over my knee and cross my arms. "How long has this been going on?"

Jules and Paycen share a look.

My temper is wearing thin, and I sneer, "Do you need his permission to answer now?"

A groove appears between Jules's brows, but she remains mute.

She's waiting for Paycen's signal. What the fuck?

He dips his chin imperceptibly, and she closes her eyes.

"About five years," she sighs.

"FIVE?" I jerk forward, my foot dropping to the floor with a thud, and Jules's eyes spring open.

The unease...the guilt she displayed a second ago disappears as she mashes her lips. I see the metaphorical shutters fall. Jules leans her ass against the edge of the table, threading her fingers and propping her chin on them. "Why don't you explain to me first how you had no idea your brother was barbecuing me?"

Her question is laced with acid. She has never allowed anyone to corner her—me included—unless it was in the bedroom and a mutual give-and-take of power.

Leaning back into the couch, I rake my hands through my hair. I sweep the ceiling for the answer. I don't think of that night. Ever. The numbness I've carefully maintained for a decade slowly seeps away. A hollow cold takes its place as images begin to flash. In order to tell her the truth, I have to relive it.

"That...night," I begin, but my throat closes. I swallow over the razor blades lodged in my throat and look at Jules. If I maintain a visual connection—seeing her in front of me, alive— maybe I can recall the events without losing my mind. "I was scheduled for maintenance."

Jules's brows pop, and Paycen chimes in, "Cleaning the guns."

"Sounds like the crime version of cleaning toilets," Jules remarks dryly.

"It is," my little brother confirms.

Words fail me. I've never heard Paycen string so many syllables together in such a short period of time.

Jules pushes off the table and slowly walks back over, sinking down next to me.

The ice in my veins has extended to my fingers, the tips almost sensationless. Needing to keep my hands occupied, I pull Jules's legs onto my lap and start massaging her calves. A gesture I have done dozens of times—*before*. I don't think about my action. It feels natural.

Jules hums her approval, reaching out and brushing her fingers over the side of my neck into my hair. The same response she would give me—*before*.

Paycen cocks a brow, and I want to flip him off.

What does he know about having a bond stronger than life or death with another human being?

It's not his fault, Jules chastises me inaudibly.

Now, I'm also hearing voices.

My head jerks in her direction, and she frowns.

Shaking my head, I continue, "I had just finished. I was on my way to the garage. To you"—I level her—"when Marshall's second caught me." Shifting my gaze to Paycen, I continue, "Something was off." He understands the meaning of my words without further explanation. For Jules, I add, "If Marshall called, he usually sent for Corbin *and* me. Or if Cor was already with him, Jenn, T, or Paycen"—I tilt my chin at him—"would get me. Never his lackey."

Jules studies Paycen, and he confirms my claim with a nod.

"Marshall was testing me." My kneading her legs becomes a distraction to keep my buzzing nerves in check.

Jules's hand leaves, and I glance to the side. Her gaze is trained on the floor, her hand fisting her Contingency. I'm side-tracked for a second because I didn't notice that she had it.

A grave mistake on my part.

I never wanted her to live with her father's actions, but the choice was taken from me. My chest tightens. I owe her the truth. I draw in a deep breath and hold it until my lungs scream for release. Exhaling, I also expel the words that changed not just my life but Jules's as well. "Marshall informed me that night that your father was on his payroll. That Grant stole money from him." I keep my tone level, prepared for anything.

Jules's shoulders stiffen, but other than that, she remains motionless for what feels like minutes. Then, her eyes slowly lift to mine, and my lips part. She's not surprised.

"You knew." I'm not asking.

"I'm sorry." Her admission is barely audible, but she might as well have shouted it in my ear—or better, stabbed her blade in my chest. The rest of that night is suddenly unimportant. I push her legs off and shoot to a stand.

I take two steps, my fingers gripping my corded neck. I apply pressure, digging into the muscles around my spine until agony shoots up my scalp and down my back. I need a distraction. Something. My rushing pulse turns Jules's pleas for me to look at her to white noise. A guttural roar builds in my core, and I don't attempt to restrain it. Letting it free, my foot shoots out and launches Jules's piece-of-shit table across the room. It slams into the wall, and one of the legs breaks off. The whole thing collapses on itself.

Like everything I ever believed in.

CHAPTER NINETEEN

JULES

MY SHOULDERS SCRUNCH TO MY EARS AS THE TABLE CRASHES against the wall. Good thing I was never attached to it.

Ethan whirls around and takes one long stride toward me. Paycen rises to his feet, his reaction slow and calculated. He doesn't say a word, but the temperature in the room drops below subzero. I'm no longer afraid of Paycen. While he may never admit it, we are friends. We have a bond I don't understand, but it's there. If there is one person I would trust with my life (next to Ethan), it's *The Coldblood*.

I hold up a palm in his direction. *It's fine.*

Paycen resembles a statue. A very dangerous statue that can swing into motion at any time.

Ethan lifts his hands disarmingly. Neither of them speaks. Betrayal and confusion mar his sharp features. It guts me to see Ethan like this.

For the past decade, I only focused on what he did to me. I never considered how my truth could affect him. Dizziness creeps up my throat, and I flick my gaze to Paycen. "Could you give us a minute?"

In true Paycen fashion, he simply aims for the door. I'm not surprised. Over the last five years, I've learned how Paycen operates. For his lack of communication, I overcompensated—and it has worked for us.

"Pace." He halts with his hand on the knob, not turning. "Don't leave." His fingers tighten around the metal, and I amend, "Please."

"I'll be downstairs."

I internally count to five before focusing on Ethan. He stares at me like I'm a stranger—which, in a way, I am. Yet, it hurts just as bad.

He looks at you like you did him when you thought he tried to kill you.

"Will you come sit?" My palm glides over the spot he just vacated. "Please."

He visibly fights with himself. The guilt of keeping my family's involvement with *The Davis Order* from him settles like a weighted blanket over me. We had been lower-class helpers. *Rens.* Nowhere near the rank Marshall would've tolerated on his son's side. And then my father decided to steal from the devil.

I expect Ethan to follow his brother—let Paycen deal with my fate. In the end, he bridges the distance. The breath I was holding escapes my lips.

He sinks onto the sofa but leaves a whole cushion length between us. His first words are more to himself than to me. "And here I thought I was keeping you safe...from my world."

I knead my fingers together as I speak toward my lap. "You never *asked* if I already was part of it."

Peering at me sideways, a thundercloud crosses his features. "And what should I have asked, Little Phoenix? Hey, are you aware that I kill for the roof over my head? And by the way, are you, or anyone related to you, on my father's payroll?"

I attempt to form a retort, informing him where he can shove his attitude. But I can't find it in me. I've spent so many years believing that he was the one sent to kill us. Now that the truth is out, an empty void has taken over the spot where the hatred once lived.

I swipe my tongue over the back of my teeth. "No, baby. You're right."

Scooting closer, I slowly lay my hand on his knee. When he doesn't push me off, I take it as a sign. "My father had worked for yours since he moved to Renneton. Grant Arrow was well known for his ability to launder one's income without leaving a trace of where it originated. Marshall gave him the capital to open the diner."

I let the information sink in, then whisper, "Why do you think I wanted to escape that town? It was his life, not mine." I recall the day Ethan walked in for the first time, like it was yesterday. "But then you hap—" The words lodge in my throat, and I swallow.

"I didn't know he was going against Marshall in some way until I overheard him on the phone. I was getting a glass of water. It was late. Dad was pacing the living room like he was training for a marathon." Pausing, I search for the right words. "The days before the fire...he was acting cagey. Kept asking if I had seen you or the other Davises recently. He was always...*tense* when it came to your father. But then, he demanded to know from the person on the other end if Marshall suspected something. He wasn't himself."

Ethan's caramel irises dull with sorrow. "I'm sorry." He carefully places his hand, palm up, next to mine on his leg. I don't hesitate, interlacing our fingers.

"I actually considered telling you once you were back," I

confess. I did plan on mentioning it to Ethan. If my father had gone against Marshall, we were all in danger—Ethan included. You never knew who would bear the wrath of the Order.

"But I never came back. Not in time," he finishes for me.

"I guess Dad thought you guys kept coming to the diner to report back to Marshall. He was too preoccupied to see what was right in front of him." A stab of sadness punctures my heart. I miss my parents so much—no matter the mistakes my father made.

"And what was that?" Ethan glances sideways.

I blink, chasing away the clouds obscuring my vision.

"That I was in love with a Davis," I say the words I had refused to acknowledge for so long. Even after everything I thought he did to me—before I knew the truth—one glance at Ethan Davis in my parking lot and I was nineteen again.

"JJ, can you take the trash out? I'm prepping the burger meat for the dinner orders," Cody calls to me in the office.

"Sure thing." I eagerly push away from my desk. I hate the book-keeping part of the job. While I love numbers, accounting is the bane of my existence. Not because I have trouble with it, I just hate the tedious paperwork part of collecting receipts and categorizing everything.

Cody hears my rolling chair clatter into the filing cabinet and barks a laugh. "Doing the books, eh?"

I enter the kitchen. Passing him to the large garbage bin in the corner, I smack him on the back of the head. He laughs even harder.

I tear on the strings, pulling the bag out. "You're fired, Mantz."

He knows I don't mean it, though. I wouldn't be able to run this place without him.

I press my ass against the push bar, swing the back door open, and aim for the dumpster we share with the scuba store next door.

I round the corner and halt. Something catches my eye. What the—?

My heart takes off in a gallop, my brain needing a good ten seconds to catch up. I stare at the Bronco tucked in the last parking spot of the lot.

It's the wrong color. But it has the same grill. The same custom light bar. The same height. My gaze slowly traces every distinct part of the body, cataloging it all yet refusing to accept the signals my eyes send to my brain.

I raise my gaze to the windshield. A dark figure slouches in the driver's seat. I don't have to see the face to recognize him. The moment the Bronco entered my line of sight, the hair on the nape of my neck tingled.

My adrenaline fires, sending every nerve ending in my body into a frenzy. No, no, no. What is he doing here?

I drop the trash and flatten myself against the wall of the building.

BUT THEN, he didn't make a move. He just kept showing up in the vicinity of my diner. My home. My initial shock morphed into confusion and grew into irritation, which was how I ended up slinking through the bushes of old Mr. Tolson's hardware store and ambushing Ethan in his car.

Ethan's gaze is on our joined hands. His thumb caresses mine. With each stroke, jolts travel up my arm, and goose bumps skirt over every inch of my exposed flesh.

I lick my lips. What do I want him to reply to my confession? Do I want him to say it back?

His eyes slowly meet mine. "For the first year after the fire... I had no idea you were alive."

My heart stutters. How is this possible?

Ethan lifts his free hand and traces the contours of my face. His fingers feather over my brow, across my cheek, until his thumb swipes over my bottom lip. His gaze follows the motion as if to memorize my features.

"I tried to get to you."

I don't dare speak. Ethan is far away, reliving the night that turned our lives into equal yet very different versions of hell.

"After Marshall threw in my face that Corbin was sent to take care of your family, I..." His voice gives out.

I wait for him to collect himself. It takes effort to bring the necessary oxygen to my lungs, each inhale and exhale a mental challenge of mind over matter. I need to breathe to survive, yet my chest is too tight to hold air.

"Cor restrained me. He was so much stronger," Ethan rasps. "I should've fought harder, but he didn't let up until the diner and your house collapsed. I screamed until my voice gave out." He rolls his lips under. His nostrils round and I watch his shoulders shake. "When the roof caved in, I could feel part of my soul break. You were gone."

Oh god. I bite the inside of my cheek to contain the sob that's choking me.

"I was numb. I remember thinking that I should feel something, but there was nothing. After that, things become hazy. I stopped paying attention. I had no reason to. Jenn and Theo showed up, and Corbin reported that the job was done. They loaded me into the back of the Bronco where I eventually blacked out."

The agony in his features becomes too much. My hands cup the sides of his face. I press my mouth against his in a mere flutter of sensation. How could I ever have believed that he would kill me?

Ethan circles my wrists, stroking my skin with his thumbs as our lips move in sync. Pulling back, he touches his forehead to mine.

He settles back into the cushion, folding my hands between his. "Jenn drove me to a motel a few hours away from Renneton. Theo followed her on his bike. To Marshall's knowledge, they were still up north and not due back until later that day. Corbin returned to the plantation. He told Marshall that I took off after he confirmed that you were all dead."

His siblings helped us survive. They betrayed the Order.

"Once I was awake, they left me with enough cash to start over." There's a long pause before he says, "I haven't seen or spoken to Corbin in ten years."

Ethan's voice breaks at the end of the sentence, and a fresh tear escapes me. His brother used to be his best friend.

"I refused to touch the money. After ditching my phone and removing the tracker from the Bronco, I started driving aimlessly. I lived out of my car. Stole to survive. Eventually, I had enough street cred to get hired for small jobs. I—"

"Why did you need to earn street cred?" I blurt. Everyone and their mother, with some connection to the less legal side of the world, had heard of Marshall Davis.

"I didn't use my name. There were days I considered giving up and going home. But then... It was the first time since I was five years old that I was free of Marshall. I couldn't risk him finding me."

Oh.

"Jenn tracked me down in Detroit almost exactly a year after you... I was scoping out a job. She showed up next to me like it was the most natural thing in the world." He huffs noncomically. "I will never forget her first words. '*She's alive, E.*'"

Ethan squeezes my fingers.

"I didn't believe her, even after she revealed how they pulled it off.

Curiosity arches my brows.

"Theo was the one who got you out."

My breath stalls midinhale. The last puzzle piece finally falls into place. I whisper, "I remember finding my mother and then waking up between the trees, watching everything burn."

Ethan thins his lips. "When Corbin got the order, he argued

with Marshall. He didn't want to kill you. But Marshall saw it as eliminating two birds with one stone. Your father stole from him, and I snuck around behind his back."

"All we did was fall— And have..." I cry, not having to spell it out. Yes, he taught me how to defend myself, but in the end, we were just two teenagers. Adults. Whatever.

"It didn't matter, Little Phoenix." Ethan rests his head against the back of the couch while angling it to look at me. "I may not have gone against his business, but Marshall had rules."

"This is fucking ridiculous," the words explode from my chest. How dare this man...

Ethan sighs. "There is no point in figuring out why Marshall Davis does the things he...well, does. He's a narcissistic sociopath. He's psychotic on his good days."

He describes his adopted father with such a lack of emotion I crawl into his lap. I shove my hands between Ethan and the couch and lay my head against his shoulder.

"Marshall threatened to put Paycen on the job. And Cor would've been disciplined. There was no way to save all of you."

Ethan hugs me, and while I hate hearing the words, I know he's right.

"Paycen wouldn't have been able to pull off a house fire. Back then, he didn't care about discretion. He was run by his demons."

Bile crawls up my throat at the thought of my friend massacring us in cold blood.

"Corbin didn't have a choice. There would've been other ways to make the bodies disappear."

"Jenn. And Carolyn." Their names are out of my mouth before I can stop myself.

Ethan slowly untangles us. His hands rest on my hips while he studies me with narrowed eyes.

"Pace filled in the blanks of your family dynamic over the years," I explain.

"I see."

That's not the answer I expected. Suddenly, I'm desperate to have the full picture of what transpired that night. "So, Corbin agreed to kill *us*. Then what?"

"Corbin brought Jenn and Theo in. He needed their help. They left me out of the loop to ensure my reactions were authentic."

My fingers dig into Ethan's sides. "That is just cruel."

He shakes his head. "They were right. I wouldn't have been able to pretend. Not with a risk of the plan failing and you potentially dying, too."

I grind my teeth. I don't like this.

"Theo and Jenn were on their way home but not due until the next evening. They always took their time, took breaks, stayed at fancy hotels. Anything to not come back to Renneton. Anyway, Cor called them as soon as he got the task." A devious smirk pulls on Ethan's mouth and my forehead wrinkles. "We all had more than one phone—a secret between the four of us. There were just things we didn't want Marshall to find. While he generally never checked the servers, the chance was there. So, we found a way to shut him out when necessary."

"Why didn't you use that phone to talk to me, then?" I accuse. Maybe Marshall wouldn't have found out about Ethan being with me.

"We stored those phones off-site. Only used them when we were not on the plantation. It would've limited my ability to talk to you," he explains.

While a nagging voice in the back of my head continues to argue that he should've found a way to use it, it makes sense why he didn't. So, I purse my lips and remain mute.

"I was busy with maintenance. I had no idea that Corbin was not home. After he... *Fuck*." Ethan looks across the room.

He doesn't want to spell it out. It hurts to think about it, to say the words in my head, but I also accepted a long time ago that my parents were gone.

"After Corbin killed them," I finish.

A muscle in his jaw tics. "Cor rigged the house and diner. T was supposed to pull you out before the fire got out of hand, but they got delayed."

"Delayed?"

"They had a flat. Of all the days we traveled, that was the one time T ran over a nail," Ethan scoffs. "They came back for you to help you disappear, but there was no trace." He studies my face.

"I ran." I settle on the broken table on the other side.

He wants to ask more questions, but I hold up a hand, a sense of betrayal slowly gnawing its way through my insides. "If you found out nine years ago that I was alive, why didn't you come for me?"

Ethan's eyes gloss over. "Because you were better off without me."

"That's bullshit, Ethan, and you know it."

"Bullshit, huh?" He lifts me off his lap and jumps up in the same fluid motion. Marching the length of my tiny apartment, he starts, "I was hiding from my father. There was always a chance of him tracking me down. He knew I wouldn't go to the authorities, but I had still gone behind his back. How was I supposed to come to you without tipping him off? To Marshall Davis, you and your family had died in that fire."

His chest is heaving, and before I can say something else, he demands, "How is my brother here?"

Ethan's question trajects me in a whole new direction. "He tried to kill me." The words are out before I can think them over.

Ethan becomes motionless. He doesn't respond and holds my gaze. He swallows once, his jaw jutting out slightly.

Well shit.

I roll my lips under. I just opened a whole new can of worms.

Ethan pivots and aims for the exit, his gun in one hand—I forgot about the damn gun—and his knife in the other.

"Ethan, stop!" I beat him to it and throw myself in front of the door like in a bad movie, arms splayed on either side, back to the thin wooden barrier. "You need to listen to me."

"HE TRIED TO KILL YOU!" he roars in my face. I ignore the droplets of spit hitting my skin.

"He didn't, though," I plead. "Please let me explain."

Ethan recoils. "Jesus fucking Christ, Little Phoenix. How is this even possible?"

He holsters the Nitro on his side and turns. With the knife still clutched between his fingers, Ethan trudges back to the couch and throws himself down. Arms stretched on the back, blade aiming in my direction, he crosses his ankle over his knee. "Let's have it. Tell me how you convinced my psychopathic brother to spare you." At his mocking, heat begins to simmer in my core.

I point a finger at him. "Stop talking about him that way."

Ethan scoffs. "Do you hear yourself? The guy downstairs would kill a puppy if Marshall told him to. He has no humanity. He was raised by the devil."

I throw my arms up. "So were you, and you turned out fine." The corner of my lips lifts into a smirk. "Well, not fine, but you know what I mean." I sober, making my way over to him. Crouching, I place my hands on his elevated leg.

"Paycen overheard Jenn and Theo one day. It was time to check in on me again." When Ethan's brows shoot up, I deduct, "You didn't know?"

He looks uncomfortable, and I slant my head, waiting.

"After the day Jenn told me the truth, I made her swear never to bring you up again. I couldn't talk about you. It... I just couldn't."

I nod. I refuse to let his words have any further impact on me. We did what we had to do to survive.

"Apparently, they took turns. I don't know how they did it since I was constantly moving. Paycen followed Jenn, and after she left, he...didn't. I was in Ohio at the time." An image of the cracked sidewalk forms in my head. Half the streetlights were broken. "I worked at a small coffee shop for cash. I was on my way home, a women's halfway house, when Paycen intercepted me."

"I still don't understand how you stopped him from killing you."

"To be honest, neither do I." I huff. "One moment, I was calculating how long I could make it on the night's tips, and the next, I was pinned against a wall in an alley. I'm pretty sure I peed myself a little."

Ethan tenses. Sensing that he wants to hunt his brother down, I tighten my hold on his leg.

"Pace had his gun to the side of my temple, but when our eyes met...something changed." My pulse slows. The same way it did five years ago. "I have no idea what. I can't explain it. All I said was, *This won't make Marshall love you.*"

Recalling that night sends icy shivers down my spine. It could've easily ended a different way.

"Paycen pressed the muzzle against my temple." I point at the spot where the phantom pain still exists. "And I said that if he needed to kill me, to make it fast. That I deserved it after everything his father had put me through."

I close my eyes, returning to the alley. I counted the seconds while waiting to hear the safety come off.

"Pace dropped his gun. I remember the shock and how my

eyes popped open. He had his head tilted the way he always does." I mimic the motion. "Then, he mumbled, '*You talk like her.*'"

A groove appears between Ethan's brows.

"Those were the only words out of his mouth for the first week. He left me standing in the dark. I remember sinking to my ass and staying in that position forever. I didn't understand why he spared me. This was Paycen. He never introduced himself, but I knew who he was from the moment our eyes met."

Ethan nods, understanding the meaning behind my words.

"After that, he showed up every night on my way home. He would randomly wait for me in different spots and attack."

"Attack?" Ethan's features contort with fury and disbelief.

I chuckle. It all seems so far away now. "He was training me. I failed. Every. Single. Night. After two more weeks of this, I lost it on him."

"We are talking about the same Davis here, correct?" Ethan drops his foot and leans his arms on his thighs, knife dangling from his fingers. "The guy who has never allowed anyone to raise their voice at him. He tried to kill me in my sleep once over a water bottle, for fuck's sake."

"The same, baby." A grin stretches over my cheeks, proud that I managed to tame the feral Davis. "He and I have come a long way since then. I was hysterical. I was tired of working twelve-hour shifts for less than minimum wage, looking over my shoulder for years, and now having to fend this teenager off every night. I punched and kicked him like a toddler throwing a tantrum. Yelled in his face that he could either kill me or help me, but I was done with his cat-and-mouse games." I pause, my eyes narrowing at a scowling Ethan. "Do you know what his response was?" A laugh bubbles up in my throat, and I deliver the punch line, "'*I am training you.*'"

Ethan pulls me onto the couch next to him. "I still can't wrap my head around this."

I drape my legs over his and lean against his shoulder. "We would meet regularly between his jobs. Sometimes, he would come to me. Other times, he'd send me coordinates, and I would meet him. After about a year, he told me that he found a place for me to settle."

Ethan inhales sharply.

"I thought he was shitting me until he showed me the deed for the diner." I sit back to make sure he sees my face. "Ethan, your little brother bought me this place. It wasn't much, and I had to come up with everything else, but he helped me start over. He is not as bad as you make him out to be. He has never learned what it means when someone cares for him."

"I don't know, Jules. He—"

Ethan's words get cut off when something flies through a window.

What the—?

Glass shatters all around us, and I try to cover my head with my hands. Ethan throws himself on top of me, and we topple off the couch. Agony shoots through my back.

Several things happen at once. Whatever came through the window explodes. My ears ring, and whenever I blink, the room fades in and out like strobe lights illuminating a rave. The cacophony of noise filling my small apartment sounds like I'm underwater. Ethan's body gets ripped off mine, and a contorted mask appears in my line of vision. I squint, recognizing the outline of a ski mask. The mouth moves, but I can't make out the words. Something glints in front of my eyes, then a shooting pain slices my neck and—

CHAPTER TWENTY

ETHAN

Darkness slowly gives way to agony as my shoulders scream, begging me to change my position. I can't.

My arms are restrained at an unnatural, upward angle. My palms face backward, pressed flat against the concrete wall. Multiple shackles mounted into the wall hold me in place, the metal biting into my wrists and right above the elbow, immobilizing any chance to diminish the torture.

I know this position well. I've done this many times. To even more people. Listened to them beg for mercy. They never got it. Once you're in *the pen*, you rarely come out.

I slowly peel back my lids, my vision fading in and out. The drain in the middle of the stained floor moves like an object in a fun house mirror—six small grates swallowing everything my father never wants to be seen again.

Lifting my head, my spine cracks, and I lock my jaw to swallow the cry my body wants to expel.

How long have I been here? Where is Jules? Jules! My eyes fly open, and I frantically search my stall. Marshall modified each cage of the old cattle pen for a specific purpose—all leading to the same end result. Of course, she isn't here. They wouldn't put us together. My stomach rolls when a new wave of torment assaults my body.

Planting my feet firmly, I attempt to take pressure off my shoulder joints. I steady my breathing, count my inhales and exhales until my pulse calms. *Pain is not real.* Growing up, that was an integral lesson of our daily training. It's nerve endings communicating with the brain, which in return interprets the signals. Without answering those prompts, there is no pain, and therefore, pain is not real. I refuse to let my brain respond the way it wants. Inhale, exhale, inhale, exhale. My mind clears from the onslaught of sensation.

The hollow emptiness in my stomach indicates that I was out for a long time. Even if they brought us to the plantation by plane, which I doubt Marshall would've risked, we would've been in transport for several hours.

My priority is Jules. After that, I simply don't care.

Scanning my confinement, nothing has changed. There is only one way in or out. When Marshall converted the cattle pens to his personal torture chambers, each stall was enclosed with a foot of concrete on all sides. One narrow window at the top of the outer wall is the main source of telling time. The steel door, complete with a food slot at the bottom, would be my only escape route. The one advantage I have is that I know exactly which of the eight rooms I am in. This particular restraint is reserved for the few Marshall fears could break free. A wave of pleasure rolls through me, knowing that my father has at least interpreted the threat I am to him correctly. If he has harmed Jules, I will stop at nothing to eliminate—

A familiar grinding sound redirects my attention. The bar securing the door from anyone going in or out is moved off its brackets. Only *the warden* has the key to the pens. In all my years, I never learned his real name—if he still had one. Even Marshall or his children couldn't come in here without him. I wonder if my father always suspected that one day one of us would turn on him. An eternity later, the door swings outward, and someone steps into my cell: Corbin.

The lingering agony melts from my muscles as surprise mingles with shock. We haven't been face to face since the night of the fire. I'd hated him for a whole year, considered tracking him down for taking Jules more times than I could count. Something had always held me back, though. After I learned the truth, the hatred gave way to betrayal. While the soldier in me understood his reasoning, he had been my brother first. And my brother had gone behind my back, letting me believe the vilest of all sins to be his doing.

My eyes meet Corbin's. I don't know what I expected for our first meeting since... An apology? He holds my gaze, unwavering and emotionless, as he steps to the side, positioning himself against the wall with his hands behind his back—like the *servant* he was trained to be.

My body goes still as the next person enters. Marshall Davis doesn't set foot in *the pens*. His prisoners are brought to him—if they can still stand. He doesn't come to them.

He has made an exception for his son.

I lift my chin and hold Marshall's gaze as he steps to the middle of the room. Contrary to his business partners, Marshall never dressed in expensive suits and imported loafers. He didn't have to prove anything to anyone. Wearing denim jeans and a black tee that molds to his physique, he intimidates everyone with his presence alone. He is the embodiment of ruthlessness and cruelty. Everything we learned, we learned from him. He molded us into who we are, fostered our skills, and perfected our strengths.

His eyes bore into mine, and I vaguely notice a third person entering. The warden.

"Son." He scans me over. "It's good to see you."

My brows arch, and I bite back the remark that wants to make its way out. Instead, I straighten as much as I can in my physical position.

"Likewise, *Father*. It's been a while." Two can play this game, and if I learned one lesson growing up under his roof, it was to never give your opponent the advantage of your weakness.

Marshall clucks his tongue. "You disappoint me, Ethan. Again." He shakes his head. "I would've expected you to learn your lesson."

I slant my head, ignoring the sting as my skin stretches from my shoulder to my ear. "And what's that?"

He curls his lips. "A Davis doesn't associate with the help. Least of all an Arrow." Reaching into his back pocket, he pulls out a pack of Silk Cuts—his only vice. Lighting one, he inhales, peering at the ceiling before exhaling. "Did you really think that I would allow you to fuck around with one of the Irish?"

What?

Marshall laughs cruelly. "Grant Arrow was a Laundromat. He sought me out when his family disowned him for marrying outside the fold. He thought I didn't know who he was since he took his wife's last name. I gave him a chance to prove himself. He did well until he decided to go rogue. There were whispers he wanted to buy his way back home."

My eyes fly behind Marshall, who still doesn't pay me any attention. Corbin's gaze is trained on me, and he shakes his head imperceptibly.

I watch as Marshall strides back and forth. "He stole from me. But when his whore of a daughter started riding my son's cock, I had to step in before Rian Donelan decided he'd accept his son's offer."

My jaw drops at the name. Of course I know who Rian Donelan is. We were raised to know all of Marshall's associates and rivals. Donelan mainly resided in Europe and was rarely seen in America.

Marshall takes in my shock and barks out a laugh. "Your little whore didn't tell you who her grandfather is?"

"Watch your fucking mouth, *Father*."

Well, shit.

Corbin closes his eyes and grips the bridge of his nose.

I fucked up.

Marshall's hand shoots out and squeezes my jaw so tight I can feel the indent of his fingers against my tongue. His nose is an inch from mine when he speaks in a low tone. "If you don't watch your mouth, *son*, I will have your brother sew it shut."

My eyes flick to Cor, who presses his lips in a thin line. Focusing back on the man in front of me, I attempt to move my head in a nod. While unsuccessful, he understands my jerky movement.

He flings my head to the side with such force my skull collides with the wall I'm attached to. Black spots infiltrate my vision.

"Where is Jules?"

Am I slurring?

Marshall takes one more drag of his cigarette before he presses the cherry against the back of my restrained hand, grinding it into my skin until the stench of burned flesh lingers in the room.

I bite the inside of my cheek, refusing to submit. Marshall holds my gaze before pivoting on his heels and disappearing through the door. The warden remains in the corner of the room, waiting for Corbin to exit next.

My brother slowly strides toward me until his feet are only a few inches from mine. He scans my face but remains mute.

Where is Jules?

He angles his body so his back is to the warden. Tilting his head, he huffs out a maniacal laugh before leaning in. "Pretend I insulted you. She's alive. Play the game."

With those words, he puts distance between us.

"Get the fuck away from me," I sneer at Corbin.

His arm pulls back, and before he lets his fist fly, he mouths, "I'm sorry."

THE NEXT TIME I come to, I am no longer restrained. My jaw throbs, but so does everything else. Facing the back wall, a black object catches my attention. Nausea climbs my throat while an unwanted sigh of relief escapes my cracked lips. Oh, goody, I've been graced with a bucket. In my time, I didn't grant many the privilege of not having to look at their piss and shit.

Rolling on my back, I swipe my palms over my face, letting them linger on my forehead. Squinting at the window, the black of night greets me. I've officially lost track of time.

The wire cages around the fluorescent tubes in the ceiling are new. Probably installed after someone used one of the tubes as a weapon. Or decided that roasting themselves was better than dying by my father's hands.

Letting my head fall to the side, my brows furrow. The food slot is open. Not that this would allow me to escape or help my case in any way, but...unease settles in my core. This is against protocol.

I push myself into a sitting position and angle my legs. Resting my arms on my knees, I stare at the opening. I don't have to wait long before footfalls echo through the hallway. Black boots appear first. A paper plate is placed on the ground and kicked through the slot. A slice of bread and something resembling oatmeal (no utensils) comes to a stop. Peering up, a clear plastic cup stands outside the slot. If I want the water, I have to get it. *Right.* I know what happens when I reach through the gap. My brothers and I once turned this into a competition. Who can shock their prisoner the most before they give up? Theo being fourteen, with Corbin and me eighteen, we didn't know better. It was how we passed the time. Revulsion at the normality that was my life climbs my stomach walls.

Rumbling reverberates through my torso as my brain sends the visual cue to my core. I break a piece of the bread off and sniff it. Smells normal—not obviously poisoned. Placing it in my mouth, my taste buds explode in a sensory overload, and I groan. I take small bites, not wanting to overwhelm my stomach and puke everything back up. That would defeat the purpose. With my hunger semi-sated, my dry mouth becomes all I can feel. I swallow every drop of saliva that pools under my tongue until I can no longer hold back. I crawl over to the food slot. I learned early on how to move without a sound, how to listen for move-ment. There is nothing. Unless someone is literally camped outside my door, waiting for me to give in, I can't make out anything out of the ordinary.

Flexing my fingers once, I shoot my arm out and grip the cup. I pull it back until my hand is safely in the cell. Nothing happened. Surprise and relief give way to utter terror when a guttural scream pierces my ears. I drop the water, the liquid soaking my front as I fall to my stomach in front of the slot.

"JUUUULES! JULES!" My throat instantly burns. "I will kill every single one of you if you—" My useless threat cuts off when another scream travels through the building. She isn't close to my cell, that much my brain still catalogs before visions of Jules being tortured fill my mind. I can smell the blood. Is there blood? Or is that just in my head? Bile shoots up my throat. One more cry drifts through the food slot, but it's a muted whimper this time. Muted by distance or— I prop myself up on all fours, the bread suddenly feeling like a rock. Cold sweat slithers over my skin, my shirt clinging to my front and back.

A mental fog obscures my ability to focus, and I heave. I retch until the little food I consumed is splattered in front of me on the concrete. Vomit covers my hands, but none of it matters. Jules's cries have etched themselves into my brain.

Empty—in every sense of the word—I swipe my hands against the floor before crawling to the opposite side of my confinement. Sitting with my back against the wall, I prop my elbows on my knees and bury my face in my hands.

It's ten years ago all over again.

THE TELLTALE GRIND of the bar alerts me to a visitor. I should fight, attempt to get out. I can't. My mind and body have shut down. For however long I've sat here, vision after vision of my dead and mutilated girlfriend has played in a loop. I never told her how much I loved her. I don't care anymore what happens to me. So, when someone enters my pen, I ignore them.

Have them kill me.

When the last voice I ever expected to hear in here speaks, my head jerks up.

"She's alive."

My eyes are swollen, and I squeeze them shut twice before I can focus.

Paycen leans against the wall next to the door. His feet casually cross at the ankles, and his hands cuff his biceps. For all intents and purposes, he appears bored. He is dressed all in black. His jeans-and-hoodie ensemble is completed by a black bandanna around his forehead and equally void of color Valentino Garavani combat boots. For the briefest of moments, I wonder if he has any clue how much money he wears.

Then his words fully sink in.

"What did you say?" I cough from the dryness in my throat.

"She's alive." I scan his features for an indication of... anything, but he might as well have informed me of what he had for breakfast.

Jules saw him as her friend, and he—

The muscles in my neck coil. Pain forgotten, adrenaline sends a renewed increase of fight through every cell of my body. Pushing myself up, I sway. My palm flattens against the wall, and I widen my stance. I'm anything but intimidating, but I'll be damned if I cower in front of him. The fingers of my free hand curl and uncurl of their own volition. "What the fuck happened, Paycen?"

"I broke her fingers."

CHAPTER TWENTY-ONE

JULES

THE DOOR OPENS.

Fuck.

My spine stiffens as a whimper escapes my cracked lips. I press my back against the wall until there is no space left, cradling my hand. The multiple deformities and bruising are a clear sign that it's broken in more than one place. If I don't get that taken care of, I can forget about my fingers ever looking normal again.

You have to make it out alive first.

IT HAD BEEN LESS than two days since I woke up in this concrete cube of hell.

When my lids peeled back, my head was throbbing. My stomach quivered, threatening to expel its contents, but there was nothing to rid me of. I curled into a fetal position and gagged, prepared to use my last bit of strength to prop my body on all fours to not vomit on myself.

Initially, I thought I was experiencing the hangover of a lifetime. That everything from the last two weeks was just a figment of my drunken imagination. I didn't go on a bender, though—I hadn't allowed myself to let loose like that in ten years. Slowly, images began to form. Glass shattering. The ski mask. The syringe.

My skin suddenly was too tight. I fought against the urge to strip out of my minimal clothing. Someone draped me in an oversized zip-up hoodie, but besides that, I was still in Cody's sweats—the ones he had left at my apartment years ago.

Whatever that fucker injected me with was worse than the time Della and I stole her dad's liquor.

Della.

I hadn't allowed myself to think about my friend in years. It hurt too much. But somehow, my mind referenced that memory.

When the waves of nausea finally subsided to a bare minimum, I yelled. Screamed for someone's attention. I demanded to know what happened to Ethan. Where was I? I got nothing.

The only human interaction was a tattooed hand shoving paper plates and a cup of water through the shoot at the bottom of the door.

My accommodations, a.k.a. cell, concrete on every side—minus the sliver of a window out of my reach—were bare except for a red bucket. What the fuck was I supposed to do with...*oh.* Then it sank in. Fucking shit. Literally. I had lived in some rundown places while on the move, but I never had to resort to... that. The mere thought, the vulnerability they forced on me, infused heat through my veins. I welcomed the new sensation with metaphorical open arms—anything to stop the shivering.

I wasn't *cold* cold, but my muscles trembled nonetheless.

Courtesy of whatever they had knocked me out with? Fuck, there were too many unanswered questions.

Eyeing my makeshift toilet, I held it until my bladder threatened to burst. Eventually, nature won out. Keeping the bucket in the opposite corner, the smell was manageable at first—not so much anymore.

I hadn't stopped gagging in hours. I could see the fumes rising from it. Of course, they weren't real. Not yet. I still *saw* them. Every time the bile rose past my throat, I pressed my tongue to the roof of my mouth and swallowed. I refused to give up the little nourishment they provided.

They. Who were they? Marshall Davis? Or someone else entirely? Someone from my father's past?

Then, I had a colossally dumb idea.

In hindsight, I blame my actions on the methane and carbon dioxide suffocating me.

I needed to get their attention somehow. So, when it was time for my food delivery, I positioned myself next to the door. The shoot opened, and the instant the hand appeared, I stomped my heel on its knuckles. A crunch echoed off the walls, and whoever was attached to that arm howled. Obscenities of the worst kind reached my ears. He withdrew his flattened digits and left the slot open.

Jules 1, Captor 0.

I retreated to the middle of the room and pressed my face to the biting floor to look through the shoot—I wasn't dumb enough to be within reach of the opening. I breathed over the icy sting against my cheek. There was nothing but more concrete. Defeat settled in. That didn't help to figure out where I was or how to escape.

Resigned, I lowered myself against the wall. When feet stomped back down the hallway, I held my breath. A pair of brown work boots appeared in the opening. My chest constricted at the noise of metal grinding on metal. Someone was coming in.

The door swung outward, an inked giant filling the gap. My eyes bulged. The guy was easily over six-five, if not taller. His shoulders measured the width of the frame. He had to duck to enter, and my breathing sped up. Trailing his body, I stopped on the bandage around his hand.

Oh shit.

The corner of his mouth lifted in a sneer as his boat-sized feet crossed the threshold. My ass scrambled across the concrete until I could shrink farther into the corner.

The giant slanted his head. "Not so brave now, you little bitch, huh?"

I mashed my lips, knowing when to keep my trap shut. Not that this would help. I was as good as dead.

"I can't punish you in the way you deserve, you little cunt, but the boss didn't say you needed all your body parts."

Wha—?

His voice was a deep timbre. Something I used to find soothing, reminding me of my father. There was no comfort now. My lungs began to burn when paralyzing fear prevented me from drawing in new air.

"A hand for a hand." The corners of his mouth stretched menacingly across his features, and he pulled out a machete from behind his back.

My heart faltered before picking up in a sprint. No, no, no.

"Warden."

The giant halted and...did his shoulders scrunch up? He side-stepped and faced the voice, giving me a direct line of sight to—

My jaw dropped.

Paycen stood in the hallway, feet apart, hands behind his

back. His all-black attire somehow enhanced his cutting features. I hadn't been scared of him in so long, but his unbothered expression by this whole situation sent new tension through me.

Realization sank in. I was in Renneton.

Meeting Paycen's gaze, I didn't find my friend. The man I had gotten to know and care about over the last five years didn't exist in this shell. Icy numbness slithered over my skin, seeping through every pore and immobilizing me.

"You are not supposed to be in here," Paycen stated with a flat tone.

He's not?

"I'm in charge of the pens. I don't owe you an—"

With two quick strides, Paycen was in the room and had his fingers wrapped around the *warden's(?)* bandaged hand.

What the fuck is a warden?

The giant slightly folded into himself, swallowing the wince, but Paycen didn't stop. A large Bowie knife appeared in his fist. Angling it under the man's chin, the warden tried to lean away. Unfortunately, that just made Paycen apply more pressure on the bandage, and I could see the giant's knees nearly buckle.

"The fuck, Payc—?" the older guy rasped as the blade broke the skin.

Paycen, however, just angled his head, flicking his eyes to mine. "I'll take care of her. I owe my big brother a message." Holding his gaze, a shiver ran down my spine. I hadn't seen this look since that first night in the alley.

"She fucking broke my—" A gurgling sound came out of the warden's throat.

Too fast for me to comprehend, Paycen had the man on his knees and the tip of the Bowie aimed at his eyeball. "Did I stutter?"

The warden's lashes grazed the knife as he blinked. "No, Paycen." His reply was laced with so much venom that you'd almost miss the real emotion behind them: terror.

Paycen lowered the blade, letting it hang loosely between two fingers at his side. "Leave."

He gave the other man his back, unconcerned that he would retaliate.

The warden hesitated one more breath before shoving to his feet. Right before stepping out of the cell, he paused and threw me a glance that promised retribution in one way or another.

Paycen pivoted on his heel, repositioning his blade anew. "Warden?"

Something told me that no one disobeyed the youngest Davis.

Humiliation and rage swirled in his irises before he finally disappeared from view. My stomach caved when the footsteps stopped outside the door. He was listening.

I swallowed over the lump in my throat.

Paycen swiveled on his heels, making no sound as he swiftly bridged the distance. My breath came in spurts, and when he squatted in front of me, I blinked, hoping that when my lids lifted, I would see the man who had become my friend over the last few years.

He wasn't there. My throat clogged with tears.

Paycen's thumb swiped away the moisture under my eyes. Bringing his finger to his line of sight, he studied the droplet with interest. "You shouldn't have done that, Jules."

Hearing his voice directed at me sent a flutter through my limbs. I opened my mouth, but he stopped me.

"Nothing here goes unpunished." There was no cadence in his words.

"What are you going to do?" I whispered despite not wanting to hear the answer.

He held my gaze. For a long moment, Paycen stared at me. My eyes dropped to his mouth, and adrenaline surged. His lips were in a flat line. My eyes flew back to his, and he closed them briefly.

Inhaling once, his hands shot out at the same time as he expelled his breath. He captured my wrist with ease from where I had my hands tucked under my armpit.

My brain ordered me to fight, but I couldn't move. His gaze never wavered when his fingers wrapped around my pinkie. A snapping sound, reminding me of breaking a twig, reached my ears before my pain receptors fired, and I screamed—every lesson he ever taught me forgotten. Pain was real. Very, very real.

Paycen repeated the motion three more times before he placed his palm against my tearstained cheek, the contact so fleeting that when I lay curled up on my side, I questioned if it had actually happened.

THE WARDEN APPEARS at the open door. His gaze penetrates mine, and I whimper.

He's here for his revenge.

Then, he steps aside, revealing a stoic-looking Jenn. My lips begin to tremble. I was never afraid of her before but after Paycen...

In this hell, my friends don't exist. In the back of my mind, a voice is questioning if anything was ever real.

Jenn strides across the room and drops something on the ground with a thump. My shoulders jump to my ears, and I force myself to control my breathing. Flicking my gaze to the side, I scan the nondescript backpack.

She lowers herself in the same manner as her little brother did not too long ago. Squatting in front of me with her elbows on her thighs, she reaches for me, and instinct kicks in. I jerk away.

Jenn rolls her upper lip between her teeth before speaking. "Let me look at it." Her tone is gentle. "Please."

"You're here to make sure the *Coldblood* didn't damage her too much. That's all the boss wants to know," The warden barks, and Jenn slits her eyes.

Peering over her shoulder, she says, "Oh, but cutting her hand off wouldn't have damaged her?" Her icy tone resembles Paycen.

The large man's fingers twitch by his side, but he remains mute.

"That's right, know your place, *Warden*."

I blanch. I've never seen her like this. The thudding against my rib cage becomes almost painful.

"Father wants to see you. I'm going to set the break," Jenn informs me as she unbuckles the top flap of the pack.

My stomach curls. *Set the...*

"Open." Jenn holds out a piece of plastic, and I stare. "You need to bite down. I'm not allowed to give you anything for the pain." When I don't comply, she adds, "This will hurt, Jules."

Suddenly, everything slows. My pulse returns to a steady rhythm, and I can think clearly. Jenn furrows her brows, studying me with interest. A new emotion pushes itself to the forefront.

"More than when your brother broke my fingers in the first place?" I hiss at the woman I considered a friend once upon a time.

"Paycen did what he knew best to de-escalate the situation," she explains calmly. She keeps her voice low, ensuring the exchange remains between us. Yet, the dismissive nature of her statement makes me draw my shoulders back.

De-escalate?

I don't bother responding. I have nothing more to say. Even

if this is all a show for them to maintain face in front of their *daddy*, they broke me once. Never again.

I open my mouth and let her place the object between my teeth. Staring at the ceiling, I focus on breathing. Her cold fingers wrap expertly around mine, and then—

I haven't screamed so much since...I found my dead parents in our burning house. The only difference is that the pain is physical this time. I failed again at severing my brain's connection to report injuries.

Sweat runs down my temple, and I can barely make out Jenn's form through my cloudy vision.

After taping my fingers, she pulls a water bottle from the pack and holds it to my lips. I'm cradling my *fixed* hand with my uninjured one and glance between the offering and her face.

"Drink. It's just water."

I doubt she'll poison me after providing first aid. My throat hurts like a mother, and I'd gulp down pretty much anything to quench my thirst.

After Jenn packs up, she motions for me to stand. It takes me several deep breaths to get to my feet. Steadying myself against the wall, I concentrate on remaining upright.

The warden comes closer with a pair of industrial cable ties, and I recoil.

"Jules." Jenn's tone is low. When our eyes lock, she shakes her head, and I feel like I'm falling.

I will get out of here. I fill my lungs to their max capacity. They will not break me. I exhale. I can do this.

I shakily stretch out my arms. The asshole grabs my injured hand tighter than needed and jerks me to him. My legs buckle as a new wave of torment shoots up my arm. Acid rises in my throat while black fuzzy spots fade in and out of my vision.

"Warden." Paycen suddenly appears in the doorway, and our eyes meet.

My tormentor's back stiffens. He grinds his teeth and slips the zip ties over my wrists.

Paycen enters, and the walls narrow. There are too many bodies in this space. He wraps his fingers around my elbow and leads me out of the cell.

CHAPTER TWENTY-TWO

JULES

PAYCEN'S GRIP IS FIRM BUT NOT PAINFUL.

The voice that whispered to me years ago that I could trust him defends him again: *He's keeping you upright.*

While that's true (my legs are anything but steady), doubt constricts my chest.

Jenn falls into step on the other side, and they lead me out of the building. I focus on the ground, terrified to find Ethan's corpse in a corner if I look around.

Stepping into the bright sun, my eyes struggle to adjust. I stop involuntarily, blinking. I would've expected to be dragged forward, but Paycen and Jenn wait patiently. I welcome the warmth on my skin, inhaling the fresh air.

Filling my lungs, I suddenly have an epiphany: my friends are with me. They just don't allow anyone to see them. They can't.

My surroundings take on shape. I've never seen the actual plantation. I only remember what Ethan divulged to me once upon a time.

The wraparound porch is cut off at the side of the house, where new additions were added to the structure. It's massive. And from what I recall, it extends underground as well.

We cross the lawn and driveway. When we hit the steps leading onto the porch, Paycen supports my weight.

"Thank you," I murmur, then snort.

He broke my fingers, and I'm thanking him for helping me walk. Two sets of eyes flick to my face with identical expressions: *She has officially lost her mind.*

Paycen kicks at the bottom of the double doors without care. Both swing inward, slamming against the walls inside. Several sets of eyes train on us. Marshall's office is on the first floor, across the entrance, and it seems we are the last to arrive.

Crossing the threshold, a hunched figure in a chair catches my eyes, and I tear at Paycen's hold.

"ETHAN!"

My struggles are useless. Jenn catches my other arm, and between the two of them, I have no chance. I'm nowhere near my full strength, not after days of minimal nourishment and getting my fingers first broken and then reset.

Ethan's head jerks up, and my bound hands fly to my mouth. The side of his face is bruised, his eye so swollen all you can see is discolored flesh. No lashes, nothing.

I round on Paycen. "Did you do this?" I snarl.

My friend only stares at me.

I trail over everyone in the room. Marshall lounges behind his desk, regarding me with interest. His fingers are steepled under his chin, and the corner of his mouth is tilted in an amused smirk. A large man hovers nearby, arms clasped behind his back.

Corbin and Theo guard Ethan's chair on both sides, expressions impassive.

Ethan holds my gaze before it drops to my wrapped fingers and then to his little brother.

I'm about to step in his direction when Paycen pinches my elbow. *Stay.* I lock my knees and bite the inside of my cheek. Remaining in place proves more challenging than forgiving him for the mutilation of my fingers.

Marshall places his palms on the tabletop of his desk and rises to his feet. He slants his head, one by one, perusing his children until his gaze lands on me. "Jules Arrow." He draws out my name.

My eye twitches at the amusement in his tone. I snub my chin. "Marshall Davis."

I will not die here.

Jenn stiffens, and Paycen's grip turns to a vise. For once, my brain sends the right signals, and I don't flinch. I ignore both, my full attention on the murderer of my parents.

His face lights up in a full-on grin, and he reaches for a pack of cigarettes. Taking his time to light one, I wrinkle my nose.

Who the fuck still smokes these days?

"Tell me, Jules..." He takes a drag and starts walking around his desk. "How are you alive?"

Marshall doesn't know that all his children are in on it.

"I got her out," Ethan slurs, and everyone's heads turn to him.

Marshall's gaze flicks to me before striding over to his son. He grips his chin, making Ethan wince. Marshall bends Ethan's head at an angle that hurts me to witness. "Son, I warned you what would happen if you lied to me again."

Ethan slants his lips, and the muscle in his neck tics.

"I woke from my mother's screams when he murdered my father." I lace my tone with venom and glower at Corbin.

His eyes meet mine. *I'm protecting Ethan, not you.*

"Is that so?" Marshall drops Ethan's chin. His head slumps

220 · DANAH LOGAN

forward before he lifts it with effort. What the hell did they do
to him?

"Yes." I curl my lips. *Fuck you, asshole.*

"Then tell me, Jules, who was the third body?" He slants his
head, lifting his cancer stick to his mouth.

Third body. *Third*...fuck. In all these years, I never considered who might have taken my place. That Corbin or Jenn might
have killed someone to—

"I never confirmed the body count," Corbin declares, and I
hear a sharp intake of breath at my side. Jenn.

Marshall goes eerily still. He pins me down as he addresses
his eldest. "Would you like to repeat that, son?"

There is a moment of silence—everyone is holding their
breath. The only sound is the violent thrashing of my pulse in
my ears.

"She was out cold. Asleep on her desk. Even checked her
pulse when she wouldn't wake up after moving her to her bed.
Assumed she had popped some pills—she was hanging out with
Greystone, after all." He shrugs casually. "I was running out of
time, so I moved on to the master. You didn't give me a lot of
head start. E could've interfered at any point; you know how
pussy-whipped he was for her." Corbin elaborates with such
indifference that I almost believe him myself.

At the mention of my former best friend, my heart squeezes.

Marshall whirls around. Drawing a gun from God knows where
he aims it at his son's head. It's not just any firearm. He holds a blind-
ingly polished chrome Auto-Ordnance 1911A1. The muzzle indents
the skin on Corbin's forehead, his natural tan whitening under the
pressure. "That doesn't explain why you didn't confirm that this
little bitch was dead. I assumed you learned how to count to three.
Why did I pay for tutors all those years, huh? You only had one job."

Jesus fuck, this man is psychotic.

Ethan's lips curl back at his father's mention of me, and Theo's fingers dig into his shoulder, silencing him.

Corbin doesn't flinch. "I was containing Ethan. He was going to rush in and fuck everything up."

Marshall chuckles. "You got some balls after all." His eyes flick to the side as he pats Ethan's cheek with his cigarette-holding hand.

A growl builds in my throat as the cherry comes too close to his injured flesh.

"Clearly, you were the one who *fucked up* in the end." Corbin doesn't move as his father lowers his gun. "Did you think you would get away with such disobedience just because you will take over the Order one day?"

Corbin's lips part, but Marshall beats him to it. "Take him to the pen."

Theo's gaze widens, but he keeps his eyes to the front. Ethan's nostrils flare, but he also doesn't make eye contact with Marshall.

"Father," Jenn is the only one daring to address him.

Two men appear from behind us and circle the room, blocking any escape routes. Corbin mashes his lips together but doesn't move. They expect him to fight. One of the goons has a Taser gun in his fist.

Once they reach Cor, the one without the Taser produces the same type of cable ties the warden had put on me. Why isn't he fighting them?

Corbin reaches behind him and hands over his weapon to Theo. The entire exchange happens without them making eye contact. When the binds are around Corbin's wrists, Marshall turns away. I assume he'll retreat to his desk. Instead, he whips around, clocking the butt of his gun against his son's head.

Corbin's knees buckle, and he collapses into himself. The two guys catch him under the arms and drag him across the floor and out the door—literally lugging him behind.

Bile rises in my throat at the unnatural angle of his restrained arms. Jenn gives out a strangled whimper, and Paycen's fingers twitch around my elbow. Theo rolls his lips under, and Ethan's spine stiffens.

Something snaps inside of me. I start tearing at my hold. "What the fuck is wrong with you? He is your son, you psycho."

"Jules." It's the first time Paycen speaks, his tone so low I doubt anyone besides me heard him.

I ignore his attempt to stop me, but I can't shut up even if I wanted to. "You turned your children into monsters. Did you not get enough hugs as a child that you have to torment your own flesh and blood? Is that how you get off?"

Marshall's head slowly twists toward me, and his eyes flare. Before I can react, he flies across the room, and his fingers wrap around my throat.

"NO!" Ethan jerks forward.

I peer at him out of the corner of my eye. Theo has both palms pressed on his shoulders, holding him down. I silently will him to stop. We can't both die here, but I'll be damned if I submit to this monster.

"You really are as stupid as your old man, you dumb bitch," Marshall sneers. His nails dig into my skin, curling around the lateral muscles in my neck as if he wants to bare-handedly tear them out—he probably does. He leans close until his nose is to mine, and I'm forced to inhale the stench of his cigarettes.

"You're lucky I cannot kill you." He slants his head. "Maybe I'm gonna go to war with your grandfather after all. It would be worth seeing the life drain from you." A disgusting grin bows his mouth up, and he squeezes harder.

Grandfather?

Saliva drools down my chin as I try to swallow, but the muscles in my throat can't fulfill my physical need.

"Where do you think my sons get their fondness for knives from?" He sinks his teeth into his bottom lip, scanning my body in a way that goose bumps ripple over every inch. My chest begins to burn, and despite my refusal to show weakness, rasped, gagging sounds spill from my lips as my body fights for oxygen.

"Over my dead body," Ethan shouts. Theo is struggling at this point, having Ethan in a choke hold. Shadows fade in and out of my vision, turning Marshall into a true nightmare in front of my eyes.

"That can be arranged." Marshall doesn't waver, his gaze lingering on my tits.

Heat flushes my cheeks. A sour taste slithers over my tongue when he licks the corner of his mouth. I do the only sane thing a person in my situation would do. I gather all the moisture I can and spit in the disgusting pig's face. Not an easy feat as my physical strength is nonexistent, and my lungs spasm. At the mere chance of this man violating me, adrenaline surges and gives me the ability to seal my fate. I'd rather die than let Marshall Davis touch me.

Paycen curses under his breath.

As fast as he'd had the gun on his son, Marshall backhands me across the face with such force that I nearly fall into Paycen. A coppery taste fills my mouth, and a smirk curls my lips.

I'm about to repeat the action—this time with a red undertone—when Ethan brings everyone to a halt.

"If you don't take your filthy hands off her, I will have your money drained from your accounts." He doesn't deliver the words with their usual power, but he's not slurring anymore.

The entire room goes still as if someone pressed pause on a video. Every single eye is trained on him.

Suddenly, Marshall bursts out laughing. He points a finger of his free hand at Ethan. "Good one, son. You almost had me there." He's about to turn back to me when Ethan speaks again.

"I found Poppy's ledger."

Who the fuck is Poppy?

A groove forms between my brows. Marshall's fingers around my throat slacken.

"It's been my insurance policy for ten years, *Father*—in case the mood would ever strike you, and you finally came after me." A weak sneer but no less threatening expression crosses Ethan's features.

The claw disappears from my throat, and I want to rub over the spot that carries the devil's nail marks. Marshall slowly pivots. He assesses his son, the air in the room crackling with violence.

"Clear the room." Those three words detonate the static, and everyone begins to move.

I can't avert my eyes from Ethan. Is he bluffing? Is he serious? If he has such a trump card, why would he use it for me? My heart rate picks up.

Jenn pulls on my arm. Though, before we take a step, a newcomer draws attention away from Ethan.

"Donelan's plane just touched down."

That voice.

I turn my head in slow motion, willing the audio signal to be interpreted incorrectly by my brain. My body sways. "Ty?" This is all too much.

His eyes flick to me dismissively, focusing on the main psychopath of the room. I haven't seen my ex since the night I stabbed him—another figure of my past that I couldn't worry about while being on the run. I held no affection for him, certainly not after the stunt he pulled in my bedroom, but I had hoped he made it. I wasn't a murderer.

Marshall clicks his tongue. "He's early. How many did he bring?"

"Ten."

My gaze trails over Ty, and I notice he stands the same way everyone approaches Marshall, hands interlaced behind his back, shoulders tense. Obedient, yet ready to fight—for their lives.

"Take her to the guest room next to Jenn's. Let's wait for Rian to make contact," Marshall speaks to the room, not Ty. "He won't just show up here. He's gotten careful with old age."

Marshall retreats to his desk and leans on the front. The vein at his temple protrudes, thudding with his silent rage. "I need to have a conversation with my son."

My grandfather is in Renneton. Why is he here? I've never met the man. He disowned Dad before I was born.

Ty nods, pivoting so his front is to my side. Jenn makes room, and I study her pinched lips. I don't think anyone noticed her hesitation, but I did. She doesn't trust Ty.

When his fingers are about to wrap around my upper arm, I'm suddenly pulled out of reach. A hard body covers my back, and for the first time since walking into this room, I feel remotely safe.

"I'll take her," Paycen announces.

I want to sink against him. My legs quiver under my rapidly draining adrenaline. Locking my jaw, I coil my limbs. I can't allow him to be compromised.

Jenn blinks, her lids staying closed just long enough for me to see that she also doesn't want her little brother to put himself at risk with this.

"Morello has history with her. He cannot be trusted." Paycen states a fact, but then, why would the *Coldblood* care? Damn it.

Marshall pauses, glancing first at Ty, then his youngest. His jaw is set in suspicion. "Ty will not harm our guest, will you?" He doesn't look in my ex's direction, watching his son for his next move.

I refuse to let another of Ethan's brothers end up in the pen for me. I angle my body forward, instantly missing the blanket of safety Paycen draped over me.

The sneer on Ty's face resembles loathing in its purest form. "Wouldn't touch our Irish princess with a ten-foot pole." He waves at me to take the lead.

I curl my upper lip.

"I'll find her something to wear. She reeks," Jenn chimes in and wrinkles her nose. She waves at me to get moving. "Let's go."

I glance over to Ethan, but his gaze is forward. His chest rises rapidly. Is this triggered by Ty's surprise appearance or his threat to bring the Order down? I hesitate, the realization that this could be the last time I see him slamming into me harder than Marshall's hand did.

Ty shoves me between my shoulder blades. "Get fucking moving, Jules."

I stumble across the threshold but catch my balance before tripping into Jenn. I grind my teeth, wanting to knee my asshole ex in the junk so hard his balls get lodged in his throat and choke him to death.

Instead, I meet Ethan's gaze one more time before the door closes on us.

CHAPTER TWENTY-THREE

ETHAN

I watch Jules leave the room with my good eye.

I don't miss her imperceptible flinch when Morello's grubby digits connect with her back. A growl reverberates in my aching chest, my physical agony momentarily evaporating. I'm not surprised to see him here. His father was Marshall's personal scrubber, a.k.a. removed every trace of a serial number from any equipment traveling through the Order. When Jules didn't take him up on his offer to run ten years ago, he probably joined the ranks in the hope of stepping out of his old man's shadow.

If he harms her in any way, I will enjoy skinning him alive—with a vegetable peeler. One limb at a time until I get to his most precious body part. I'll stop right before he passes out, wait for him to recover, and then continue. I haven't killed anyone (like that) in a very long time, but to finally get my hands on Ty Morello, I will break the oath I made to George when he offered me a future.

. . .

MY SOLE FOCUS was on staying seated when every muscle in my body screamed for me to curl into a ball on the floor. I felt her before she crossed the threshold between my brother and sister. The tingling sensation in the back of my head started like a low hum and slowly built until it resembled a million insects invading my mind. As soon as I laid eyes on Jules, I could breathe again.

Jules wore the same clothes as the night my father's men had overpowered us. The only addition was a black hoodie I recognized immediately. It was mine. Leaving all my belongings behind, I didn't care what had happened to them. I expected Marshall to toss everything. He probably did, and one of my siblings saved a few precious items—*Jenn*.

Seeing her swallowed by the fabric gave me comfort—knowing I was with her.

Paycen had informed me that she was alive, but having grown up here, alive and *alive* could be two very different things.

After my little brother left my pen, the warden paid me a visit. One look at his hand, and I couldn't stop my grin, which ignited his already smoldering rage. Paycen hadn't given me any explanation as to why he had hurt *his friend*. Things now clicked into place. The warden had underestimated my girl. She bested one of the most brutal men on the plantation, and Paycen intervened before he could execute his revenge. Thank fuck. In the short time I observed the two, I could see that she'd changed him. Jules had accomplished what none of us had ever managed.

The satisfaction of *The Davis Order* slowly but surely crumbling, piece by piece, gave me the will to push forward. To let the warden have his revenge.

I still had my trump. And I would play it to get Jules and myself out.

Despite Jules's unquestionably suicidal actions since entering my father's office—no one talked back to Marshall Davis—pride expanded my broken ribs. She was a true phoenix—my phoenix.

No matter how many times her life got burned to the ground, her wings clipped and broken, Jules Arrow rose from the ashes stronger than before.

Jules held her chin high when my father hit her. She walked in front of her ex she stabbed ten years ago with her shoulders drawn back. If she was concerned, she didn't show it. She displayed more courage during those twenty-some minutes than most people living on this property did their entire lives.

My sister's contempt for Jules was visible to everyone and proved how much she had perfected her acting over the last decade. Jenn signaled to me with one shift of her eyes that she wouldn't let anything happen to Jules.

THE DOUBLE DOORS CLOSE, and I'm alone with my father, his second, and my two remaining brothers as the only witnesses to what I'm about to reveal.

Marshall lowers himself behind his desk. He sits motionless for several breaths before reaching for his Silk Cuts. Lighting another, his gaze is unfocused.

He flicks his wrist, sending ash flying across the tabletop. T steps to my side and waves his hand. I understand their silent commands.

Fuck, this will hurt.

I inhale deeply and push to my feet with the exhale. I swallow the agony that shoots through my body. My ribs hurt like a mofo. Self-assessing, I'm guessing the warden broke at least two with his last kick.

T guides me over to the chairs in front of the desk. I don't lower myself into the plush leather until Marshall gives us his attention and dips his chin—more at T than me, but the signal is there.

My brother remains at my back while I drop ungracefully on

my ass. Preserving my strength, I don't need to be upright to deliver my ticket out of here.

I don't bother looking for Paycen. I haven't lost my ability to sense where my siblings are in a room. He retreated to the wall by the door—the spot he has taken ever since he was allowed to actively participate. He prefers the shadows, blending into the background.

Which makes it even more miraculous how he kept seeking out Jules.

Marshall curls the fingers on his free hand on top of the desk. "I'm listening."

That's it. No threats, no questions. I have him by the balls, and he's trying to figure out if I can cut them off. I can.

"Poppy kept a ledger," I repeat my earlier statement. "She recorded every job. What was requested, by whom, and what she delivered." I let him process the information. "I have a record of every piece of paper she ever forged for you, *Father*. Including the offshore accounts under your aliases."

With each word, my heart rate slows, and memories flood my brain.

I FOUND the book taped under the sink in Poppy's crapshoot apartment the day we murdered her. Without looking into the black moleskin, I shoved it in the back of my pants and covered it with my shirt. Something compelled me to.

The first time I scanned the pages, sitting on the toilet of the motel room Cor and I shared, I bit my cheek. Swallowing the metallic taste, I flipped through the notes. It didn't just contain Marshall's business dealings and security measures but every single job Poppy ever took payment for, including which ones her apprentice was hired to do. She was a paranoid bitch. This would come in useful one day.

Thank you so much, P.

I couldn't keep it on me or anywhere on the plantation. That much was clear. I would've been dead on the spot if anyone had found it. So, I gave it to the one person who was as much at risk if the notebook ever saw the light of day: Poppy's associate. She was a mere teen at the time, but she would've surpassed her master soon. She was incomparable.

I put my faith in a person I had never met and probably wouldn't lay eyes on again unless one of us had to execute our contingency plan. One could've considered my trust suicidal.

Little did I know then that our paths would cross before I needed to remove the ledger from the safety-deposit box we shared under pseudonyms she created.

She took a job for one of Marshall's rivals. If on purpose or by accident, I never asked. Marshall didn't tolerate it either way. But instead of killing his best forger, he put her in her place— locking her up at Twin Lake Psychiatric Hospital until he saw fit to release her.

Unfortunately for my father, he didn't consider who else was locked up there. Fate has a curious way of coming full circle.

A SLIGHT SMILE plays on my lips. "Did you know that she's no longer at TLPH?"

Marshall's eyes flare. I don't need to elaborate on who she is. She has too many names to narrow her identity down to one. I have no clue which one she used before her incarceration. Of course he's aware that she isn't, but his surprise at my knowledge on the matter is what I wanted to see. That I am familiar with her, know her personally.

From the day I found out that the man who took me out of the foster system and brought me into his home wasn't your average Samaritan, Marshall ensured that we only knew what he wanted us to. And interacting with the people who kept the secrets that could bring the Order down was not part of it.

"She wasn't too happy with your form of house arrest. She was more than willing to provide me with the necessary documents to withdraw every single cent from your accounts."

I let the information sink in. I count seven breaths before Marshall shoots to his feet and swipes everything off his desk with a guttural roar.

I've got him.

I gingerly cuff my arms, careful to rest the weight on my abs instead of my ribs. Marshall's chest heaves. He wants to shoot me. He can't.

"If I don't walk out of here, you will lose everything." I get comfortable in the seat. "What will it be, *Father*?"

It's that moment the door opens, and Ty walks in.

"Sir—"

Whatever he wants to report, he doesn't get to it. Marshall draws his Ordnance and shoots him between the eyes.

Well shit.

Marshall slams the gun on the desk. "Get this cleaned up." Spit flies, accompanying the flush of fury coloring his features.

His second jumps into action and moves for the first time since I was dragged in here.

"Rian already demanded the release of your little whore." Marshall slits his eyes. "You're negotiating for yourself." There is bustling behind me, but I ignore the commotion of whoever removes Morello's lifeless form and begins to scrub his brains off the wall.

"I will always negotiate for Jules," I state calmly—not that there is something to negotiate. He has no choice. "Who says you won't start a war with the Irish just to stroke your broken ego?" New energy infuses my veins. "I don't want your money, but if you so much as come after Jules or me, I will take it all."

"How do I know you're not bluffing?" Marshall's hands flatten against the tabletop, his weight supported by his locked elbows. He's grasping at straws.

I gesture at the sole pen next to his palm that survived his temper tantrum. A groove forms between his brows, but he hands it over. Lining it up with the inside of my arm, I write down four rows of numbers. Account and routing numbers to Marshall Davis's offshore accounts.

Holding my arm up for him to read the digits, his eyes round. His nostrils flare, and his fingers twitch for his gun. He refuses to look at my face. "You have thirty minutes to grab your whore and leave the property."

BURSTING THROUGH THE DOOR, I find Jules sitting on the edge of the mattress. Jenn has her daggers ready and positions herself in front of my girl before I can take two steps. Warmth infuses my body.

As our eyes connect, Jules flies into my arms. I fold her in my embrace, and she clings to me. Letting her emotions overwhelm her—no doubt for the first time in days—her shoulders shake. I grit my teeth as she puts pressure against my ribs, but I don't tell her to loosen her hold. I need the connection as much as she does.

I must've made some sound because Jules pulls away, her fingers holding on to my arms. "What's wrong?" Her eyes fly over my stained clothes.

"I'm fine, Little Phoenix." I take a few shallow breaths. "Nothing ibuprofen won't cure." Cupping her face, I drink her in.

Her brows arch. She wouldn't be my Jules if she couldn't see through my false mask of bravado. I fucking hurt. Everywhere.

"Who was shot?" Jenn inserts herself into the reunion, and I hollow my cheeks.

Making sure Jules's eyes are on me, I answer my sister's question. "Morello."

Jules sucks in a sharp breath, and Jenn digs the heels of her hands (with the daggers between her fingers) into her eyes.

"We have to go."

Jules's lips part, but no sound comes out.

"Marshall gave us thirty minutes to get off the plantation," I explain.

"Twenty-four now. You're wasting time." Paycen appears.

I glance over my shoulder and nod.

I reach for Jules's hand, interlacing our fingers. "Any chance we can borrow one of your cars?"

My siblings exchange a look. "Ty's Jeep is available." Paycen shrugs.

Jules chokes, and I squeeze her hand. She wasn't close with her ex by any means, but she is a far better person than any of us. He means nothing to me, and neither does his mode of transportation. He was just a body to the Order. No one of consequence.

"It's the blue Wrangler. He always parks—uh, parked under the far carport near the bunks. You remember the way?" Jenn inquires. The bunks are the old servant quarters where Marshall keeps the muscle. Only the family and his second sleep in the main house.

My siblings can't be seen helping us. My insides turn cold. This is the second time I have to say goodbye to Jenn in less than a month. This time feels different, though. Final.

Jenn steps up to me, placing her hand on the side of my cheek. "I'll find a way to come see you." Her voice cracks at the end, and I swallow over the lump in my throat.

Turning to Jules, Jenn wraps her in a hug. Sobs come from

both girls, and my heart breaks for them. Jenn's circle of friends has never expanded past Jules, and Jules couldn't make friendships for the last decade out of fear of exposing them to the Order.

"Jules." I hate to interrupt them, but we're running out of time.

Jenn is the one who untangles herself first. She retreats to the bed, and Paycen takes her place. He peers down at my girl with an expression I've never seen on him before: affection.

Jules cranes her neck, her green irises darkened with tears. "Tell me I'll see you again." She sniffs and wipes with the sleeve of my hoodie under her nose.

"You will see me again." Paycen steps forward, and my chest constricts when he opens his arms. He rests his chin on the crown of her head while Jules clings to my little brother. "I'm your shadow, remember?"

I assume the meaning behind his statement originated somewhere during the five years Jules slowly but surely chipped away at Paycen's fortified walls. Had it been any other male, I would've ripped them apart by now. Greed demands that I be the only one she turns to for comfort after we've been separated for so long. Instead, clouds impair my vision as Jenn and I witness the bond the two have formed. Jenn covers her mouth, stifling her own emotion.

"Promise me, Pace," Jules mumbles into his body.

"I promise." Suddenly, he recoils and whirls around.

Paycen disappears into the hallway, and I press my lips together.

T materializes in the doorframe. "You gotta hurry, man. Marshall is on a warpath downstairs."

I jerk my head up and down once and then reach for Jules. Stopping next to my brother, I place a hand on his shoulder. "Don't be a stranger, T."

His eyes meet mine, mirroring my regret for missing ten years of his life. "You, too."

I hesitate. "Tell Cor—" my voice cracks. Tell him what? He is currently in the pen because he took the fall for me. For us.

"I will."

THE JEEP WASN'T hard to find. It was as obnoxious as Morello himself—metallic cornflower blue with tires that made it resemble a wannabe monster truck.

After I helped her into the passenger seat, I retrieved the keys from the board and left. I would figure everything else out later. My priority was to put as much distance between Renneton and us as possible.

WE'VE BEEN DRIVING for two hours when Jules speaks for the first time. During our mutual silence, I devised the best course of action. We'd be safe, and it would allow us to rest for a few days.

"Where are we going?" Her question is just above a whisper.

"Atlanta."

We just passed a sign telling me we are about two hours out. A quick glance at the gas needle makes my mouth run dry. We'll be cutting it close.

"Atlanta?" she repeats our destination with an incredulous undertone.

"Atlanta," I confirm. "It's the closest location where I can contact my boss." Peering over, I say, "We have no money or phones. We need clothes, and as much as I hate to admit it, I need painkillers and a bed."

Jules frowns. I didn't mean for my words to sound patronizing, but I'm fading. The soreness in my torso has expanded to a pounding headache, which makes it difficult to focus on the road ahead.

"And Bax will find a way to get in touch with your grandfather," I say more to myself than Jules.

Her head whips around. "Why on earth would I want to talk to my grandfather?" The disbelief in her voice makes me chuckle.

I reach over and hold out my hand, palm up, and wait for her to twine her fingers with mine before explaining, "Because he flew to the US for you. Paycen was the one who got a message through to him."

Paycen divulged that much during his short visit to my pen. He cares for Jules. If there was a doubt in my mind, it's gone now. My little brother would do anything for her, and for that, I am in his debt.

"Rian had no idea you survived. He's your fam—"

"Do not finish this sentence, Ethan Davis. You are my family. You, Paycen, and Cody," Jules snaps, angling her body away from me.

At the mention of the kitchen help, my jaw locks. I keep my thoughts about that to myself, though. She's been through more than a person should endure. While I will happily bury Cody Mantz alive if he so much as makes a move on my girl, he was there for her when I couldn't be. I'll give him one chance to prove his worth—and one chance only. Let's hope for his sake that Jules is right about him like she was about Paycen.

With her facing away, I roll my lips under.

I spot an emergency pullout and swerve across two lanes, cutting off a Mercedes in the process. The driver hits the horn, not letting up until he's way past us. I have other priorities, though, rather than chasing that idiot down.

Putting the Wrangler in park, I turn the hazards on and swivel my body to face Jules. "Please look at me."

Her shoulders rise and fall with her inhale, but in the end, she faces me. Jules eyes me warily, and the car suddenly feels too small.

I place one hand on the middle console. "You and me, Little Phoenix, we were meant to be from the moment I walked through the doors of your father's diner." I peer at the ceiling as I speak my next words. "I never told you why we came there the very first time. It wasn't my place to tell." I hold the air in my lungs. She's going to castrate me for this. Expelling my breath with a whoosh, I drop the bomb on her. "Corbin had just found out that he would be marrying Della."

I slowly lower my gaze to Jules, finding her staring at me with her jaw in her lap. She closes her mouth, shakes her head, and then opens it. "Come again?"

"There is a whole story behind this. One I will tell you sometime." I press my tongue to the roof of my mouth. "My point is... you and I have always been real. I never came to the diner to spy on you or your father. The first time may have been for a different reason, but I returned for you. Only you."

Tears pool in her eyes, muddling the green in her irises. Jules inhales a shaky breath and then climbs over the center console into my lap. She doesn't give me time to move the seat back before her mouth descends on mine. Her tongue swipes over the seam of my lips. I groan between wanting more (so much more) and the stabbing sensation in my chest. Tongues tangling, lips mashing against teeth, I ignore the pain and pull her closer. Thrusting up against her sweats-covered pussy, Jules whimpers. Her uninjured hand dives into my hair, and she tugs. God, I want her so bad. Not here. We both need a shower and proper medical attention. And lots and lots of painkillers.

I slow our heated kiss and nip at the corner of her mouth. "There is something else I've been wanting to say for a very long time."

Jules leans away, scanning my face. She doesn't ask what I'm talking about. She knows.

"I should've told you ten years ago, and I'm so sorry it took me this long." I drop my gaze.

Jules's forefinger finds its way under my chin and angles my head back up. "We had to burn to rise from the ashes. But now that we have, nothing can stop us, Ethan Davis."

I touch my forehead to hers, letting our breaths mingle. Inhaling her exhale, my chest expands. "I love you so goddamn much, Little Phoenix."

"And I love you."

CHAPTER TWENTY-FOUR

JULES

TWO MONTHS LATER

I SIT in *my* brand-new Lincoln Navigator—courtesy of my also brand-new grandfather—behind *my* diner. *Rezoned.*

When Pace presented me with the deed so many years ago, I accused him of playing a cruel joke. But in his usual noncomical way, he just stared. "I thought it was fitting." That was all he commented on it.

And fitting it was. I moved around so much for so long that I never remembered the zip code I was in. Sometimes even forgot the time zone. I was rezoned for half a decade. And now I own it.

I look down at my hand. Wiggling my fingers, the phantom ache of the breaks still lingers. I've been pain-free for a few weeks, but whenever I curl my fist, I still feel where Paycen snapped them like brittle twigs.

Two months ago, I didn't know if I would walk out of my pen alive. Now, I am free, can use my name again, and slowly build a relationship with my grandfather.

THE DAY MARSHALL let us go, Ethan drove us to some fancy hotel in Atlanta. The Altman. I had never heard of it. He handed the valet the key to my dead ex-boyfriend's car, took my hand, and walked us into the lobby. Thank God there weren't too many witnesses present, but the ones that were there gaped at our blood-stained attire, his swollen face, and my broken hand.

I remember having my heart sit in my throat, waiting to get kicked out. Ethan strolled up to the front desk girl and flashed her his trademark smirk. If his face hadn't looked like he just came from an underground fight (and lost), she probably would've wet her panties.

"M-May I help you?" Blondie stuttered as she scanned us up and down. She peered around, no doubt searching for security.

Ethan dropped his gaze to her name tag. "You sure can, Grace. My name is Ethan Davis. I work under Marcus Baxter for George Weiler's security team in LA. My girlfriend"—he lifted our joined hands as if to emphasize our relationship—"and I ran into some...issues. I lost my phone. Would you be so kind as to call my boss? We could use a place to clean up before heading home."

Have his teeth always been this brilliant white?

Poor Grace resembled a fish who had just experienced the orgasm of her life. Apparently, Ethan's name meant something—even if he didn't look like himself at the moment. "Um, oh my gosh. Mr. Davis. Of course. Uh, we didn't expect you. One moment." She began to scramble, flipping through some ancient phone directory.

What the actual fuck?

"Mr. Davis?" I couldn't keep the disdain out of my voice. "Why does some random chick in Atlanta know your name?" I blamed my immature jealousy act on the torture and lack of sleep over the last few days. My clothes stuck to me in ways that sent bile up my throat. It was a miracle we hadn't attracted flies yet.

Ethan draped his arm around my shoulder and leaned close to my ear. "Because Bax and I work personal security for the owners of this nice establishment." His breath fanned over the shell of my ear as he chuckled, sending signals to parts of my body that had no business being awake right now.

There was so much I had to learn about his new life.

"Mr. Baxter would like to speak to you." Grace held the phone out to Ethan. He placed a kiss on my temple before reaching for the receiver.

Lifting it to his ear, Ethan's first words sent a pang to my heart. "We're alive." While I couldn't make out the response of the person on the other end, I did gather that he wasn't happy.

Poor Grace watched us with something flip-flopping between interest, awe, and fear.

"Paycen?" Ethan snorted, then sobered up quickly. "Sorry, man. I know you're not a fan." More listening. "Copy. Thanks for handling that." Pause. "I see." Ethan hollowed his cheeks and puffed out a breath. "We need a place to crash for a day or two and sort some things out. Then, I'm coming home. I'll call you later and explain everything. Just let me shower first, 'kay?" He nodded to himself. "Sounds good. Yeah, tell everyone I'm fine. I'll call you later."

He handed the phone back to Grace, who, in return, held out a key card. She didn't elaborate on the room number, and Ethan didn't ask. I understood when I saw the PH stamped in the corner.

Who are these people?

. . .

W e   s h o w e r e d, and I passed out draped in a fluffy white robe—
that was softer than anything I'd ever felt on my skin—as soon
as my head hit the pillow. By the time I woke up, the sun was
high in the sky, judging by the rays gleaming through the gap in
the blackout curtain.

Everything hurt, nausea rocking my stomach. When was the
last time I ate?

Padding out of the bedroom, I found Ethan dressed in clean
sweats and a tee with a phone to his ear. He was marching the
length of the suite's living room. Where the hell did he get all
that from? Letting my eyes drift over my surroundings, I spotted
several bags stashed by the front door. An assortment of
pastries, fruit, waters (sparkling and not-sparkling), juice, coffee,
and tea covered the dining room and bar top to the kitchenette.
Holy shitballs.

Ethan halted, his eyes locking on me.

Did I say that out loud?

"I'll call you back." He didn't wait for whoever was on the
other end to respond. Dropping the device on the coffee table,
he strode over with the same confidence I'd seen radiate off him
from day one.

His arms wound around my midsection and his cheek settled
against my temple. "Good afternoon, Little Phoenix."

Afternoon? My arms hung by my sides as I processed
everything.

Ethan pulled back, his hands resting on my hips. "Let's get
you something to eat. The doctor will be back soon to check on
your hand. I didn't want to wake you."

"Huh?" My brows were near my hairline.

"Coffee first. I didn't forget."

"Uh." Clearly, my ability to articulate was still in the other room.

Settling at the table—*Jesus, even the chairs are out of this world*—Ethan served me coffee and piled food on a plate in front of me. "Take small bites. Your stomach needs to get used to it again after..." He trailed off, and I pulled my upper lip between my teeth.

Ethan informed me that the hotel's physician had already checked him out, taped his ribs, and given him the good stuff—which explained why you wouldn't suspect at all that he was nursing two broken ribs. The swelling of his face had gone down enough to reveal his eye. Shades of purple and black marred his body from head to toe.

I want to crush the warden's hand all over again.

I nibbled on a croissant, losing the battle with my anxiously bouncing leg. My body had its own form of processing...this. Ethan was back in my life. I had been kidnapped and tortured. I lost Paycen. This hotel.

He placed his hand on my knee. "Your grandfather will be here this evening." At that, my leg paused, and I sprayed the coffee I was about to swallow across the table.

"Excuse me?" My pulse sped up.

"I have to get back to LA. And while I'm fairly certain that Marshall won't come after you anymore, I'd feel better if you were with someone I can trust."

"And you trust the Irish Mob?" Was he for real?

"He's your grandfather," Ethan argued.

"That doesn't mean shit. You know best that family cannot be trusted. I've never met the man in my life." My body began to shake uncontrollably, adrenaline surging through my veins.

"Shhh." Ethan reached for my wrist, pulling me into his lap. "I won't take off without making sure you're safe. But I have to go back to Los Angeles."

My heart sank at his words. He was leaving me?

"I have to pack up my apartment," he clarified with a wink, sending a flutter in my stomach that made me sit straight. "I owe it to my boss to give him my notice in person." He lifted our joined hands to his mouth and gently kissed my knuckles. "I'd be in jail if it wasn't for him. I had gotten arrested during a job. The guy who hired me threw me under the bus to cover his worthless ass. George pulled some strings and offered me a future as long as I would leave my old life behind. I took it, and I never looked back." Ethan propped his chin on our hands. "Until Jenn told me that Marshall found you."

The hitch in my breath was audible. "What are you saying?" I needed to hear the words.

"I stayed away for a decade to keep you safe. You're safe now, and I'm selfish." Ethan wet his lips. "Even if you don't want to be with me in...that way anymore—which would suck hairy monkey balls, just saying—I would still be close by. You've always been it for me, Little Phoenix."

I drowned in the caramel of his eyes, the sincerity of his words too much for my already overwhelmed emotional state. Instead of responding, I answered him with my body. Straddling his lap, I rested my forearms on his shoulders. The tips of my fingers played with the strands of his hair. Ethan's lids drooped, and he shuddered.

"What are you doing, baby?"

I held his gaze, sinking my teeth into my bottom lip. Slowly bridging the distance, never dropping my eyes from his, our mouths fused in a kiss that answered the question—both of them.

A low groan rumbled in Ethan's chest as he dove under the loose terrycloth of my robe. Parting it, he exposed my naked body to the cool air of the AC. My nipples hardened, and a moan slipped past my lips as his thumb swiped over one in a feather-like caress.

Breaking the kiss, he moved to lick and nip along my jaw. "Is that a yes?"

A light pinch with his teeth at the sensitive skin under my ear and my hips responded of their own volition. Rocking against him, my pussy made contact with his hard length. The friction of his sweats teased my clit and elicited a whimper from my mouth.

How could I be this needy for him after everything we—

Ethan abandoned the discussion of our future. "Lift your ass." The husky tone of his command sent my nerve endings into overdrive before anything happened. The corner of his mouth quirked, and I arched a brow. His eyes turned devious. "On your toes. Do as I say."

A tremble between my thighs compelled me to press them together, which proved impossible in my current position. Shit, I loved when he took charge. Heat shot to my core, the wings of butterflies filling my chest, accelerating my breathing. Obeying his command, I rose. Taking a step back, Ethan's head shook with disapproval. "I said up, not leave."

My brows furrowed. He arched his back into the chair, hooking fingers into his waistband. Lifting his hips, he pushed them over his ass and down, letting them pool at his ankles. His arm snaked around, guiding me forward from the small of my back. "*Now* sit." The way he emphasized the *now* made me laugh.

My amusement quickly got overshadowed by a stronger sensation as I watched him stroke his cock with his other hand. Precum glistened at the tip, and I couldn't stop myself from licking my lips in anticipation. He swiped it away with his thumb before making several painfully slow, methodical pumps with his hand down his shaft, inviting my pussy to replace his fist.

He didn't have to tell me twice. With everything that happened to me, to us, this was exactly what I needed to forget what was still to come.

I aligned myself with his dick, resting my palms on his shoulders. Ethan parted his lips for another order as I sank down, burying him deep inside my pussy. Ethan groaned as I moaned at the fullness.

Exactly what I needed.

WE HAD sex twice more before the hotel physician showed up again. According to the man, Jenn had set my fingers expertly, and all he had to do was put a proper splint on and prescribe me the same good stuff.

Meeting my Irish Mob grandfather was another story. When the front desk called, informing us he was on his way, my knee went back to speed bobbing. I jumped off the couch and patrolled between the door and back to the living room, peering through the peephole each time. I repeated that track three times before a knock echoed through the suite. Two precise taps. Not too hard yet conveying a strong presence.

I chewed on the pad of my thumb. What would I say to the man who had disowned my father?

Ethan squeezed my arm before he approached the door, a large knife held behind his back. As soon as he opened the door and Rian Donelan stepped over the threshold, my breath stalled. He looked like an older version of Dad. My lips began to tremble, and his eyes glossed over as well.

"I'll give you two some privacy." Ethan gestured for Rian to take a seat. Stopping next to me, he placed a kiss on my cheek. "I'm in the bedroom. One word and I'm at your side. I have no problem killing the head of the Irish Mafia if he tries anything."

Ethan didn't bother lowering his voice, which made Rian chuckle.

I slowly walked over and sat down opposite my grandfather.

"I like him," were his first words.

I peered over my shoulder, meeting Ethan's gaze before he closed the door to the bedroom. "I love him," was my reply.

Rian Donelan was nothing like the people I grew up with. The Rens. The Order. I didn't doubt that he was ruthless in his ways. Ethan had given me the CliffsNotes version. But Rian didn't let me see that side of him. He was my grandfather, plain and simple—as simple as it could be for us.

He followed me to Maine, where he temporarily rented a house outside Montson.

He never apologized for disowning my father. The only time the topic got addressed was when he confessed that he missed too much time with me, and now that he knew that I was alive, he would see to it that I got to know my Irish family—if I so wished. Did I?

We remained in Atlanta for two more days before getting picked up by a private jet. By now, I understood who Ethan worked for, though I couldn't get used to the abundance of luxury. None of this was mine (or Ethan's), and I didn't trust anyone's intentions that easily—no matter how genuine they seemed.

Rian had his own mode of transportation and traveled separately.

When we arrived at the small private airport, Cody was already waiting.

Ethan arranged for him to pick me up and take me home. Ethan would head to LA. The way the two eyed each other, it was clear there had been more discussion than, "Can you pick Jules up?"

Cody hugged me briefly, nothing like he used to, and then stepped back. "I'm glad you're back, JJ."

"Was everything taken care of?" Ethan leveled my friend, who in return gave a curt nod.

"As we discussed."

I would've expected some type of alpha-macho remark of, *If you touch my woman in any way, blah blah blah*, but Ethan surprised me once again.

He stretched his hand out to Cody. "Thank you."

Cody seemed as surprised as me because he hesitated for a fraction of a second before placing his palm in Ethan's.

"I'll wait in the car," my friend informed me before heading to a white Lincoln Navigator.

"What was that about?" I turned to Ethan.

"Cody oversaw the repairs of the diner." At my blank expression, he amended, "The broken windows and doors."

Oh.

"I also had an alarm system installed."

My face flushed. I'd been taking care of myself for so long that I forgot how it felt... And Ethan going so far as forming a truce with Cody turned my insides to mush. Not willing to dive down the emotional rabbit hole, I deflected. "Whose car is this?"

"Yours." He smirked. "Papa Donelan figured you could use an armored SUV after rising from the ashes."

I slugged his arm, then glanced at the tank of a vehicle. "Mine?"

"I'm sure you can return it if you don't want it." Ethan shrugs.

"Oh, shut up." Like I would return that beauty. I wasn't that stubborn. Wrapping my arms around his neck, I glanced at the jet behind us. Rising to my toes, I pressed my lips against his, the man who was my first love and would be my last. "How long will you be gone?"

Ethan sighed. "Not sure. A few weeks probably. Packing up won't take long, but we have to find a replacement for my position and train him. It wouldn't feel right to just leave after everything they did for me."

A pang of guilt settled like a rock in my stomach. "Are you sure you want to quit? We could try long distance for a while and see if we even work out." Not that I meant any of it. Ethan and I would work out, and I sure as shit didn't want a long-distance relationship after being apart from him for ten years.

"Never been surer in my life, Little Phoenix." Ethan leaned his forehead to mine. "I'll call you when I land."

TODAY IS the day Ethan finally comes home.

Finding a replacement for his unique position with the Altman Hotel Group took longer than expected. Apparently, a lot was going on with one of the owners, and Ethan wanted to assist. That was all he divulged over the phone. How could I say no to that?

Confirming the time, I chew on my cheek. It's only one. He wouldn't land for another few hours. At least that would allow me time to clean the apartment a little bit—not that there is anything to clean. All I have is a couch, one chair, and my bed. I never replaced the table Ethan had kicked across the room.

I ran errands all morning, met with some of my local suppliers, and Cody insisted I should get my hair and nails done after moping around for weeks. Fucker. But he is right. I've missed Ethan like crazy—worse than when we were first together and he left for his *job*.

I open the driver's side door and jump onto the gravel.

Pulling the back door of the diner open, I'm met with a

cacophony of sounds. What the——? Rooted to the floor, I glance around as if I will find the answer stapled against the wall of the hallway.

I approach the front to see if everything is okay there. What is this noise? The diner is buzzing with people, which isn't unusual for the time of day, but the hammering from the floor above is definitely not normal.

Kaitlyn, one of my two waitresses woman-*ing* the main room, is busy with customers, so I decide to take measures into my own hands. My feet carry me toward the back of the building.

Passing the kitchen, I see Cody at the stove. I should check in with him, but since he has played security for me for the last month after Rian headed back to Ireland, whatever is happening in my apartment wouldn't be without his knowledge.

Just in case, I reach behind my back and clasp the wasp handle of my Contingency. Unsheathing it, I take one step at a time, making sure to miss the one that would give my approach away. Reaching the top, a female voice drifts through the wooden barrier. A crease forms between my brows. With my heart hammering in my throat, I reach for the knob and slowly twist, not wanting to alert whoever is inside my home. I let the door swing inward, fighting the physical need to stumble back. My entire living room is covered in tarps. White tarps. My minuscule amount of furniture is gone. My eyes fly to the female staring at me with a phone to her ear.

"Uh, I have to call you back," the stranger says and hangs up. She's wearing dark skinny jeans paired with a loose-fitting, three-quarter-sleeve silk blouse.

"Jules, hi. We didn't expect you so soon."

"Um..." I tilt my head, my gaze drifting over my apartment and back to the woman. I still have no idea who she is. My fingers tighten around the handle of my knife, and her gaze flicks to my hand.

Is she smiling? What the—?

"Who are you?"

She squares her shoulders. "I'm Denielle. I'm—"

My bedroom door flies open, and Ethan comes into view with a sledgehammer in hand. "Fuck, I love smashing—"

He halts when he sees me, and his mouth forms an *O*. At the sight, my heart skips a beat before it takes off in an unnatural sprint. I don't think twice before flinging myself into his arms.

A thud reaches my ears before he cups my face. "Hey, Little Phoenix."

"Why are you already here? I was going to pick—" My question gets cut off when a blond Viking god of a man steps up behind Ethan. He's a little taller than my man, with his hair tied back in a bun. My eyes bulge, and Ethan throws a glance over his shoulder.

Dropping his palms, he clasps one hand in his. Leaning down, he whispers, "You can put the knife away now."

Oh.

My spine stiffens, and Ethan chuckles. He pulls me to the side so that the male stranger can walk past us. He heads straight over to...Denielle?

"Jules, this is Denielle Keller and Marcus Baxter. Bax is my boss."

Marcus drapes an arm over Denielle's shoulder, and she nestles into his side.

"It's nice to meet you...I guess," I stammer like an idiot, then level my boyfriend. "Um, what happened to my apartment?"

"You mean our apartment?" Ethan points out, and I throw him a droll glare.

"We're renovating." The duh is inaudible, and I want to punch him in the throat.

"We came with Ethan to ensure he is all set for his first day next week," Marcus states.

I flick my gaze between the three figures.

"You didn't tell her," Denielle accuses with pursed lips.

"It was supposed to be a surprise." Ethan scowls.

"Whoops." She grins in a nonapologetic way.

I like her.

Ethan places his palms against the sides of my neck. His thumb strokes my skin, sending goose bumps down my spine. "One of the reasons it took longer to get back was that George and Bax didn't accept my resignation." We both look over. Marcus shrugs as unapologetically as his woman.

"I am taking over the security department for the new Altman Hotel in Boston. I'm gonna have to be in the city a few days a week, but other than that, I'll be home." He grins, then places a kiss on my lips.

"Home?"

"Home, Little Phoenix."

EPILOGUE

JULES

ONE YEAR LATER

"LAZY PIECE OF SHIT," I mutter as my hands scrub the pots in the sink.

"Stop being a bitch, JJ," Cody counters, throwing onion rings into the frying pan.

What the fuck is he even cooking?

Ethan has to stay an extra day in Boston, and I am in a shit mood. Then Cody called me into the kitchen to help with the dishes. Two of my three servers called in sick. They usually rotate helping with the kitchen duties while two are in the front.

The kitchen door swings inward, footsteps approach, and someone halts beside me. I focus on my hands in the soapy water, too annoyed to ask what Lina wants. She knows how to do her job.

"He's back," a voice that's not Lina's says beside me. A

scream tears from my lungs, and I rip my hands from the water, spraying suds everywhere.

I whirl around, grasping for my Contingency in the back of my jeans while trying to pick my jaw up off the floor. What the—

"You're needed in the front." Della smiles while wiping the droplets off her face.

"Della?" I mean, yes, I would recognize my childhood best friend any day, but... "What are you—" I gesture between her and the door with the tip of my blade. I haven't seen her in over a decade, even after I was let in on her *relationship* with Corbin.

Corbin. He remained in *the pen* for months before Marshall let him out. Theo had been getting messages through to Ethan. He never said it out loud, but his face spoke volumes when we finally got the news that Corbin was safe.

"Just play along, Jules." She winks, takes my knife, and hands me a notepad and pencil.

Tears prick my eyes. "Della?"

"We have time to catch up later. For now, you have an order to take." She pulls me into a brief hug and turns, striding out of my kitchen like she's here every day.

I slowly pivot and stare at Cody. Am I hallucinating? He's moved on to placing buns on the grill, ignoring me completely.

I glance down at the items in my hands and then at the swing door.

Just play along.

Setting one foot in front of the other, my flip-flops patter against the floor. I exit into the hallway and turn toward the front of the diner. Crossing under the arch, my feet root to the hardwood, and the notepad and pencil slip from my grasp.

The entire diner is empty except for the largest booth. It's U-shaped and situated at the far end of the room, taking over the whole corner.

Several sets of eyes are trained on me. I can't move.

Della stands next to the bench seat, her hand on the back of the booth and her eyes twinkling.

Theo sits at the edge. Next to him lounges Corbin, with his arms stretched over the back in both directions. His fingers graze Della's, yet neither of them acknowledges the other.

Jenn is nestled into her big brother's side, grinning like a loon.

My eyes meet Ethan's. He has one foot propped on the bench and his upper body angled toward me.

"Took you long enough," someone whispers behind me, and I close my eyes.

"You're here."

Paycen steps up beside me, glancing down. "You're my only friend." The corner of his mouth twitches imperceptibly before he strides with his hands in his pockets over to his family.

Ethan scoots out, letting Paycen take his place.

My boyfriend makes his way over and stops only when our feet almost touch.

"What's all this?" I breathe, unable to speak at a normal volume. My lungs constrict with emotion, and I swallow over the lump in my throat.

"This was the moment I knew I would marry you." He licks his lips, slanting his head. "Plus a few modifications."

Is he nervous?

"Is this safe?" Having them here? "What if—"

"We took the necessary precautions," Jenn announces a little too loudly from the background.

"Let the man get on with his plan, Jules," Corbin chimes in, and Theo's laughter drifts over.

I can't avert my eyes from Ethan.

He reaches into his front pocket and extracts his fist.

Holding it between us, he opens his palm in excruciating slowness.

My heart stutters before taking off at hummingbird speed. There, in the center, lays a black titanium engagement ring. Instead of a traditional diamond, it holds an obscenely large cushion-cut ruby.

I flatten my palm against my chest, absorbing the vibration from my erratic heartbeat.

Ethan takes my free hand and interlaces our fingers. "Jules Arrow, you are my power, my strength, and my certainty. Before you, I was physically strong but didn't know what true strength meant. I had the power to take a life, but you stole my soul the moment I laid eyes on you. With you, I saw a future worth living for. You are my phoenix. Fiery, passionate, and indestructible. Will you do me the honor of becoming my wife?"

Tears are streaming down my cheeks. I remove my hand from my rib cage and cup Ethan's face. My thumb caresses his cheekbone. "Full of beauty and passion. Laced in the desire to survive. You've pricked my heart." I bring our lips together before murmuring, "I do."

ETHAN & JULES

The End

Make sure to keep reading for
an exclusive preview of Deadzone.

Ethan
& Jules
You don't want to miss
Theo meeting his match!

KEEP READING

Deadzone
The Davis Order, Book One

Prologue

Note:
This chapter is subject to change in the final version of *Deadzone*.

NAT

AT NINETEEN YEARS OLD, I'M AHEAD IN LIFE AND ALSO SO FAR
behind that the normalcy of being a teenager is the equivalent of
a fictional novel. Ahead, because I live a life of wealth not many
get to experience. Behind, because it comes with the price of a
solid rhodium cage outfitted with motion sensors and cameras.

I'm not an ungrateful, spoiled princess. I appreciate everything I've been given—the necessity of the security measures
understood. People are ruthless. Not because they want your
money or valuables, but because they want *you*, on a silver plat-

ter, preferably spread-eagle and ready to dissect. They want to find your flaws, any shred of information that could make them a quick buck.

Which is one of the reasons I switched to online schooling at the age of twelve. I attempted one more year of normality after my family's lives changed. It didn't work out. Kids are cruel. They eavesdrop on their parents' hushed conversations and repeat the verbal stabs back at you with a devious grin. I shrugged them off for the first few months. I had a best friend who had my back and a bodyguard who followed me everywhere. The worst they could do was talk. But eventually, it got to me. I ate less, slept more, and the most alarming sign: I stopped reading.

Books have been my escape since I was able to sound out letters and form words. I can get lost in fictional worlds for hours...days. But the stories lost their meaning when *my story* became others' entertainment.

The second my feet crossed the threshold of my school, my shoulders hunched of their own volition. My clammy palms stained the fabric under my armpits, where I would tuck them away to hide the trembling. When I got cornered in the girls' bathroom one day, my lungs seized up. No matter how desperately I tried to inhale, the oxygen wouldn't reach its target. I passed out. And that was when my parents pulled me from school.

Mom and Dad informed my brother and sister, who flew in from California for a family intervention—disappointed I hadn't confided in them sooner. But what did they expect? My family had been riddled with secrets from the day I was born. They were never mine, but in the end, it didn't matter.

My father, retired Colonel Tristen McGuire, is a renowned name in his field and is sought out by many for his expertise. He had—correction *has* connections that shouldn't exist. My mom,

Heather, has worked as a corporate attorney for as long as I can remember. However, she took a step back over the years and now handpicks her cases.

What they hid from everyone was the reason our family almost fell apart: my brother's and sister's secrets. Secrets, plural. What Lilly and Rhys discovered was what changed all our lives. Not that it was their fault, either. Lilly's life wasn't her own. She'd been a pawn in a game that had spun over years. Lilly isn't my sister by blood, though I will always see her as one. She is my best friend and closest confidant. She'll never betray your trust.

I gave up a long time ago trying to explain their story. If someone wants to, they can Google them and read it on their own. It literally covers hundreds of pages. But usually, people just make up their own disturbingly erroneous narration of Lilly and Rhys McGuire's story. While they are an inseparable package deal these days, it wasn't always like that.

Lilly is also the reason we now have wealth. It is technically hers, but she said from day one that Mom and Dad saved her life, and what's hers is ours. Unfortunately, that comes with the other side of the coin: the paparazzi, the whispers, the glances, the fake friends who want to reap the benefits of the money, the bodyguards...the list goes on. There were times I felt resentful toward her; I wanted it to be how it was before. But that will never happen. So, I've become careful about who I trust, rarely venturing out of sight of my personal detail, and have finished high school in the security of the four walls of my room.

Now, for the first time, the door to my cage is open.

I lower the window of my silver Range Rover and let the wind whip my dark-brown hair around my face. The strands tickle my skin, and a squealed laugh escapes my throat. I click the button on the steering wheel to turn up the volume of "This Corrosion" by *In Extremo*. My taste in music is questionable, as my best friend, Olivia, tells me on the regular, but that's one thing I inherited from my sister. Dancing ballet to classic metal gives you a rush like no other. Movements you never thought your body was capable of.

I raise the window enough for my hair to stop obscuring my vision. The landscape rushes by, and I feel free. As free as one can be with trackers in her phone and car, a PSA Dagger in the glove compartment, its twin under my seat, and a hunting knife the size of a small machete tucked in the driver's side door.

Just because I've studied ballet since I was four doesn't mean I didn't also practice other *skills*. My siblings were trained in MMA since they were ten, weapons training shortly after. Inevitably, I was as well.

But for the next two weeks, I will be by myself. On. My. Own. No bodyguard, no parents, no brother or sister. Just *me*.

I am on my way from Westbridge, Virginia, to our family vineyard in Northern California, where I will attend online college. It took me months to convince my parents and our head of security—Uncle G, as I call him—to let me drive alone. I conceded to the extra trackers, one more gun than I usually carry, and frequent check-ins. Surprisingly, Lilly was the one taking my side and putting up a stand to let me do this. I loved her a little more for it.

I'm on day two of the drive. I have it all mapped out. I am going to spend some time in the national parks, soaking up the peace of being surrounded by nature with no cell reception. My trackers will remain operable—Dad and Uncle G made sure of that.

I decide to pick up more snacks. I'm on a less-trafficked part of the highway, and with no rest stop in sight, I take the first exit in search of a grocery store. According to the map displayed on the car's navigation, there is a small town about two miles down the road. My phone lights up in the cup holder, and I peer down, seeing Olivia's face grin back at me on the screen. A smile tucks at the corner of my mouth, and I reach for it. Flicking my eyes back to the road, a guy crosses the asphalt right in front of me. Our gazes collide, and his lips part. The distance between him and my car rapidly closes, yet he doesn't move. At the last moment, I jerk the wheel and—*crash*.

A crunching sound of metal registers in my ears right before my forehead hits—

Deadzone is currently planned to release in 2024 after *I Am the Dark*, book six in *The Dark Series*.

It's set about two years after the last chapter (not the epilogue) of *Rezoned*.

KEEP READING

New to my books?
Want to find out how it all began? And maybe meet some of the
Davis siblings before we knew about the Order?
Check out the prologue and first chapter of *In the Dark*, the first
book in *The Dark Series* and a dark, new-adult,
romantic-suspense trilogy.

In the Dark
The Dark Series, Book One

Prologue

HIM

*I WALK INTO HER ROOM FOR THE NIGHTLY CHECK, EXPECTING THE
usual crying and pleading to let her go home, but when I open the door
and hear nothing, I know something is wrong. I rush to her small form on*

the bed, calling her name, but she is not responding. I shake her, but she's completely limp in my arms. Checking her pulse, I sigh in relief. She's alive. What have I done? I scoop her up and race outside to my car which, thankfully, is still in the driveway from my earlier errand. Making sure she is secure in the backseat, I break every speed limit to the nearest emergency room. I can't lose her, too. Making sure my hat is low, hood covering my hair and most of my face, I race inside the double doors and nearly throw her at the first nurse I can find. "HELP! HELP HER!"

Back in the car, I lean my forehead against the steering wheel and try to catch my breath, chanting, "She will be fine. She will be fine. She will be fine. I'll get her back."

Chapter One

LILLY

IT'S MID-NOVEMBER, and everyone is talking about the upcoming Thanksgiving break. Denielle and I sit with Emma and Sloane at our usual lunch table. Our cafeteria is a huge, rectangular hall located in the center of where the three wings of Westbridge High meet. Two sets of double doors lead in from the east and west wings. The south wing is connected via two walkways to the east and west wings. Technically, it is its own building, not a wing, but since it's south of the main complex, everyone calls it the south wing. I'm sure someone put *a lot* of thought into it before making that decision, or it was just the most logical, who knows. The south wing also leads to the parking lot and houses the administration offices, health office, and all of the art-related classrooms—best lighting and all.

Our lunch table is in the heart of the room, next to floor-to-ceiling windows overlooking the outdoor seating area and green space. We have the perfect view of everything and everyone. When I'm not required to pay attention to my friends, I tend to just stare outside at the trees framing the school grounds. We are the only mixed table of gymnasts and cheerleaders. Emma and Sloane are the cheerleaders. Denielle and I are on the school's gymnastics team and train at the local academy during our off-season. The rest of the cheerleaders flock around the far corner table by the east exit, and the rest of the gymnasts are spread over different tables on the west side. It's like an unspoken agreement, but since the four of us have been friends since middle school, we refused to conform to that rule when we entered high school. The jocks claim three of the middle tables and are the center of attention, no matter where in the room you are—you can't miss them. This includes my brother, Rhys, quarterback of the school's football team as well as reigning wrestling champion, and his best friend, Wes.

I'm chewing on my turkey-avocado wrap, tempted to let my gaze wander outside and stop listening to Den going on incessantly about her boyfriend, Charlie. They have been together for two years, and this will be the first time he's coming home since he left for college in August. I peer at my watch—twenty-three minutes and counting. I quietly sigh to myself but try to be a supportive best friend and pay attention. Denielle and I have been friends since my family moved back to Westbridge, Virginia four years ago. We lived here when Dad did his tour at the Pentagon, but he ended up taking command in North Carolina for three years, so we moved again. When he retired from the Marine Corps after twenty-some years, he took a government contractor position. His new job requires him to travel, so he doesn't care where we live. Mom has been a corporate attorney with the same firm for as long as I can remember. She is able to commute between her local office and the firm's main office in Alexandria easily. Living in North Carolina, she had to travel for days at a time, and she never liked leaving us kids for that long—especially when Natty, our little sister, was younger. But it wasn't just that. Both my parents had lived in the Virginia area when they went to school, which was where they met, and a lot of their college friends are still here. Rhys had immediately voted for Westbridge, as you would've thought he'd lost a limb when we left there three years earlier and he had to say goodbye to Wes. The two had been inseparable since Rhys's first day at Westbridge Elementary. My brother had dropped his lunch, and Wes shared his grilled cheese sandwich with him. The bond they formed over two pieces of bread resulted in a lifelong friendship. With so many ties to Virginia, my parents figured moving back was a win-win for everyone. Oh, and of course there is Butler Gymnastics Academy where I had trained for years before we moved.

I've done gymnastics my entire life, so it was a no-brainer to rejoin Butler's as soon as my boxes were unpacked. I kept up with it in North Carolina, but it wasn't the same. Every academy has its individual training method, and I remember being so nervous that I wouldn't make the cut. Denielle took one look at me during my first practice session and flashed me a grin. "I like you. I think we'll be best friends." And that was it. Luckily for us, we also attended the same middle school, and she's been by my side ever since. There was never a question we would compete for spots on the school team as soon as we started high school.

I finish my wrap, and Denielle is coming up on thirty-four minutes. My attention is fading quickly. My mind drifts again, and I remember the second week of our freshman year when Charlie literally ran Denielle over. He was coming out of the cafeteria, late for his next class, and we were about to enter for our lunch period. His head was turned, talking to one of his buddies, when he plowed her down. It was comical; her books went flying, and the contents of his opened backpack went everywhere. Den was about to let him have it when their eyes locked. Both of them just stared at each other, slack-jawed. They went on their first date the following weekend and have been together ever since. They have one of those relationships you only read about—*the perfect couple*. They complement each other in every way: where she is spontaneous and temperamental, he is calculated and level-headed. Even their fights make you want to gag at how perfect they are. Sometimes, I wonder how they make it work. Anyway, Charlie left for college this summer, and they are working their way through a long-distance relationship. So far, it's been going well, but Thanksgiving will be the first time he's been back, and to say Den is excited would be like saying the sun is *kinda* warm.

"He'll regret sending me all these naughty texts and then not acting on them."

Emma and Sloane laugh at Denielle's comment, and I just roll my eyes. "You are so full of it. First of all, how could he act on it, being three states away? And second, the minute you two are alone, you'll jump his bones."

Den grins at me sideways. "Wasn't that what I was referring to?"

I just shake my head and gather my things. "Grab your stuff. I don't want to be late for journalism again. Mr. Davey said we'd get our research assignment today."

"Geek."

"Love you, too. Get your ass moving."

"YOU HAVE until after break to finish your paper. We've talked a lot about the news in the last few weeks—how subjectively things are being presented based on the presenter. I want you to pick a current news topic. It can be anything from economics, politics, even a recent criminal case, and research the entire subject. What is being reported and how is it presented versus what you believe is being left out and why."

Mr. Davey mentioning a criminal case immediately intrigues me. Economics and politics have never really interested me. I'm more a math and computer science kinda girl. Plus, our household is composed of an attorney and a former Marine. Heated discussions over politics are a given, which is a reason I stay clear of it as much as I can. Criminal case it is.

RHYS

I GLANCE toward the table by the windows where Lilly and her friends had taken up residence during the first week of freshman year. As much as the three middle tables are ours, that one is *property* of Denielle, Sloane, Emma, and Lilly, with the occasional visit from a random student. Lilly is staring out the window while Sloane and Emma hang on Denielle's every word. I press my lips together to hide the smile that wants to creep across my face from seeing Lilly's bored expression. I wonder what the topic of Den's monologue is that evokes such an opposite reaction in Lilly versus her two friends. Not that I would ever dare ask. If I did, the answer wouldn't extend beyond Denielle's middle finger. Turning back to my table, a chuckle escapes me at the visual in my mind, and Wes gives me *the eyebrow*. Purposefully ignoring my best friend, I shove another forkful of the disgusting *and* cold spaghetti in my mouth. How the cafeteria folks can fuck up something simple like spaghetti is beyond me.

The last two classes are dragging. All I can think about is

today's practice since Coach decided to jam extra sessions in before break. I walk between Wes and Jager toward the gym when my girlfriend appears in front of us. Kat gives my friends her usual sultry eye flutter before she wraps her arm around mine and pulls me toward the guys' bathroom we just passed.

"Excuse us, guys. I need Rhys to take care of something for me *really* quick."

She gives me a sidelong glance, and I know exactly what goes through my best friend's and teammate's heads.

Awesome.

Wes fist bumps me as I'm being dragged away, and Jager hoots loudly. However, before we get to the bathroom door, I stumble into someone, which is followed by, "What the fuck, McGuire?"

This is getting better by the minute.

I turn toward the voice and come nose to nose with Lilly's best friend and *my* archenemy. With her four-inch heels, Denielle is almost at eye level with me, and we stare at each other—neither of us budging. I put my most bored expression on, one I have mastered over the last few years, but before I can say anything, Kat sneers from my side, "Watch where you're going. You're holding us up."

Kat intimidates ninety-nine percent of the school's female population, but not Denielle Keller. She just raises an eyebrow and looks between her and me before settling on Kat.

"Oh, you mean now you have to finish him off in three minutes versus five?" Her gaze travels to me, and with a smirk, she continues, "I think you'll be fine. From what I've heard, you two never need more than two."

Instead of walking around me, she bumps her shoulder into mine with as much force as she's able to gather in the short distance between us.

As I follow Den's retreating form, a hiss comes from Kat that sounds something along the lines of *bitch*, but instead of engaging, Den just flips her the finger and keeps walking. I bite the inside of my cheek not to burst out laughing and let Kat drag me the rest of the way into the bathroom.

After ensuring we're alone, she rounds on me. "You've been ignoring me this week."

She can't be serious.

This time, I don't even have to pretend to be bored. "What are you talking about?"

"During lunch *and* practice!" With both fists on her hips, all that's missing is her stomping a foot to complete the temper tantrum.

The urge to turn and walk out is overpowering, but after a calming inhale and exhale, I simply say, "I've had extra practice, and you know that. What do you want from me? Walk you to the other end of the gym in the middle of everything so that we're seen together?" I almost expect her to say yes, but instead, she switches gears altogether.

"Don't forget Emma's party on Friday. I expect you to be there."

It's not like I have anywhere else to be—like home.

"I will."

My answer pacifies her, and she presses a quick kiss on my cheek. "That's my boyfriend."

I sigh inwardly. Yes, it is.

Continue reading Lilly & Rhys's story in
In the Dark, The Dark Series, Book One.

ACKNOWLEDGMENTS

It's that time again. Diving into this new world was as exhilarating as it was scary, and I hope you enjoyed getting to know all the Davis siblings. Some of them surprised me once again. As I always say: *I don't write my books. My characters do*.

While this is Ethan and Jules's story, Theo, Jenn, Paycen, and Corbin all played a big role in it, and I can't wait to give you their books.

If you read *Followed by the Dark,* you may remember the trackers, which could cause a few questions for part two in *Rezoned*. You will get the answer to that in either a bonus scene or in one of the other books.

I have one bonus scene planned for Ethan and Corbin at this point, but as usual, if there is any bonus content you would like to see (for any of the books or characters), please feel free to email authordanahloganpa@gmail.com, and my PA will add them to my list.

Did you know you can ask my characters questions and their answers will be posted in my newsletter? Scan below QR code and select "*Ask the Characters*" if you want to chat with them.

Now to the thank-yous:

My husband: You always have my back when I need to disappear into my head and sort out something my characters decided to spontaneously change. I couldn't do this without you.

My daughters: You won't read my books for a VERY long time. With that being said, your suggestions for new book titles and what I should put on my covers always make my day. I love you to the moon and back.

My family and friends: Thank you for cheering me on and recommending my books all over the world. Your support blows me away.

Mary: My PA and friend. Thank you for letting me throw new tasks at you at all hours of the day, always listening to my rambles about new ideas, and especially for saving our text conversations. Without you, I would still be sitting here, trying to figure out how *Rezoned* was supposed to end. I couldn't do any of this without you.

Sammi: Thank you for always being there, no matter how busy you are yourself. Your friendship means the world to me.

Jim: We make one hell of a team. Thank you so much for proofreading Ethan and Jules's spicy scenes and giving me pointers about the male anatomy I did not know. ;-) I can't wait to hear your feedback on the next project.

My alphas: Mary D. and Lil. Thank you so so much for reading this story chapter by chapter, allowing me to jump back and forth and upload changes to something you already read because, once again, the plot changed. You need to blame the characters, not me—just saying.

My betas: Lyndsey, Ellie, Loren, Robyn, Emma, and Tiffany. Thank you for taking time out of your busy lives to beta read this *novella*. *cough cough* I know, I told you it would only be 25K words, but what are another 50K, right? You are an integral part of my process, and I can't begin to tell you how grateful I am for you.

Bethany from Weaver Literacy Agency: Thank you so much for getting me my first foreign deal this year. You are a rock star, and I am beyond grateful to have you as my agent.

Jenn from Jenn Lockwood Editing: Thank you for, once again, adjusting to my crazy schedule and making my words clean and pretty.

Rosa from My Brother's Editor: Thank you so much for proofing Ethan and Jules's story and ensuring *Rezoned* is ready for the world.

My ARC Readers & Street Team: THANK YOU!! Thank you for reading and reviewing my books before they're out in the wild and spreading the word. I'm blown away by your support and wouldn't be here without you!

And finally, you, my readers: Thank you for reading my words and escaping with me into the world(s) my crazy head cooks up. Seeing you fall in love and like (or dislike) my characters makes me so happy because it means I created something you can identify with in one way or another. I can't wait to give you many more books and to hear what you think about them.

All my *TDS* readers have been patient with me, letting me get Ethan out of my head before writing *IATD*. Now, it's *HIS* turn, though. And once you get *HIS* book, you'll understand why I had to write Rezoned first. **Did you find the Easter eggs?**

Let's go finish *The Dark Series*.

xoxo

Danah Logan

STAY CONNECTED

Born and raised in Germany, Danah moved to the US, where she
met her husband, eventually trading downtown Chicago's city
life for the northern Rockies.

She can be seen hanging with her twin girls and exploring the
outdoors when she's not arguing plot points with the
characters in her head.

But it's that exact passion that has produced *The Dark Series* and
continues to keep her glued to her laptop, following her dreams.

Scan the below QR code to sign up for Danah's newsletter and be the first to know about her upcoming releases, sales, and new arrivals.

Add me on Facebook
www.facebook.com/authordanahlogan/

Follow me on Instagram
www.instagram.com/authordanahlogan/

Visit my Website for more content
and other places to stalk me
www.authordanahlogan.com

Or scan this second QR code for all the links:

ALSO BY DANAH LOGAN

The Dark Series

In the Dark, Book 1
Out of the Dark, Book 2
Of Light and Dark, Book 3
(Lilly and Rhys)
A Dark, New-Adult, Romantic-Suspense Trilogy

Because of the Dark, Book 4
(Wes and King)
A Dark, Hidden-Identity, Romantic-Suspense Novel

Followed by the Dark, Book 5
(Denielle and Marcus)
A Dark, Enemies-to-Lovers, Age-Gap,
Romantic-Suspense Novel

I Am the Dark, Book 6
(HIM)
A Dark, Age-Gap, Romantic-Suspense Novel

The Davis Order

Rezoned, Prequel
(Ethan)
A Dark, Hate-to-Love, Second-Chance,
Romantic-Suspense Novel

Deadzone, Book 1
(Theo)
A Dark, Age-Gap, Romantic-Suspense Novel

Coldblood, Book 2
(Paycen)
A Dark, Touch-Her-and-You-Die, Romantic-Suspense Novel

Cleaner, Book 3
(Jenn)
A Dark, Why-Choose Romantic-Suspense Novel

Firestarter, Book 4
(Corbin)
A Dark, Enemies-to-Lovers, Romantic-Suspense Novel

Printed in Great Britain
by Amazon

23177292R00169